Peter Jangle
AND THE
NEW MADRID
DISCOVERY

ISBN: 0985259000
ISBN-13: 9780985259006
Library of Congress Control Number: 2012910806
CreateSpace, North Charleston, SC

Peter Jangle

AND THE
NEW MADRID
DISCOVERY

(2ND IN THE PETER JANGLE SERIES)

JOHN W. MARSKE

ACKNOWLEDGMENTS

The publishing process for the first two Peter Jangle novels has been fun, frustrating, and immensely educational. I acknowledge my need for better writers than I to review my work. As such, I want to thank my friend, Katy Harbison, for agreeing to read, edit, and suggest changes to my first novel, *Peter Jangle Uncorks the Inflation Genie*. She agreed to this task without pay, did a great job in a short amount of time, and inspired me to write.

Not wanting to burden Katy with another project (My goal was to maintain our friendship), I decided to run a contest for editing "privileges" for this novel. I listed certain qualifications—needed to be an English major, willing to put in long hours at below-market wages, and must be a Notre Dame graduate.

I asked each interested candidate to read the first novel and give me feedback and suggestions. The comments and qualifications from all the respondents were impressive. I chose Andy Schilling. Andy brought over 20 years' experience in the Foreign Service, editing language drafts for transmission back to Washington. This full-time speechwriter from Omaha, Nebraska stayed focused while dealing with a change in jobs and a death in his family. I thank him for his good work.

I also want to thank the people who wrote reviews on Amazon. Reviews are always flattering, even if they're not positive. It means someone is taking the time to read your work. Finally, I want to thank my wife and family, who accepted the fact that I was getting up early and leaving home on weekends to write. I also want to thank my parents who encouraged me to keep writing and keep learning. God blessed me with a great support group.

CHAPTER ONE

One solitary blade of beach grass stood apart from the rest, ten feet below the top of the sand dune called Mount Baldy. On this muggy evening in Michigan City, Indiana, Mount Baldy melded in perfect symmetry with the heavenly bodies above. The dune offered comfort to those willing to nestle in its bosom.

A young couple lay snuggled at the top of the dune, admiring the night stars, while being serenaded by the harmonious sound of the lake caressing the beach below. Their coiled bodies formed a gentle imprint in the sand. Far below the dune, a family of four deer darted through the woods, as if fleeing from a dangerous predator. A pair of Rottweilers, guarding a dimly lit shack, suddenly pierced the night silence with their barking. Within minutes, Jim Webb and his young bride, Karen, felt the dune vibrating beneath their outstretched bodies. They would soon realize why Peter Jangle feared this magnificent mountain of sand.

A rumbling sound, originating from the southwest, caused each of their bodies to tense. The ground began shaking, and fine grains of sand started cascading down the east side of the dune, with increasing speed. Jim and Karen tried in vain to get to their feet to avoid being swept away in the avalanche of sand. It was too late. Jim desperately reached out to Karen, yelling, "Hold on to me!" as both bodies went tumbling down the dune. The trembling of the earth lasted a total of one minute. Within that minute, the landscape was drastically altered.

Jim brushed the sand out of his hair and frantically called, "Karen…Karen, where are you?!"

He quickly rose to his knees, intent on searching for his bride. Grains of sand clung to the sweat of his body. Jim surveyed the landscape, looking for any sign of Karen. His heart leapt when he noticed movement in the sand, just beyond his reach. A sense of relief crossed his face, as he lunged forward to provide assistance. He stopped abruptly when he saw the cause of the sand displacement. A chipmunk dug itself free, shook the sand out of its hair, and scurried off to safety. Jim looked about anxiously, until he heard a faint gasp of breath, followed by coughing. His gaze fixed on his wife, who was desperately trying to clear her mouth of the sand partially blocking her air passage. Rushing down to where Karen was half-buried, Jim reached out for her hand, while at the same time trying to free her from the weight of the sand.

"Thank God! Karen, are you okay?"

"I think so," Karen replied, still trying to get her bearings. "What in the world just happened?"

"I don't know. But let's hurry and get off this dune before it happens again."

Looking up, they noticed they had tumbled halfway down the dune. The sand at the foot of the hill looked like it had covered an additional eight inches of the parking lot below. The two stumbled hand in hand toward their car. Still gasping for breath, Jim looked at Karen and said, "We've got to tell someone about this."

"What are we supposed to tell them?" Karen asked.

The lone blade of beach grass, which once stood proud near the summit of the dune, was nowhere to be found.

On the other side of town, a small ranch home adjacent to the seventh fairway of the Long Beach golf course, had just ceased shaking. Long Beach was a suburb of Michigan City that nestled against Lake Michigan. The mature trees and winding, hilly roads offered a Cape Cod-type atmosphere, in the middle of Indiana. Many of the surrounding home sites offered a summer escape for the "new wealth" from Chicago. But the Jangle family had lived there for generations. Their family finances had experienced the past booms and busts of the local economy. And it was their house, on the seventh fairway of the golf course, which had just ceased shaking.

"Did you feel that?" Claire Jangle asked her husband, staring at the dining room chandelier that was slowly rocking back and forth.

"I felt it," David replied, looking around to check for damage. "I don't think that was Peter dropping his weights on the floor this time," David joked nonchalantly.

Claire smiled nervously. She admired her husband's wry attempt at humor. "No... that definitely wasn't Peter. I actually think that was an earthquake."

"An earthquake? Here in the Midwest?"

"It can happen. Remember all of the talk about the New Madrid fault line in Missouri? They've been warning us about this for years. Turn on the TV. Let's see if there's anything about it on the news."

As soon as they turned on the television, Peter Jangle sprinted up the basement stairs.

"What's up?" he asked.

"Peter, couldn't you feel the house shaking? We're checking the news to see if there are any reports of an earthquake."

"Is that what that was? I figured you guys were just stomping on the floor to get me to turn down my music." Peter had obviously inherited his father's humor.

It took a full forty minutes before the national news picked up the story of the earthquake in the Midwest. As the story broke, the facts surrounding the catastrophe were incredible. The earthquake had registered 6.8 on the Richter scale, and it had delivered a dramatic and devastating blow to the surrounding area.

Gathering around the television, David and Claire Jangle turned up the volume. The network news reporters based in St. Louis, Missouri, were commenting that they were unable to reach New Madrid, the epicenter of the earthquake.

"From what we are currently hearing, Tom, at approximately 10:58 p.m., an earthquake measuring 6.8 on the Richter scale struck near the city of New Madrid, Missouri. We haven't had any contact with the people in New Madrid, but we are hearing there is considerable damage in Memphis, Tennessee, which is located approximately 100 miles down the Mississippi River from New Madrid. In addition to the structural damage, one of the bigger problems in Memphis seems to be flooding from the Mississippi River. Geologists fear that the quake might have actually changed the course of the River. However, we won't be able to confirm that speculation until daylight. Once daybreak occurs, it is expected that FEMA will dispatch aircraft and helicopters to make a full damage assessment."

"Tell me, Steve, is there any damage where you're located in St. Louis? And exactly how far are you from the epicenter of the quake?"

"St. Louis is about 170 miles north of New Madrid. The earthquake certainly did make an impact here. We have broken glass downtown, from some of the large office buildings. And we're hearing reports of significant property damage in some of the outlying suburbs. They've announced that there will be no public access to the St. Louis Arch until they've had time to check for any structural damage."

"Are there any reports of fatalities?"

"While we don't have any confirmed fatalities yet, the quake clearly affected a large area, and fatalities are going to be a concern. Right now, emergency personnel are still being deployed. It will be quite a while before we know the full extent of the damage."

"Thank you, Steve. For those of you just joining us, it appears that a 6.8 magnitude earthquake has struck the Midwest along the New Madrid fault line. While we have yet to assess the full extent of the damage in the New Madrid area, or in Memphis, Tennessee, geologists are concerned about the magnitude of the earthquake. We already have reports of some damage in St. Louis, which is 170 miles north of New Madrid. In fact, reports are now coming in that the earthquake's impact was felt as far north as Chicago, almost 390 miles north of the epicenter. We are now joined by Kae Estes, a seismologist at the Mid-America Earthquake Center at Washington University in St. Louis. Tell me, Kae, does the magnitude of this earthquake surprise you?"

"For an area that has been relatively dormant for so long, the magnitude is a bit surprising, but it is certainly not unprecedented. One of the things that many of our viewers might not know, Tom, is that the highest earthquake risk in the United States, outside the West Coast, is along the New Madrid Fault. Damaging temblors are not as frequent as in California, but when they do occur, the destruction covers over 20 times the area of the California quakes due to the underlying geology."

"Kae, could you explain the extent of the fault line? And when is the last time that we had an earthquake in this area?"

"Sure. The New Madrid fault crosses five state lines and cuts across the Mississippi River in three places and the Ohio River in two places. The fault is active, averaging more than 200 measured events per year. Of course, most of these events only register 1.0 to 2.0 on the Richter scale. Every eighteen months the fault releases a shock of 4.0 or more, capable of local minor damage. Magnitudes of 5.0 or greater occur about once per decade, and can do significant damage and be felt in several states. It is very likely that this most recent quake will cause significant damage and unfortunately, it is highly likely there will be some loss of life."

"That's what I was going to ask you, Kae. Obviously we hate to speculate on casualties, but has there ever been an earthquake of this magnitude in the area?"

"There has...but certainly not in recent times. Histori-cally, this area has been associated with some of the largest earthquakes in North America. Four catastrophic earth-quakes, with magnitudes estimated in excess of 7.0, occurred during a three-month period between the years 1811 and 1812. Hundreds of aftershocks followed over a period of several years. The largest earthquakes that occurred since then were on January 4, 1843, and October 31, 1895, with magnitude estimates of 6.0 and 6.2 respectively."

Peter's eyes widened as he looked at the scenes unfolding on the television. Without saying a word, he cuddled up close to his mother and father on the couch, just as he used to when he was a little boy. All three of the Jangle family members spent the next two hours in near-silence in front of the television, before finally retiring to bed. Peter stared up at his ceiling as he lay in bed. "Please, God, don't let the Sandman come back," he whispered as he closed his eyes and went to sleep. It was a prayer that Peter recited often. Fear of the Sandman had consumed him since that fateful summer three years ago.

CHAPTER TWO

Two friends were traveling to Chicago; Jerry was heading south, and the women were staying in their hometown for the summer. Sarah Banks and Kathy Cohen were in the large kitchen of the Banks' house, preparing ham and cheese sandwiches for their friends at the beach. After spending time discussing the previous night's earthquake, the two girls turned the conversation to their plans for the summer.

"So...Are you and Peter planning on seeing a lot of each other over the summer?"

"You bet," Sarah answered with a smile. "We actually discussed us both working in Chicago this summer and sharing an apartment."

"Yes! Why don't you do that? It would give me a great place to crash on the weekends."

Kathy and Sarah had been best friends since the second grade. While Kathy knew that Peter cared for her friend, she had always been a bit put off by his smug attitude. She still resented the times when he had treated her mother, a schoolteacher at Michigan City High School, with disrespect. Kathy was fiercely loyal to her family and friends, and she was known to hold a grudge.

"Believe me, we seriously considered the Chicago thing, but the more we looked at the cost of apartments, it just wasn't that practical. At first Peter thought he would live at home and take the train in to Chicago. But now his plans have changed. He told me that Tom found a cheap apartment in the city they can share. So everything worked out well—they found a cheap place to live, and my dad's happy that I won't be in Chicago. He's excited that I'm going to be working with him at the bank this summer."

"Yikes! How do you feel about working with your dad?"

"I'm actually looking forward to it. I want to prove to Peter that he's not the only one who can spout economic theory at will. He's so consumed by high finance. I figure this will give me a chance to participate in his career aspirations."

Kathy turned away and threw her hands up in disgust, shaking her head. "Sarah, if you weren't my dear friend, I would swear that Peter was slowly sucking all the personality out of your pretty head. Remind me, what is 'captain economy' planning on doing this summer?"

"He's going to be working for a company called American Dinero."

"What's that? Some kind of Mexican restaurant?" Kathy replied sarcastically.

Sarah tried to hide her smile. She didn't want to encourage any more disparaging remarks.

"No. As a matter of fact, Peter told me that they're one of the largest institutional money managers in Chicago. Actually, it sounds like a great opportunity for him."

"Wow...the banker and the money manager...your dinner table conversations will be fascinating."

"You should talk, Kathy. Who would've ever believed that you'd be working for a law firm this year?"

"Well...I figure I need the training to keep all of you people who control the money out of jail."

Sarah smiled. Kathy Cohen had become increasingly liberal since going away to college. She continued to think that her mother, a divorced schoolteacher, was a member of the most under-appreciated class. She had also become very distrustful regarding money and politics. She believed that anyone choosing a banking or political career was driven by greed rather than passion.

Sarah neatly placed the twentieth ham and cheese sandwich snugly in the cooler, commenting, "I think this ought to be enough sandwiches."

"Should we take anything to drink?"

"You can grab some water if you want," Sarah replied. "I'm sure the boys will have brought plenty of beer." She rolled her eyes in a disapproving manner.

"Beer, sun, and boys. Thank goodness summer is upon us."

Kathy grabbed the beach towels, leaving Sarah to carry the cooler.

"Let me get the door," Kathy offered, as she pulled the sliding glass door open. Sarah Banks' house stood on a large hill on the east side of Lake Shore Drive. The large glass windows that lined the back of the house offered the type of beachfront views usually reserved for residents of the Atlantic and Pacific coasts of the United States.

The two girls paused to admire the unencumbered view of Lake Michigan. The three-foot high dune grass that was growing on the opposite side of Lake Shore Drive obscured most of the beach. The girls carefully walked down the thirty-three steps that led from the house to the road. A man in his forties jogged by and waved at the girls crossing the street. His lingering gaze didn't go unnoticed. Both girls smiled, without having to say a word. The sounds of loud music and laughter could be heard in the distance as they navigated their way through a narrow path in the dune grass that led down to the beach.

"The food's here!" Tom Nelson cried out.

"And a mighty fine presentation, I might add," offered Jerry Parker, his eyes fixed upon the supple young bodies of Sarah and Kathy. If anything, Sarah's body had firmed even more through her three years of college, and Kathy's shorter frame was chiseled like a long-distance runner's. This tight-knit group of friends had gathered at the beach each summer since graduating from Michigan City High School. All had elected to attend colleges in their home state of Indiana.

Although Peter trusted each of his friends, he had never discussed his secret encounter, three years ago, with the genie he called "Sandman." He had hoped to put behind him the awful events that had taken the lives of many people. Sarah Banks and Peter's dad were the only ones with whom he had shared the story. The experience had been enlightening, educational, and terrifying for him. The mere remembrance of the past events sent chills down his spine. The genie had helped Peter influence the U.S. economy through his covert position as the Chairman of the Federal Reserve Board. Peter had always been a star athlete, but as a result of his experiences with the genie, Peter had refocused on his education.

He finished his senior year of high school ranked in the top five percent of his class academically. Perhaps more significant than his educational growth, was the increased spiritual growth Peter had realized over the year. He learned how easily he could be fooled into rationalizing his actions. He vowed he would never be deceived by evil again. He had just finished his third year at the University of Notre Dame, and he was assuming a summer intern position at one of the largest institutional asset management companies in the country. He was determined to use his knowledge to advance his career.

"Let me help you with that," Peter offered, grabbing the cooler from Sarah's hands. Peter looked into Sarah's eyes and whispered, "Are you sure you don't want to share an apartment with me in Chicago this summer?"

"Peter, you know that none our parents really wanted us to share an apartment. Besides, I thought that Tom was going to be living with you this summer."

"He is. It just scares me a bit. I think Tom's planning on us hosting a party apartment in Chicago. To be honest, I don't want people frolicking through our apartment at all hours of the night. I'm incredibly lucky to have landed my job this summer. It's exactly what I want to do after I get out of school. I don't want to risk messing it up."

"Well, you better make sure you behave yourself," Sarah said, as she put her arm around Peter's shoulders. "I don't want you messing up, either."

Tom Nelson and Jerry Parker trotted toward the two to retrieve a sandwich from the cooler. "So Sarah, did Peter tell you that he and I are going to be housemates this summer?"

"I don't know, Tom. Maybe you should stay here and work for my dad, and I'll live in Chicago and work for your dad's company."

"No, Sarah, I really think your dad wants you at the bank." Tom smiled. "The neat thing about my job this summer is that I'm not really going to be working with my dad. As a pharmaceutical rep, my dad's main job is to drive around and try to get doctors to prescribe the company's products. I'm going to be helping out at the headquarters in Chicago. They said that I might even be able to do some work at their plant in Joliet. Talk about a neat experience. I'll get to see how all of the drugs are made."

"Just be sure you don't help yourself to any of the samples," Jerry joked, pushing at Tom's shoulder. "That's how my old man ended up in prison."

Feeling left out of the conversation, Kathy Cohen grabbed Jerry by the arm. "I haven't even heard what *you're* doing this summer, Jerry. Are you going to stay around here and keep me and Sarah company?"

"I wish." Jerry smiled. "No. I'm going to be working with Hoosier Insurance down in Indianapolis this summer. One of my profs from IU helped arrange the job for me. And Sarah is going to let me stay at her apartment in Indy at a very reasonable rent. I'm looking forward to it. Indy is a neat city."

"Any city is a neat city compared to Bloomington, Indiana," Kathy said. "Maybe I'll meet you down there some time this summer to take you on a tour of the 'premier' state university in West Lafayette."

"Oh, Boiler up, Kathy," Tom shot back.

Not wanting to listen to another school rivalry debate, Sarah intervened. "I'm just glad you can use the apartment, Jerry. Just be sure you don't trash it. I'll need to find a roommate for next year when school starts."

"I'll tell ya, buddy," Tom said, putting his arm around Jerry. "When I met you three years ago, I never would have imagined that you and I would be going to the same college together."

Tom was a white kid from the suburbs of Michigan City; Jerry was a black kid who grew up in a tough section of Gary, Indiana. Their first encounter was on the football field their senior year of high school. They immediately clashed. Despite their initial hostility, the two had become close friends over the past three years.

Tom Nelson and Jerry Parker had both just finished their junior year at Indiana University. Jerry was the first in his family to attend college, and he maintained a solid "B" average as a finance major. Tom, a marketing major, was holding his own, with a 2.75 grade point average. Kathy Cohen, who started at Purdue University intending to graduate with an education major, had shifted her focus and was now contemplating law school after graduation. While her mother had not discouraged her from pursuing an education degree, she *did* encourage her to explore other options.

Sarah Banks, meanwhile, was studying communications at Butler University in Indianapolis. She was initially reluctant to accept a job with her father at Michigan City National Bank. She had always been a bit self-conscious over the fact that she was blessed with good looks and money. She went out of her way to avoid being labeled as pretentious. While she understood that her parents wanted her to earn money after college, her real passion was serving others through charitable work and community service. Her father recognized her passion and assured her that he would not grant any preferential treatment at the bank. He promised that the job would provide her the opportunity to use her communication skills in the community relations and marketing areas of the bank.

Although each of the five young adults had chosen to study at Indiana-based colleges, Peter still believed that a brighter future awaited him on one of the United States' coasts. While the other kids were talking behind him, Peter grabbed a beer from one of the coolers and looked out across the lake. The waves gently lapped up on the shore. The Lake Michigan shoreline played a prominent role in some of his fondest memories. He remembered his parents bringing him down to the beach as a young child. The immensity of the lake was both intimidating and an inviting respite from the hot summer sun. In his youth, Peter and his friends often escaped to the beach to avoid the watchful eyes of their parents. Although he loved his parents dearly, the beach offered a world of independence for a teenager trying to discover himself. This was his home. He knew it would always provide a certain comfort.

But the beach also rekindled memories of horror. He remembered that the beach was where he had first encountered the genie that he called "Sandman." He remembered the "inflation creation monster" that he himself had been responsible for unleashing in the waters of Lake Michigan. He remembered the last terror-stricken moments of his friend, Steve Shindler. Steve had struggled in vain to keep his head above water, fighting the tight grip of the monster intent on pulling him down to the depths of the lake.

Looking down, Peter saw the broken fragments of shells that lined the part of the beach where the sand meets the water. Grabbing a flat, round stone, he tilted his body, cocked his arm, and hurled the rock over the motionless body of water. He counted eight times that the rock skipped up from the surface of the lake before finally plunging out of sight. A soft touch upon his shoulder suddenly interrupted his quiet thoughts.

"You still think about him, don't you?"

Without turning away from the lake, Peter recognized Sarah's voice. "I don't think that I have the right to forget him."

"Are you talking about Steve, or are you talking about the Sandman?" Sarah asked, recalling the self-appointed name that the genie had declared.

"Both," Peter replied. "I can't forget either one of them. They were both my responsibility."

"Well then, let's not forget them." Turning to face the others, Sarah raised the clear plastic bottle of water in her hand and exclaimed, "Here's to Steve Shindler! The unforgettable kicker of the Michigan City Red Devils, and an unforgettable friend." They all raised their drinks, and a chorus of "Hear! Hear!" echoed over the stillness of the lake.

For a brief period of time, Peter's mind was once again at ease, as he and his friends discussed both their past and their futures. They knew the next week would offer a test—they would find out whether their college education had prepared them for the real world.

CHAPTER THREE

The Jangles routinely started their Sunday morning by attending church together as a family. After mass and a bountiful Sunday brunch, Peter packed his bags for his new job.

"Come on, Peter, if you're all ready, I'll drive you to the train station," David Jangle called from the kitchen.

Peter's parents had convinced him that there was no reason to have a car in Chicago, since his apartment was a short seven blocks from the Randolph Street train station. Although few words were spoken, there was clear pride in David Jangle as he and Peter exchanged glances on their way to the train station. Upon reaching their destination, Peter said his good-bye. David reached over to pull Peter close.

"I'm incredibly proud of you. You know that, don't you?"

Peter smiled in response and said, "Thanks, Dad. I'll let you know when I get settled."

Peter wondered if he should discuss the genie with his dad before he left. He decided against it. The genie was in the past. He was now embarking on a new beginning.

After opening the car door, Peter grabbed his suitcase in one hand, strapped a garment bag across his shoulder, and walked into the train station with nervous anticipation. He stopped for a moment and wondered if he should have said more to acknowledge his father's pride. Perhaps he should have told his father how much he loved him. *He knows I love him*, Peter thought to himself. *I don't need to say anything.* His thoughts quickly shifted to the opportunity that awaited him in the Chicago financial district.

As he looked around the train station, Peter's thoughts once again drifted from the future to the past. He remembered the hometown pride in his father's voice as he told him about the origins of the South Shore Railroad. At the beginning of the 20th Century, the east coast and midwest relied on electric interurban railways to travel from one urban center to another. However, competition from the steam railroads and the newly popular automobile soon drained ridership. Most all of the original electric rails went bankrupt. The South Shore Railroad was bankrupt until a man named Samuel Insull purchased the railroad at a public auction in June, 1925, and renamed it The Chicago South Shore and South Bend Railroad. The rail connected Chicago with South Bend, Indiana. Mr. Insull upgraded the cars, built new stations, and converted the railroad from AC electric system to its current 1500 volt DC system. Unfortunately, the improvements could not overcome the challenges of the market economy.

The railroad's history continued to mirror the economic history of northwest Indiana, and the SouthShore Railroad entered bankruptcy during the days of the Great Depression. The eventual economic recovery once again breathed new life into the railroad. It was operating profitably by 1938.

Today, the South Shore is controlled by the public transportation sector; profit is no longer the overriding motivation. In 1977, the Indiana General Assembly created the Northern Indiana Commuter Transportation District (NICTD) to rescue the ailing South Shore. NICTD operates the rail as a public service because it was determined that the people and the economy of northwest Indiana needed an alternative, reliable form of transportation to get to jobs, schools, museums, and recreational opportunities found in the great city of Chicago.

Stepping onto the train, Peter realized that he had now joined the many northern Indiana commuters riding into Chicago for job opportunities not available in their own hometowns. He was thankful that the state had saved the train system, and happy that some of his friends from high school were now employed at the South Shore station. In fact, the original Chicago South Shore & South Bend Railroad had now morphed into a strategically located shoreline carrier connecting northern Indiana's industrial complex with twenty various transcontinental, regional, and local railroads. The freight business was headquartered in Michigan City. Although the freight line is not affiliated with the passenger service provided by the NICTD, Peter was happy that it was providing jobs for local residents.

After approximately eight minutes, the train stopped at the Ogden Dunes station. Peter knew that the large sand dune, Mount Baldy, resided just beyond the trees. Peter remembered the dune as the place where he had first encountered the genie who had caused him so much trouble years ago. Nonetheless, the genie had inspired Peter to learn about the economy and study harder in school. Peter supposed that the genie had indirectly helped him in an unintended manner.

Peter laid his head against the window of the gently swaying train as it continued its scheduled stops on the way to Chicago. The train was not particularly crowded on this Sunday afternoon, since it was a day of rest for the workforce. A few families with small children boarded the train at Gary, Indiana. Peter figured they must be headed to some of the museums in Chicago. As the train passed the large steel mills of East Chicago, Peter once again recalled the stories his father had told him. When America entered the Second World War, the railroad experienced its best years ever. Trains operated around the clock to take riders to work in one of the many steel mills lining the south shore of Lake Michigan. Today there are far fewer steel mills in operation. The noise of the train wheels against the steel rails lulled Peter to a restful state. He was proud that despite drastic changes in the economy, the South Shore Railroad continued to roll on.

As Peter slowly drifted off to sleep, he remembered some of the other stories his father used to tell him. His father loved telling childhood memories of growing up in Michigan City, and meeting Don Larsen. At least one time each year, his father would sit down with Peter and play the tape of Game Five of the 1956 World Series between the New York Yankees and the Brooklyn Dodgers. Larsen set a major league record that day by pitching the only perfect game ever recorded in post-season play. Peter loved to hear his dad describe the final out. *With two outs in the ninth inning, Larsen faced pinch hitter Dale Mitchell, a .311 career hitter. Larsen quickly put Mitchell in the hole, with a ball one, strike two count. Larsen's next pitch was perfectly positioned on the upper, outside corner of the plate. A called strike! Mitchell stood with his bat on his shoulder for the third and final out.* David Jangle used to tell stories of how his older brother played in little league baseball games with Larsen, before Larsen and his family moved out to San Diego in 1944. The memories brought a smile to Peter's face as he drifted off to sleep.

After a few more stops, Peter was awakened by the train conductor's announcement that they had reached the Randolph Street station in Chicago. The end of the line. For Peter, however, this was just the beginning.

CHAPTER FOUR

J erry Parker turned off Interstate 94 to head south on Interstate 65 towards Indianapolis. A few miles more on Interstate 94 and he would have been at the exit of his hometown, Gary, Indiana. Although it had been only five years since his mother had moved him to Michigan City, it seemed like an eternity since he had been a full-fledged member of the Vice Lords gang in Gary. He was now in his third year of college, and soon to start an internship at an insurance company. He laughed at the irony, while turning up the volume of the "Snoop Dogg" disc spinning in the CD player.

After leaving the outskirts of Merrillville, Indiana, Jerry knew that most of the remaining trip was nothing but rustic farmland and open plains. He stopped to get a cup of coffee, to make sure the drive would not put him to sleep. Jerry had met a few kids from small rural farm communities on the campus of Indiana University. He would laugh as they described the drunken mischief that amused them in their provincial hometowns. He understood the major difference between his childhood and theirs. *They had nothing to fear as they wandered the streets of their hometowns. At the same time, he knew that they feared his hometown. And despite their false bravado and outward signs of kindness, he couldn't help but think that they secretly feared him.* "We all distrust that which we don't know," he recalled Tom Nelson telling him. He knew Tom was right. He also knew that he had a responsibility to make a difference.

People seem to focus on each other's differences until they find a common purpose. He now was fortunate to be one of those who had a purpose. He was going to be a college graduate, and he was destined for a successful business career. *No one would be able to take his accomplishments away from him.*

The three and one-half hour drive from Michigan City to Indianapolis seemed like an eternity. Upon arriving in Indianapolis, Jerry exited onto Meridian Street. He reminisced about the first time he had seen the large mansions that lined the street. The Michigan City Red Devils were preparing for the state football championship, and he had secretly wished that one day he would be living in similar luxurious surroundings.

Reaching his destination, Jerry stepped out of the car and looked up at the Indianapolis skyline. Though not as grand as Chicago, Indianapolis offered opportunity not available in Michigan City. Slamming the car door shut, Jerry nodded his head in quiet confidence. He knew that this was a place where he could make a difference.

✳ ✳ ✳

The streets of Chicago were bustling with people as Peter tried to navigate his way with a suitcase in his left hand and a large blue and gold garment bag strapped over his right shoulder. He didn't want to look like a tourist, and he realized that his suitcase would likely signal that he was not a Chicago native. He walked quickly—and proudly—down Randolph Street, trying to avoid prolonged eye contact with the strangers who passed in front of him. Still, the energy of the city was already beginning to invigorate him. The sudden rumbling sound of the Chicago "EL" above his head suggested the power behind this great city. Crossing State Street and heading toward Dearborn, he couldn't help but notice the diversity in the people. Poles, African-Americans, Germans, Latinos, Jews, and Indians – the city welcomed all, and gave everyone an equal shot at success and failure.

Walking south on Dearborn, Peter resisted the temptation to look up and stare at the architectural magnificence of the Daley Center, the Chase Building, and other large skyscrapers that lined the street. Nonetheless, he could not prevent a smile from crossing his lips as he realized the tremendous opportunities that awaited him in the city of big shoulders. Continuing south, past Adams Street, he began wondering when he would finally reach his apartment for the summer.

He grinned and tried to stifle a laugh as he caught sight of the building that Tom had secured for the summer. *This is living,* he thought to himself. With his suitcase in hand, he jostled his way through the revolving door, proceeded to the elevator, and pushed the button for the 17th floor. After Peter knocked three times, the door swung open, revealing Tom who exclaimed with a smile, "Welcome to your new digs, bro!"

Tom immediately handed Peter a beer and proudly spread out his arms and asked, "Dude, what do you think of the place?"

"Not bad," Peter replied. "How'd you get this place so cheap?"

"Care4 leases a couple of apartments here for executives. Their main headquarters is in the Chase building up the street. My dad was able to get us in here at a subsidized rent level."

"Cool. What do you say we give Jerry Parker a call and see if he's at his place in Indy yet?"

Jerry Parker's cell phone rang, temporarily interrupting his efforts at unpacking his belongings. "Jerry! It's Peter. Tom and I are both here at our place in Chicago. Did you get to Indy yet?"

"Yeah. I just got here a little while ago. I'm unpacking."

"You won't believe this place. I'm looking out our window at the Chicago skyline right now. We're right in the middle of the financial district. I can see the Chase building where Tom's going to work." Jerry started laughing.

"What's so funny?"

"I'm staring at another Chase building here in Indy. These banks are getting as big as Starbucks, Walgreens, CVS and McDonalds. They're everywhere."

"Yeah...too big to fail." Peter replied.

"It's kind of ironic that all of these big cities have lost their local banks, and yet... Michigan City National Bank stands tall in our home town."

"Yeah, that's about the only thing we still have at home."

Jerry was used to Peter's negative spin on his home town. Quick to change the subject, he asked, "Have you called

Sarah yet to find out if she's fired up about starting her job at the bank?"

"Not yet. I'm sure she's doing fine. She'll probably come here or I'll go home most weekends to see her. What about you? Are you planning on going home much on the weekends?"

"Sure. I'll want to check in on my mother. But it's a much longer drive for me to get home than it is for you. So, do you start work tomorrow?"

"Yeah. Of course, it looks like Tom has already started the party tonight."

"Well, give him my best. You guys be careful up there. Thanks for calling."

Hanging up the phone, Peter thought about calling Sarah to see how she was doing. However, he was quickly interrupted. Tom pulled Peter by the arm, prodding him. "What do you say we go check out the scenery at Grant Park?" The two boys immediately grabbed their keys and left the apartment.

CHAPTER FIVE

Peter Jangle woke up two hours early for his first day of work. Getting out of bed and dropping to the floor, he completed thirty push-ups and fifty sit-ups before entering the shower. Peter was the type of kid who lived in his body instead of his head. Physical activity gave his life measurable results. He cared about winning, whether it was on the football field or in the boardroom. But the genie had taught him something new. He now realized that he needed to gain knowledge, not just muscle, in order to be successful. He was looking forward to his first foray into the corporate world.

After finishing his shower, Peter went to his closet to pick out his best suit and tie. He wanted to make a good impression on his first day. He sat down and applied black polish to his new dress shoes. He grabbed an iron and a new can of starch to press a perfect crease in his white dress shirt.

Thirty minutes later, Peter eagerly opened the large mahogany door to the entrance of American Dinero, conveniently located one block from the Chicago Board of Trade. He was immediately greeted by the thundering voice of a large man striding confidently toward him. "You must be Peter!" The man glanced quickly at his watch and exclaimed, "Right on time! Follow me to my office so we can talk a bit about what I'd like you to work on this summer."

Peter walked briskly to keep up with the pace being set by Francis Solli. He remembered their initial interview on the campus at Notre Dame, when Mr. Solli spent most of the time talking about his old college football days. Immediately behind the reception area was a large glass-enclosed conference room. There were two smaller conference areas to each side of the large room. Mr. Solli led Peter down one of the aisles separating the large conference room from the smaller client areas. They passed through a maze of open-walled cubicles. Peter kept close to Mr. Solli to hear his voice over the loud chatter of collegial conversation. Peter could see that the desks inside the cubicles were buried under piles of newspapers and research reports. A long oval-shaped table was positioned directly behind the large conference room, directly in front of Mr. Solli's large corner office. Six young men were seated around the oval table, with phones plastered to their ears, and their eyes fixed on the Bloomberg terminals in front of them. Along each back wall, extending from Fran Solli's office, were rows of glass-enclosed offices. Fran strode purposely ahead of Peter to his office, without any introductions to those in the room. Upon reaching his office, Fran motioned for Peter to sit down, as he closed the door behind them. The windows behind Fran Solli's desk looked out at the Chicago skyline. Fran took a seat in his tan, high-back leather chair and propped his Cole Haan loafers on the edge of his mahogany desk. Peter was impressed.

"You guys have a great view of the skyline here, Mr. Solli!"

"Thank you," he replied. "And please, call me Fran."

"So what do you know about the money management business, Peter?"

Remembering the experience the genie had given him as Chairman of the Federal Reserve, Peter answered, "I've never worked for a money management firm, but I'm pretty familiar with the workings of the Fed, and how they adjust the money supply to affect the economy."

"Oh really? Well, I'll tell you, Peter, if you think that you can predict interest rate movements, you can certainly make a lot of money in this business."

Peter remembered the lessons the genie had taught him regarding interest rates. Peter pictured a seesaw. If interest rates go down, bond prices rise; If bond prices rise, bond investors make money. He also remembered it was not easy to predict interest rates. He remembered being confused when the financial markets were driving long-term interest rates higher, despite his efforts, as Chairman of the Federal Reserve, to lower short-term rates.

"I never said that I could predict interest rates. I just think that I have a pretty good grasp about why they move."

"Well, good for you. And do you know what causes stock prices to move?"

"Well, I follow the markets, and I've read a lot of invest-ment books. Stocks move for all kinds of reasons. They might move for macroeconomic reasons, or fundamental reasons within the company, or events within the industry. I've even studied a bit about technical analysis, and learned how stock prices might move based on historical stock charts."

Peter wondered if he had answered Mr. Solli's question correctly. Thankfully, the response he received seemed encouraging.

"Good for you. You seem to have a pretty good knowledge of the markets. I think I'm going to have you initially assisting our stock and bond analysts this summer. But first let me explain a bit about our company and how we're set up. As you probably know, American Dinero is one of the largest U.S-based money managers. We manage over $450 billion in assets. Approximately $100 billion is managed here in Chicago. We passed the trading area on our way to my office. I'll introduce you to those guys later. Of the six guys gathered there, we have one mortgage-backed trader, two corporate bond traders, one municipal bond trader, one guy who trades government and agency bonds, and another who trades equities. The desk is headed by a guy named Tony Salami."

Wanting to impress his boss for the summer, Peter asked, "Does American Dinero trade any private placement securities?"

"We buy traditional privates for some of our accounts, but those are mostly buy-and-hold. They don't trade much. As far as 144A-securities, those are traded by our corporate traders."

Realizing he was reaching the limit of his knowledge, Peter just nodded in acknowledgment.

"As you can see, the traders are situated in the middle of the floor. The portfolio managers sit in the offices along the walls to my left. This gives them easy access to the traders. Each portfolio manager has an assistant. Those are the people sitting in the cubicles to the left of the traders. The traders also have a couple of assistants who settle the trades. On the other side of the floor, to the right, are our analysts. Those are the people you'll be working with. We currently have four fixed income analysts and six equity analysts. Our analysts all report to Terri Tanaka. We also have our research library over there."

"Does everyone work together? Or do they work on separate projects?" Peter asked.

"Good question! It's extremely important that we all work as a team. Our analysts talk to sell-side analysts to come up with new ideas, or to get insight into companies that we own. Both our traders and our portfolio managers have contact with sell-side brokers to get ideas. The traders, portfolio managers, and analysts all hold separate meetings to discuss ideas. Then they bring their best ideas to meetings where we all gather to discuss overall strategy and tactical adjustments. I think you'll find the whole process very interesting."

"I look forward to it."

Fran Solli then removed his feet the the top of his desk and leaned forward toward Peter, looking him in the eye as if trying to probe his very soul. He said in a soft whisper, "You know what you have to remember, Peter?"

"What?"

"We're all pigs."

At first Peter didn't know how to react, but then Fran broke into a smile and started laughing. "Okay, you're a Notre Dame student. I'm sure you've read the George Orwell novel *Animal Farm,* haven't you?"

It was one of Peter's favorite books, and he quickly answered, "Yes."

"Good. That's what we've got here. Think of me as Old Major, the old pig whose visionary dream inspires the animals with their first concept of revolution."

Growing more comfortable with his new boss, Peter interrupted, "But Old Major died early in the book."

"Okay. I'm not quite that old. I'm a Young Major." Fran shot a quick glance at Peter to make sure he understood the humor. "The point is that I've got to instill the vision. I need to inspire these other animals to work as a team. It's not always easy. Our revolution in the money management business is to discard the 'efficient market theory' you read about in your textbooks. We look for trading advantages that we can exploit. The trick is to work around everyone's individual ego. What I want to do is minimize the competition among ourselves, and use our competitive spirit to beat other market participants. You need to remember that for every trade, there's usually a winner and a loser. We obviously want to win more than we lose."

Peter sat opposite Fran, trying to recall the novel. He remembered that after Old Major died, Napoleon and the other pigs took control. Peter also remembered that the pigs reinterpreted Old Major's original philosophy for their own self-benefit. Peter didn't know why Fran would use this analogy to describe a firm where he was still in control. Peter felt compelled to ask the question.

"Are any of the people here similar to Napoleon in the novel?"

Fran smiled and replied. "That's a scary thought, isn't it?

Fran stood up and pointed out to the trading desk.

"See those traders out there? Our head trader, Tony Salami, best resembles Napoleon. He's a good guy. But he's very opinionated. The traders have the biggest egos, because they battle with the street every day, always trying to get a better price. They regard this business as a war. They come to work every day prepared for battle.

"Tony would love to have full control over the portfolios. The traders believe that every trade they make is going to be a good trade. I want them to believe that! But I also need to control our risk. Risk control lies with the portfolio managers—the guys with the client contact. It's their responsibility to ensure that the traders don't take unnecessary risk. Remember, in the novel, Napoleon is overcome by greed and becomes too power-hungry. I don't want that to happen here."

"So who would represent the portfolio managers in the book?"

"Okay, no one really controlled Napoleon in the novel, so my analogy is a bit flawed. Nonetheless, I do believe that there were some interesting characters that might match our portfolio managers. Remember the goat, Muriel? She was the farm animal who read better than the 'common animals.' Her advanced reading ability gave her authoritative control over the other animals. That same 'authoritative control' strokes the egos of our portfolio managers. They like the limelight. We work hard to promote them on the business channels, like Bloomberg or CNBC, to tout their 'investment expertise.'"

"But Muriel never restrained Napoleon from assuming power," Peter objected.

For the first time, a sincere look of disappointment crossed Fran's face.

"No, that's the problem," he replied. "Muriel wasn't inspired enough to take action to oppose the pigs."

"So who controls the traders?" Peter asked.

"Hopefully, by the time you're done working here this summer, you can tell me. The analysts tend to be the ones least influenced by the traders."

Peter mentally prepared himself for another character analogy. He wasn't disappointed.

"Do you remember the gloomy, cynical donkey, named Benjamin, in the novel? He never embraced the Revolution. Our bond guys usually look skeptical when our stock guys start singing the tune of a 'new paradigm.' You'll notice a philosophical difference between our equity analysts and our bond analysts. Our equity analysts tend to be overly optimistic. They always think the economy will overcome any temporary obstacles. It's probably psychological. As long as the economy does well, their stocks will do well. They typically prefer to play offense, rather than defense. This means that sometimes they purchase stocks based on price momentum, rather than fundamental value. It can work for a while, but it's a dangerous game."

"So how are the bond analysts different?"

"They aren't sucked in by the traders' propaganda as quickly as the equity guys. They tend to be more pessimistic. A slow economy doesn't bother them. A slowdown usually means lower interest rates, which translates to better bond returns. In addition, even if the companies that they invest in do extremely well, the positive investment return is limited by the face value of the bond they receive at maturity. So they don't get overly optimistic. Rather, they worry over any potential risk that might result in their bonds failing to pay in full at maturity."

Peter glanced at his watch. He was enjoying the conversation, but he was eager to meet the other folks on the floor. He didn't want to form too quick an opinion of the others without meeting them. He couldn't wait to relay some of this conversation to his professors at Notre Dame. It certainly offered a view of the money management business unlike anything he had read in his school textbooks.

"And this brings us to our final cast of characters," Mr. Solli continued. "Remember the two horses, Boxer and Clover, in the novel?"

Fran didn't wait for Peter to answer.

"They were the two faithful workhorses. The problem was that they didn't think things out for themselves. Once the horses accepted the pigs as their teachers, they absorbed everything that they were told, and passed it on to the other animals by simple arguments."

"Yes, I remember," Peter replied. "How does that apply here?"

"Sometimes I worry that our analysts aren't coming up with enough original ideas. I hope that's not the case. Nevertheless, I want to be sure that the traders aren't pressuring our analysts to write positive research reports, just because the trader thinks a certain stock or bond is cheap. I want our analysts doing their own independent research."

Fran leaned forward on his desk and looked intently at Peter.

"Peter, I want you to challenge the traders and portfolio managers on their ideas. And I want you to come up with good ideas on your own."

"I don't know how many of your people will listen to a summer intern," Peter replied, hoping that Fran would reconsider the request.

"Don't you worry about that," Fran replied. "I'll make sure they listen. Here's what I want you to watch for. I'm concerned that some of our analysts have career aspirations to be portfolio managers. I don't want to discourage their aspirations, but I worry that they hesitate to contradict the existing traders and portfolio managers out of fear that it'll damage their career. It's my job to ensure that they remain independent. Do you remember what happened to Boxer in the novel?"

Peter nodded. He recalled that Boxer's life ended with a trip to the glue factory. Peter could think of nothing more to say.

Likewise, for the first time in what seemed like two hours, Fran Solli fell silent. As the two stared at each other, Peter nodded his head, as if to acknowledge his charge for the summer. "Well… Okay then," Fran summed up. "What do you say we go meet the cast of characters?"

Peter swallowed hard. He knew that the world he was about to enter differed dramatically from the supportive family environment he had just left.

CHAPTER SIX

"Welcome aboard." Mitch Gaffigan extended his hand as he met Jerry Parker in the main lobby of Hoosier Insurance. The company headquarters was prominently located on Monument Circle, the epicenter of downtown Indianapolis. Jerry knew that Mr. Gaffigan had graduated from Indiana University. He quickly sized up Mitch as a stereotypical rural Hoosier, undoubtedly raised on some Indiana farm. Jerry hoped that he would not be viewed as the token minority at the company.

"So you live in Michigan City, is that correct?"

"Yes," Jerry replied as the two boarded the elevator to go up to the fourth floor executive suite.

"Did you feel any impact of the earthquake up north?"

"We felt the tremors. In fact, the newspaper ran an article about two people lying on a sand dune when the earthquake hit. They were nearly buried alive. They said that the dune actually moved a few inches as a result of the quake. Did you feel a stronger impact down here?"

"There was minor property damage to some homes, and they're still not letting folks back into some of the older office buildings until they check for structural damage. Still, we certainly didn't suffer the devastation they experienced in southern Missouri, Illinois, Tennessee and Kentucky. I think the most recent death toll I've heard is 238 people. And they're still experiencing significant flooding around the Mississippi River."

The two continued to talk as they walked out of the elevator and entered the reception area through two glass doors. Jerry smiled as they walked past a young and attractive blonde receptionist. Jerry noticed the name plate, indicating that the receptionist's name was Linda. He made a mental note of her name and then continued to follow Mr. Gaffigan to his spacious corner office. The office offered a panoramic view of the reflecting ponds that accented Monument Circle. The clear, blue sky shimmered brilliantly in the water. Jerry noticed various groups of people congregating around the park-like setting. Not wanting to get distracted, Jerry continued the conversation.

"Did the earthquake have a big impact on your company?"

"Well, we don't write property and casualty insurance, so it won't have much of an impact on us. I'm sure we'll have some death claims and some health-related claims. To be honest though, this isn't the time to be worrying about the financial impact on our company. The main thing is to ensure that we care for our policyholders as best we can. We also have our employees to consider. Some of our employees have family in the area, and we also have some agents who live in the area. We're obviously concerned about their well-being. This is the first business day since the quake, so we won't know much more until we have time to get an accurate assessment."

"Is there anything I can do to help out?"

"Well, we might have you fill in for some of the people planning time off to check on their loved ones. My original plan was for you to work in the investment area, down on our third floor. I want you to assist our credit analysts. Why don't you give me an idea of what you know about the life and health insurance business?"

On the defensive, Jerry replied, "Well, I've taken an insurance course in school. So I know the basics, but that's about it."

"Well, like many financial institutions, our largest balance sheet asset is our investment portfolio. When we collect premiums from our policyholders, we need to invest those dollars in a profitable manner. The earnings on our investments are used to build our capital base and pay our policyholders when they have claims. Like I said before, we write both life insurance and health insurance. Each of these different types of insurance has different claim characteristics. When you write health insurance, you can expect claims every year. Each year a certain percentage of people are going to get sick. Additionally, you have people who are going to go to their doctors for a check-up, and you have people who are prescribed certain medications on a regular basis. Since these claims are short-term in nature, we tend to invest the associated premium dollars relatively short-term, and relatively conservative."

"On the other hand, life claims tend to be longer-term in nature. If someone buys life insurance at age thirty, you hope that person will live well into his seventies. That gives you forty years to invest the money before you have to pay any claims. In addition, we also sell investment products where the policyholder gets to participate in our investment performance. Obviously these funds are invested consistent with the description of the product being sold. At present, we have an eighteen billion dollar investment portfolio. You'll be working with our analysts to determine appropriate investment alternatives. Do you have any questions?"

"No, I look forward to it."

"Good. I'll take you down to the third floor and introduce you to the people that you'll be working with."

CHAPTER SEVEN

Sarah tried on three different outfits before selecting the perfect business attire for her first day of work. She decided to pin her hair up in a bun to cast a more professional appearance. She rode to work with her father. It was just past 7:15 a.m. when they pulled into the bank parking lot and parked in the first spot, reserved for Steve Banks.

"Now I don't want you to embarrass me." Sarah chided her father playfully as she tugged on his arm.

"Don't worry, my sweet. I expect big things from you. I want to see the results of all that money I'm paying for your education." Steve Banks held the door open for his daughter as they walked into the main lobby of Michigan City National Bank.

"Good morning, Mr. Banks," came the greeting from Ms. Sanders, personal assistant to Steve Banks for the past twenty-one years. Ms. Sanders was an overweight, matronly-looking woman with a stoic face. Sarah always thought that she looked much older than her 58 years of age. An extremely high cholesterol level had resulted in three stents being placed in her heart over the past five years. Having never been married, and living alone, Ms. Sanders depended on her job for health care. As a result, Steve Banks felt a moral responsibility to keep her employed, even though current technology had more or less passed her by. Ms. Sanders was grateful for the opportunity, and dutifully protected Mr. Banks. Despite her struggles with all the new technology, she served well as gatekeeper to the President of the Bank.

"And how are you doing, Sarah?" Ms. Sanders firmly grasped each of Sarah's shoulders with her over-sized hands. Sarah was surprised by the strength of Ms. Sanders' grasp.

"Are you looking forward to working with us this summer?"

Sarah just nodded her head, not wanting to say anything that might cause the grip on her shoulders to tighten.

"Sarah is going to be working in the Trust Department with Doug Keyster," her father proudly replied. "I was wondering if you could go show her where Doug sits."

Ms. Sanders led Sarah to the elevator for a ride to the fourth floor trust department. Sarah smiled at her father as the elevator door closed, relieved that she would not be escorted as daddy's little girl for the remainder of the day.

Upon reaching the fourth floor, Sarah followed Ms. Sanders through a maze of cubicles before finally reaching a walled-in office at the northeast corner of the floor. Through the glass, Sarah spotted Doug Keyster, the President of Lakeshore Fund Management. Doug confidently had his feet propped on the corner of his desk, intently reading *The Wall Street Journal*.

"Excuse me, Doug. I thought you might want to meet Steve Banks' daughter, Sarah. She just completed her junior year at Butler University, and I understand she's going to be working with you in the Trust Department this summer."

Doug Keyster removed his feet from his desk and, with quiet conviction, proceeded to stand up, never taking his eyes off Sarah. Walking over to her, he cupped Sarah's extended hand on both sides and looked directly into her eyes.

"It will be a great pleasure working with you this summer, Sarah. We have a lot of exciting projects going on here, and I'm sure we'll be able to get you some interesting work." Returning Doug's gaze, Sarah took notice of his beautiful blue eyes, charming face, and Cheshire cat grin. The fifteen seconds he held her hand seemed like fifteen minutes.

"I look forward to it," Sarah responded, fixing her gaze on the handsome young man in front of her.

"So, Sarah, has your dad explained to you what we do here in the trust department?"

"Well, I know that you invest money for people."

"Well then, I guess you know all there is to know," Doug Keyster said with a smile. Sarah's gaze remained fixed on Doug's eyes. Although he was twelve years her senior, Doug had obviously kept himself in shape since his college days. Doug stood six feet-five inches tall and was an avid basketball player and exercise junkie. In fact, he was more than willing to engage in stories about his college basketball days at DePauw University, where he had been a two-year starter. Sarah also noticed that Doug didn't wear a wedding ring.

Growing self-conscious at the realization she was staring, Sarah quickly added, "Actually, my boyfriend is working in the investment area at American Dinero this summer."

"Wow! Good for him." Doug moved closer to Sarah, peering into her eyes. "So you have a boyfriend, eh? How serious are you two?"

Sarah was growing increasingly uncomfortable with the conversation. Her heart was beginning to race, and she instinctively looked away to break eye contact with Doug. "We're pretty serious. We've been going out with each other since high school." Wanting to change the subject quickly, Sarah interjected, "So... what do you want me to do this summer to help you?"

She hoped that she did not sound too forward. Doug smiled and sat down in his long-backed chair, gesturing for Sarah to sit in the chair across from his desk. She immediately felt more at ease with the desk between the two of them.

"Well, let me explain a bit about the way we're set up here. We have eleven people who work in the trust department. There are three portfolio managers, as well as two lawyers who work in the probate and estate area, and one business development professional. They all report directly to me. In addition, your father was kind enough to give me an assistant. So I have seven direct reports.

"The estate area obviously handles people's estates. Often our bank will be named in someone's will as the trustee for that person's estate. Our Estate Group makes sure that all the assets of that estate are collected, the taxes paid, and the remaining assets are distributed as directed in the will. It's our hope, of course, that some of the beneficiaries of the estate will choose to have us help manage their inherited assets. In other words, if the beneficiaries of an estate each inherit a million dollars from their parents, we want to help each of them manage that newly inherited money."

"Doesn't a lot of that money get taxed by the government?" Sarah remembered her father griping about estate taxes when his father-in-law passed away.

"It depends on the degree of estate planning that the individual does before his death. We work with estate lawyers to try to minimize the taxes paid. That's the beauty of setting up a trust account. When you set up a trust account, you effectively take that money out of your estate, which is taxed, and transfer it into a separate legal entity called a trust. As trustee, the bank holds those assets, separate from the estate, and then transfers the assets to the beneficiaries, as outlined in the trust agreement. The trustee pays taxes on the assets in the trust. But this is a much lower dollar amount than the beneficiaries would have to pay if the assets were still in the estate of the deceased."

Doug's conversation sounded as exciting as a snail race. Nonetheless, Sarah was still captivated by her new mentor.

"That's interesting," she replied, trying to suppress a yawn.

"There are all kinds of interesting tricks in the U.S. tax code. But that's another story altogether. Anyhow…as I was saying, I have three portfolio managers who report to me. Two of them work on personal accounts. These might include beneficiaries of estate accounts that I mentioned earlier, or it might be a new account that our business development officer brings in to the department. In other words, we're competing with banks and other brokerage firms like Merrill Lynch, Smith Barney, Edward Jones, and the mutual fund families, to help manage people's assets. We compete based on our investment performance and our fiduciary knowledge."

"What do you mean by fiduciary knowledge?"

"It basically means that there's a bunch of government regulations to ensure that banks work in the best interest of their clients.

"In addition to the personal money we manage, we have a portfolio manager who helps me in managing the money of large institutions. These include tax-exempt foundations like the United Way, the American Cancer Society, the American Liver Foundation, or it can include school endowments like Indiana University, Purdue University, or Notre Dame. We also manage the investment portfolios for some small insurance clients. In the institutional marketplace, we often compete with the larger money managers, like your boyfriend's firm, American Dinero."

"Isn't it difficult to compete with the larger firms?"

"Not really. Most accounts value our consultative style. We compete by offering more customized solutions. And obviously, we have to compete on investment performance. Despite our small size, we've compiled an extremely competitive investment record over the ten years I've been here. You might want to remind your father of my spectacular performance," Doug said with a self-assured smile.

CHAPTER EIGHT

It was a hot Friday afternoon. Two weeks had gone by since the schoolmates from Michigan City had started their summer jobs. They had previously planned to meet this weekend on the beach in front of Sarah Banks' house. Although eager to share stories of their work experiences, they would have to endure three more hours of work.

"Son of a bitch!" Tony Salami swore as he slammed down the phone. "That's it! Lehman Brothers is in the penalty box." Tony abruptly pushed himself up from his chair, chomping on the gum in his mouth, as if trying to grind it into oblivion. He stomped over to a white board, hanging on one of the cubicles opposite the trading desk. Grabbing a dark blue marker, he quickly scribbled, **"LEHMAN TRADERS**

ARE UNREASONABLE AND SELF-CENTERED. NO TRADING WITH LEHMAN FOR TWO WEEKS."

The words on the white board reminded Peter of the easel the Sandman had used to highlight his lesson plans. A chill went up Peter's spine as he leaned aside and whispered to one of the other traders, "What's up with Tony?"

The other trader merely smirked, watching Tony walk to a long table that stood perpendicular to the trading desk. While the whiteboard reminded Peter of the Sandman, Tony Salami's appearance was in stark contrast to the genie. The Sandman was scholarly-looking, and thin. Tony bore a much closer resemblance to Tony Soprano, of the old HBO television series, *The Sopranos*. The other trader's eyes remained focused on Tony, as he whispered a reply to Peter.

"He's been trying to sell some illiquid bonds to Lehman Brothers for about a week now. He basically told Lehman that he would sell the bonds for a yield of 130 basis points over the ten year treasury bond yield. Lehman, on the other hand, bid the bonds 138 basis points over the ten year. But Tony stuck to his guns, and Lehman agreed to try to work the bonds at Tony's price. Anyhow, now Lehman has come back to him and said the best they could bid the bonds is 145 basis points over the ten year. Tony thinks the Lehman broker shopped the bonds all over the street and realized that no one was willing to buy the bonds. Since Lehman doesn't want to hold the bonds in their inventory, they backed up their bid. Watch Tony... this is where the action gets good."

Peter didn't understand *everything* the trader had told him, but he understood that Tony felt Lehman had made a commitment and then backed out of their commitment. He further understood that Tony believed that Lehman had muddied the market to such an extent that Tony would be unable to sell his bonds to anyone else at his desired price. Peter watched Tony as he hovered over the table. He could see Tony was furious, and he wondered what would happen next. Was Tony going to take his anger out on someone else?

On top of the table was a large aquarium holding some oval-shaped fish with protruding lower jaws. Next to the aquarium was a second, smaller fish bowl, containing seven medium-sized goldfish. Plunging his fist into the bowl, Tony grabbed a hapless goldfish and plunked it into the aquarium. Immediately the oval-shaped fish opened their mouths to expose their razor-sharp teeth. The piranhas devoured the goldfish within seconds. The other traders clapped in approval.

"That's what we're going to do to anyone who tries to screw us." Tony menacingly spit his gum into the trash can. Striding back to the white board, Tony sneered at the written name of Lehman Brothers. He rubbed out his previous commandment and replaced it with a new one. "**IF YOU'RE HONEST AND UPFRONT, YOU'LL BE EATEN ALIVE.**"

"It's a freakin' jungle out there," Tony muttered as he stalked out of the room. The show was over. Peter quietly retreated to the other side of the floor to finish working with the analysts. Now he realized why Tony was the perfect portrayal of Napoleon, the pig.

✳ ✳ ✳

The next day, each of the five friends gathered on the beach in front of Sarah's house. Tom tossed Jerry a red Frisbee that had been lying on the sand.

"So—how are things in Indianapolis?" he asked.

"Things are going well. I like the company, I like the people I work with, and I like the city. In fact, the first week I was there, my boss gave me a ticket to sit at the Hoosier Insurance table for an event called the Pathfinder Awards. It was great! They honored Peter Ueberroth. Ueberroth started going into great detail what a terrific sports city Indianapolis had become."

"Who's Peter Ueberroth?"

Jerry looked at him incredulously.

"Dude, he was the guy who organized the 1984 Summer Olympics in Los Angeles. Anyhow, he started talking about how Indy is scheduled to host the NCAA men's Final Four basketball tournament, the World Swimming Championships, the USA Outdoor Track & Field Championships, the Solheim Cup, and the Super Bowl in 2012. I mean, Indy is scoring all of these world-class sporting events. They're known for much more than the Indy 500 these days. It's pretty cool. I might actually try to get a job down there when I graduate. So, how's *your* job going?"

Tom wasn't sure how to reply. He was a bit jealous that Jerry had obviously been embraced at his workplace. Tom, on the other hand, felt a bit lost.

"It's kind of weird. I've been there for two weeks, and I haven't even met my boss. The guy I'm supposed to report to helps supervise Care4's labs. I think he's some kind of chemist. But I guess his family was visiting relatives down in southern Missouri when the earthquake hit. I heard he lost them all: his in-laws, his wife, and two daughters. Right now most people don't even know when he's going to be back to work. In the meantime, they don't really know what to do with me. So I just kind of hang around my cubicle and try to look busy."

"You should talk to your dad. I'm sure he could get you assigned to work with someone else."

"Are you kidding? He's got the perfect job," Peter replied.

Pointing to Tom, Peter said, "This guy goes out and parties all night, and then he pretty much decides when he's going to show up for work the next day. I'm not even sure that they'd notice if he *didn't* show up."

Tom poked him playfully for the smart remark and said, "Come on, man. I help out anyone who needs me. Everyone loves me." The glint in Tom's eye and the grin on his face led Jerry to question Tom's sincerity.

"From what I've heard, the people at Michigan City National Bank love Sarah, too," Kathy said in a manner inviting further inquiry. Sarah gave Kathy a sharp look. She knew that Kathy was only trying to make Peter jealous.

"Well, I hope her dad loves her," Jerry said. "Despite all my problems, my momma still loves me."

"What's not to love?" Peter added with a proud grin.

"Oh, I'm not talking about her dad," Kathy continued. "I think that her new boss in the Trust Department would like to get to know her a little bit better. Isn't that right, Sarah?"

"Kathy, be quiet!" Sarah hissed, tilting her head towards her friend and gritting her teeth. "She's just trying to get you jealous, Peter." Sarah then walked over to Peter and clutched his arm playfully. "I told Mr. Keyster that I already have a boyfriend who's becoming an incredibly successful money manager in Chicago. In fact, he was quite impressed that you're working at American Dinero. I think he's kind of jealous of *you*," she said with a smile.

"Mr. Keyster, huh? Maybe I ought to meet this Mr. Keyster one of these days and reinforce the fact that you're already spoken for."

Although Sarah smiled at Peter's statement, she couldn't help but be a bit offended by the remark. She cared for Peter, but she didn't care for his possessive tendencies.

"Don't worry, my man. I'm your buddy," Tom said, putting his arm around Peter. "Jerry and I can go rough the guy up a bit if you want us to."

"Stop it, guys," Sarah said, seeking to put an end to the conversation. "Mr. Keyster is like ... 35 years old, and he doesn't have half the body of my guy here. Now, who's in the mood for a sandwich? We have ham and cheese, roast beef and cheese, and turkey."

Sarah opened the cooler she had brought down from her house and started handing out sandwiches. Much to Sarah's delight, the conversation about her and Mr. Keyster was quickly forgotten. Forgotten by all but Peter, who remained uncharacteristically quiet for the rest of the afternoon.

CHAPTER NINE

On Sunday morning, Peter and his family attended Mass together and went out to breakfast. This was one of Peter's favorite rituals whenever he came home. It added stability to his life. Dipping his toast into the yolk of his egg, Peter asked his father, "So how's work going at the Lake Michigan Research Institute?"

Peter was referring to the entity that he had helped create. Three years ago, the genie granted Peter his wish to improve the lives of those he loved. Not only did the genie enable Peter to assume the position of the Federal Reserve Chairman, he had also allowed him a brief stint as the President of the United States. Munching slowly on his toast, Peter remembered sitting in the soft leather chair of the Oval Office and signing legislation approving the creation of the Lake Michigan Research Institute. It was all about job creation in his part of the country.

While Peter now recognized the genie as an evil influence in his life, he was still tempted by the genie's magic. Even today, he often found himself craving that power, like a crack addict longs for a fix. Like the crack addict, he knew his addiction would eventually lead to his downfall. He had never forgiven himself for succumbing to the allure of power. Each night before climbing into bed he prayed to God that he would be able to resist any further temptation by greed. He was fully aware of his vulnerability.

The Lake Michigan Research Institute was a new joint program of the EPA and the FDA to clean up the Great Lakes. The cleaning process also allowed for conducting medical research on some of the biomass that filtered down to the tip of Lake Michigan. The legislation that Peter had signed as President unexpectedly resulted in his dad's employment as manager for the building project.

"The project's going well," David Jangle answered. "One of the small labs is complete and we are working on two larger facilities that we expect to be finished by next summer. In fact, they've already collected some biomass from the lake, and they've been testing it for a few months now. From what I've heard they're pretty excited about potential medical uses for some of the new compounds they've discovered."

"And how is Mr. Shindler doing?"

This question took David Jangle by surprise. David knew his son still blamed himself for his classmate's death. Steve Shindler died because of the Inflation Monster that Peter had unleashed. David and Sarah Banks were the only two people with whom Peter had shared this secret. Ironically, Bruce Shindler, Steve's father, had become close friends with David Jangle. It was Bruce Shindler who had offered David his current job after a five-month period of unemployment. Sensing the pain of his son's guilt, David Jangle looked reassuringly at Peter and replied, "Mr. Shindler is doing fine. He really is doing fine."

Noticing the sudden forlorn attitude of her two men, Claire Jangle quickly changed the subject. "And how is *your* job going, Peter?"

Peter forced a smile, while looking down at the table. He speared two sausage links with his fork and guided them into his mouth. His mouth full, he replied between bites, "It's interesting. I'm working with a bunch of pigs."

"Well, that's not a very nice thing to say."

"Mom, the thing is...the traders *like* to be called pigs. The guy who runs the place gave me this whole treatise comparing the employees at American Dinero to the characters in Orwell's novel, *Animal Farm.*

"Well, I didn't read *Animal Farm,*" David Jangle replied. "But I want you to be sure to treat those people with respect. You don't want to burn any bridges. They might be able to get you a good job when you graduate next year." David stabbed at a couple of sausages and then continued with his lecture. "But I certainly don't want you to start acting like a pig, either. I don't know much about Wall Street, but I've heard how they operate. And it makes intuitive sense."

David swallowed his food and then looked Peter in the eye. "Bulls make money. Bears make money. But pigs get slaughtered."

"You heard that on Cramer!" Peter replied, referring to the often animated CNBC commentator.

"It doesn't matter where I heard it. The important thing is that you heed those words."

Not ready to let the subject drop, Claire asked, "What do you mean ... when you say they are a bunch of pigs?"

Peter smiled. "I don't know… they just have big egos. Actually, most of them are pretty funny. This one trader— Tony Salami—thinks he's in charge of setting the rules for the other traders and the analysts. He's always writing new rules on this whiteboard set next to the trading desk. I was talking to one of the analysts, Terri Tanaka, the other day, and she said that one time Tony actually forbid her from getting anywhere near the traders for a two-week period."

"Why would he do that?"

"I guess Terri gave a negative report on a company that Tony convinced the portfolio managers was a great buy. Anyhow, at Tony's insistence, the portfolio manager bought a bunch of the company's bonds. After reading Terri's research report, the portfolio manager got pissed off at Tony."

"Peter Jangle, you don't need to use that language! I don't want you becoming a pig," Peter's mom sternly replied. After taking a sip of her orange juice, Claire Jangle asked, "Did this Terri Tanaka do her job correctly?"

"Yeah. I think she's the smartest analyst they have."

"So you mean this guy Tony punished Terri for doing her job?"

"Yeah, basically."

"Well, I guess he does sound like a pig," Claire replied, as she pursed her lips and shook her head in disgust.

✣ ✣ ✣

After returning home from lunch, Peter grabbed the Sunday *Chicago Tribune*, stuffed it in his duffle bag full of freshly washed clothes, and rushed out the door with his father to meet Tom Nelson at the South Shore train station. Boarding the third car of the train, Peter spotted Tom slouched in his seat. Taking the seat across from Tom, Peter said, "You look a mess. How late did you guys stay out partying last night?"

"Oh, man," Tom said, slumping further in his seat, "I don't know. I think Jerry and I left around two. I let him crash at my house. I wasn't going to let him drive home. What was up with you last night? You left kind of early."

"I don't know. I guess I was tired."

"That whole business about Sarah and her new boss is bugging you, isn't it?"

"No. It doesn't bother me. I trust Sarah."

"Yeah, but do you trust *him*?" Tom smiled and closed his eyes to sleep as the train rolled out of Michigan City.

Peter pulled out the paper and began reading. The lead story continued to focus on the aftermath of the earthquake in the Midwest. The official death count, as a result of the earthquake, now stood at 487 people. Many died as a result of flooding along the east bank of the Mississippi River, near Memphis. The effects of the quake were such that it widened the mouth of the Mississippi River, extending it to the Wolf River Harbor. The flooding effectively wiped out the Mud Island River Park and the community of Harbor Town, a relatively new urban neighborhood. It was reported that the death toll could have been much higher in the city of Memphis, which was also flooded, had the earthquake not taken place in the late evening, after most of the workforce had gone home for the day.

Placing the paper in his lap, Peter once again began to think of the genie. Thoughts of the genie haunted him each time a natural disaster occurred. His eyes were half-closed as the train rolled past the loading platform in East Chicago. He was suddenly startled by an image out of the corner of his eye. Terrified, he bolted upright and quickly turned to look out the train window. He pressed his face square against the glass as the train starting pulling away. Peter could not be certain of what he had seen. His heart started racing faster as beads of sweat formed on his forehead. Was it a dream, or had he, in fact, seen a man dressed in a black suit, with a black fedora, laughing as they passed the train station? Peter feared it was the same black suit and fedora worn by the Sandman three years earlier.

CHAPTER TEN

Sarah and Kathy sat eating lunch outside of Swing-belly's, a casual diner near the Michigan City harbor. The warm wind forced them to hold their napkins in place. They sat in silence for a moment, only listening to the distant waves crashing on the shore. Sarah was still feeling a bit betrayed by Kathy's comments at the beach. "Why did you have to bring up that whole conversation about Doug Keyster in front of Peter the other day?"

"I'm sorry, Sarah. I didn't mean to make you uncomfortable. I was just kidding. Besides, I didn't want Peter to think that he could take you for granted. I mean, did you hear that crap he was saying about how he was going to tell Doug that you're 'spoken for'?"

"I'll admit, that wasn't the brightest thing I've ever heard him say. Still, you've got to quit being so hard on him. He's a great guy. He takes care of me."

Sarah crossed her arms as if to hug herself. She wanted Kathy to know that Peter made her feel comfortable.

"Oh, come on, Sarah! You can take care of yourself. You can't let Peter try to control you. Sometimes I think he's just a bit too over-protective." Kathy looked down and used her straw to stir the lemon in her water. Raising the straw to her lips, she asked, "So how are things going with you and Mr. Keyster?"

"Good. I mean…I'm learning a lot," Sarah replied defensively.

"I bet you are." Kathy said with a grin.

"Seriously, Kathy. The guy's really pretty smart. He manages a fixed income bond fund, a value equity fund, and a growth equity fund; and they're all performing really well. He's teaching me a lot about investing."

"Be still my heart. And he's good looking too, huh?"

Sarah blushed and looked away, wanting to change the subject. "And how are things going with you at work?"

"Hell, I don't know. I thought this would be a great opportunity to find out if I wanted to pursue a law career. Now I'm not sure what I want to do. One of the things I'm learning is that there's a tremendous amount of pressure on young lawyers to increase the billable hours they charge their clients. It's all about making money!"

"Come on, Kathy! Is that a surprise to you? Everything is about making money. That's the American way."

"Yeah, but listen to this. One of the things I'm supposed to do is keep track of everyone's billable hours. So at the end of each week, the lawyers in the firm turn in a report that details the hours they spent on their various clients. It's my job to take that information and bill the clients. The thing is…I watch these lawyers all day. I know what they're doing.

They spend half their time in committee meetings and in the hallways talking about sports. Then they turn in these reports that claim they spent eighteen hours a day working solely on client projects. Half of the time the hours they report would imply that they sleep only four hours a night!"

Sarah could tell that Kathy was upset.

"What are you saying? Do you think they're lying on their reports?"

"They have to be. I watch some of these guys every day. There's no way that some of them are spending as much time on client work as they're reporting."

"Well, have you talked to anyone about it?"

"Who am I going to talk to? Their bosses know about it. And I think they encourage and condone it. Meanwhile, the lawyers know that if they don't report a certain amount of billable hours, they're likely to lose their jobs. Besides, if I try to report it, there's no way I'm going to get any kind of recommendations for my future law career."

"I don't know, Kathy. If it's wrong, it's wrong. You need to do something about it. I know it's hard. Have you talked to your mom about it?"

"Yeah. All she said is that I don't need to convince her that some lawyers are dishonest. She says she experiences dishonesty every day with her teachers' union attorneys. However, she also pointed out that you'll find dishonesty in just about any profession. She says that she spends half of her class time not only trying to teach economic principles, but also trying to instill moral principles. Unfortunately, she regrets that some of those lessons are lost when her students eventually enter the competitive workforce."

Sarah didn't know exactly how to respond. She certainly didn't believe that her dad was ever dishonest. Likewise, despite her high regard for Kathy's mother, she wasn't sure that the education industry was always above reproach. Sarah raised her glass of iced tea, and looked Kathy in the eye. She summed up the dilemma the only way she knew how. "Well, let's hope we'll be a little different, huh?"

✿ ✿ ✿

While Sarah and Kathy were finishing their meal, Peter was hard at work on the other side of the lakefront.

"What are you working on, Peter?"

Peter looked up to see Terri Tanaka, the senior analyst at American Dinero, looking over his shoulder.

"David Koslow asked me to do a report on Consumer Media."

"Good! I'm glad to hear that you're working with Dave. I think he's one of our best portfolio managers. Of course, one of the reasons I say that is because he insists on good research from his analysts." Terri smiled.

"So how can I make Dave happy?" Peter asked.

"First off, you have to understand how Dave works. I would consider him a good, fundamental value manager. Do you know what that means?"

"It means he likes to buy things cheap." Peter replied.

"That's probably a decent description. He's usually interested in stocks and bonds that have recently declined in price. He believes the markets tend to over-react, unfairly punishing the stocks and bonds of certain companies, based on one quarter's earnings performance, or some adverse news event. When he sees sudden, sharp drops in prices, he looks to us for research that can give him a compelling reason to buy."

"Do you know anything about Consumer Media?" Peter asked.

Terri seemed a bit surprised by the name.

"Consumer Media? That's a new name for us. What's he interested in buying, the bonds or the stock?"

Terri leaned closer to Peter, placing her right hand on his shoulder. Her long, silky black hair fell within inches of his face. Peter inhaled the enticing scent of Terri's perfume. For the first time he noticed Terri's dark penetrating eyes, sparkling like black opals behind her round, wire-framed glasses. Flustered, Peter knocked over a cup of water that was on his desk. He clumsily lunged at the research reports, trying to save them from getting wet. Reaching for his research, he accidentally elbowed Terri in the shoulder, causing her to flinch. Jumping from his chair, he tried to rectify the situation.

"I'm sorry, Terri. Are you all right? I'm sorry."

"Don't worry about it, Peter. I'm fine. Now, what are you researching, bonds or stock?"

Regaining his composure, Peter remembered the original question.

"Dave wants me to look at the bonds. They recently got downgraded by Moodys to a B2 rating, based on the announcement of a small acquisition and a stock buyback."

"So they have public stock outstanding?"

"Yeah. It's pretty cheap. It only trades at $4 a share."

"Be careful, Peter. Don't ever say a stock is cheap unless you think it's worth buying. After all, a $4 stock can be expensive, and a $150 stock can be a bargain. It all depends on the earnings and growth potential of the Company. You know that, don't you?"

"Sure, I know that." Peter replied in a tone betraying his uncertainty. Terri smiled, not wanting to embarrass Peter by asking too many difficult questions.

"Well, good. We had an intern here last summer who didn't know the difference. Anyhow, this guy went to Tony suggesting that he buy a $3 stock 'because it was cheap.' This particular stock had 100 million shares outstanding, it was trading at $3, it was losing revenues, and it was struggling to make profits."

"What did Tony do to the guy?"

"I think he fed him to those piranhas in the tank by the trading desk." Terri laughed and grabbed an extra chair to sit next to Peter. His eyes immediately fixated on Terri's muscular thighs that were exposed as she crossed her legs next to him. Peter was certain that she must be a runner.

"Do you want to know how I value stocks, Peter?"

"Sure. That's why I'm here. Teach me." Peter was beginning to feel more at ease in Terri's presence. Since his encounter with the genie, Peter had become more guarded when meeting new people. He didn't feel the need for false bravado with Terri.

"The first thing to realize is that you can't properly value a stock without knowing the value of the total company. After all, a stock is nothing more than ownership in the total company. Right?"

"Right," Peter replied. "I actually had this professor at Notre Dame who explained this concept pretty well. He told our class about his twelve-year old son. He told us that the teachers at his son's school gave detention slips to anyone in the class who wasn't prepared with a pencil to take notes. Knowing this, the professor's boy went out and bought a pack of twelve pencils for a dollar. Whenever a student would forget his own pencil, the prof's kid would be willing to sell one of his own pencils for a dollar. Since the total cost of the whole pack was one dollar, and since he was able to sell each of his twelve pencils for one dollar, the boy was able to make a profit of eleven dollars for each pack of pencils he purchased. The boy bought nine packs of pencils over the school year and was able to make a total profit of $99.00."

Terri had a puzzled look on her face. "What does this have to do with what we're talking about?"

"My prof used that as a case study for valuing a company. He told us that his boy wanted to sell stock in his company. Then he asked us to value the company, to determine how much we would pay for the stock."

"I hope I won't regret asking you to continue your story." Terri smiled encouragingly at Peter. He was surprised at how eager he was to please her. "I will warn you, though," Terri said. "I'm out of here if you start singing the Notre Dame Fight Song. But, go on with your story. How did your class determine the value of the stock?"

Peter wondered if he was starting to sound like a nerd. He continued nonetheless.

"Well, first we had to determine how many shares of stock the company was going to issue. The prof said his son was willing to sell 100 shares of stock, representing 100 percent ownership in the company."

"In other words, each share of stock represented 1 percent ownership in the company."

"Exactly." Peter wasn't sure if Terri was trying to hurry him along.

"So how much did you say that you were willing to pay for one share?"

"We figured that if the company made approximately $100 profit, and if one share represented 1 percent of the company, one share would be worth about 1 percent of the profit, or $1."

"Wait a minute," Terri interjected. Didn't you say the company made $99 profit on the nine pencil packs?"

"Yeah, I'm just rounding to $100 for simplicity."

"That's one way to create value," Terri mused. "But go on with the story. You told your professor that you would pay $1 to the boy for each share of stock? Did his boy accept the offer?"

"No. This kid figured that his company was a growth stock. He figured that he could have sold twice as many pencils last year if he had tried harder. Selling twice as many pencils would give him a profit of $200. So he figured that each share of stock was worth at least $2."

"So did you buy his stock at $2 a share?"

"No, because then the kid said he was going to start hiring other kids who would sell pencils in the younger grades. This way the business would grow even larger and he would have a plan in place to continue the business for years. Basically, he said that the business would make ten times as much money in five years. So he wanted us to pay $10 a share."

"Now I see where you're going with this. So how did you determine the value of the stock?"

"Well, we had to determine a realistic growth rate for the company."

"Good for you, Peter! You've grasped the basic concept of valuing a company. Unfortunately, I think your professor might have stolen that example from another investment book I read. The book goes on to ask questions such as: What happens if one of the other kids starts his own pencil-selling business? Faced with competition, the professor's boy might have to sell his pencils at a lower price. Maybe the boy's employees will start asking for more money. That will lower profits. Or maybe, the other kids will change their habits. They won't forget their pencils anymore. They'll always bring their pencils to class and they'll have no need to buy the boy's over-priced pencils. As you can tell, there are many uncertainties. There's no science to determining growth rates out over twelve months."

It was evident that Terri was now enjoying their conversation.

"But we digress. Let's get back to your current assignment. You need to determine whether David Koslow should buy the Consumer Media bonds. We'll talk about stocks later. The main thing you need to know is whether or not Consumer Media will have sufficient cash to pay off their bonds when they come due. It's just like paying back a loan. Do they have sufficient cash flow to do it? Of course, from a trading perspective, and an investment performance perspective, you want to know more than whether or not we'll get our money back. You want to know whether or not their financial future will get worse before it gets more certain. In other words, assuming that you do think they'll pay the money back, should you buy the bonds now, or will you be able to buy them cheaper later? That's the type of analysis Dave will expect from you."

Terri stood up to leave. "I'll see you later, Peter. Let me know if you need any help." Peter smiled as Terri walked away. He had not known many women in his life with such intensity and enthusiasm for investing.

Peter's smile soon faded and a feeling of anxiety began to take hold. He was a bit unsure of whether he was capable of performing the work that was expected of him. Desparate for information, Peter bent down in his cubicle and reached for the black leather briefcase his parents had given him. Opening his briefcase, he searched for an object hidden under a couple of folders. It looked like a calculator. Grabbing the object, he peered through the opening in his cubicle to make sure that no one was near him. He then began composing the following phrase in the hand-held device: "Describe the difference between a 'cheap stock' and a 'rich stock.' Example: a $4 stock versus a $150 stock."

Again, checking to make sure no one was approaching, Peter saw the following scroll across his screen:

"A stock is often considered 'cheap' if the following conditions are met:

1. *the cash component of the balance sheet of a company represents a large percentage of the market capitalization, or*
2. *the expected earnings over the next twelve months represent a large percentage of the market capitalization."*

Peter then typed in the following phrase: "Explain market capitalization."

The display on the screen read: *"Market capitalization is the stock price multiplied by the number of shares outstanding. This is the 'value' the stock market assigns the total company. In your example, one company had a $4 price per share, and the other company had a $150 price per share. Assume that your $4 stock has 100 million shares outstanding. The market capitalization would be $4 x 100,000,000 shares = $400,000,000. This means that the stock market values this company at a price of $400 million.*

"Assume that your $150 stock has 1million shares outstanding. The market capitalization would be $150 x 1,000,000 = $150,000,000. Despite the higher stock price, since the company has less shares outstanding the market capitalization is lower than the company with the $4 stock.

"*Using rule (1), assume that the $4 stock has $20 million cash on the balance sheet. We know that 20,000,000 / 400,000,000 = .05 or 5% of the market capitalization. In other words, if you buy this company for the current value of $400 million, you will get a cash return of 5% of your purchase price.*

"*Suppose that the $150 stock also has $20 million cash on the balance sheet. We know that 20,000,000 / 150,000,000 = .133 or 13.3% of the market capitalization. The first definition for a cheap stock would lead one to believe that the $150 stock is relatively less expensive than the $4 dollar stock. This is because you receive a higher percentage of your purchase price guaranteed by cash.*"

Peter smiled. He knew that the device in his hand was unique to him. It could not be bought in any store. The genie had called it an "econometer" when he presented the gift to Peter. Peter considered it his knowledge tree. Despite the genie's disappearance, the econometer still worked. Over the past three years, Peter had relied on this econometer as a great reference source for almost any question he could imagine. This was one gift from the genie that Peter was still thankful for.

Peter seemed relatively satisfied with the explanation of how to value companies. Hoping to discover a simple rule on how to buy stocks, he typed on the keyboard, "Should I always buy stocks where the cash, or liquid assets of a company, represent the greatest percentage of the market capitalization?"

Peter was stung by the sarcastic reply of the econometer:

"*Wrong! Guess again! Imagine a company that has no assets other than cash. The company makes no products and it doesn't invest its cash. Suppose this company had $10 million in cash on the balance sheet, and the market cap was $11 million. Your logic would buy the company because the cash represent a large percentage* *of the market capitalization. You'd pay $11 million and you'd get $10 million back. That doesn't sound like a great deal, does it? In addition, what if that company is paying employees? You will be losing your cash in the future as you continue to pay your employees. You need to think about the future, Peter! You need to think about future earnings that your company will generate when you purchase a stock. That's the problem with you humans—you're so short-sighted!"*

Peter watched the disparaging words scroll across the screen in amazement. He immediately started looking around to see if someone was playing a joke on him. He remembered who gave him the econometer. Could the Sandman be trying to contact him again?

Meanwhile, the econometer continued with its written lecture:

"The first definition of a 'cheap stock' is incomplete without applying the second definition. You need to analyze the expected earnings of the company over the next twelve months. You can then divide those earnings by the number of shares outstanding. The result is the expected earnings per share. A cheap stock does not have a price per share that is significantly higher than the expected earnings per share. This is called the P/E ratio. P stands for price per share, and E stands for expected earnings per share. In general, we want to pay the lowest possible price for the highest expected earnings. Why would you buy a stock that has no expected future earnings? That only makes sense if you plan on liquidating the company and selling the assets for more than what you paid."

Peter found himself getting a better grasp of the finance classes he had taken at Notre Dame. Glancing at his watch, he decided to take the rest of his work home.

✫ ✫ ✫

Peter walked briskly through the Chicago rush hour crowd. He realized he was surrounded by a city of strangers. He yearned for the safety of his apartment. For some reason he felt very uneasy about his experience with the econometer today.

The phone was ringing when Peter arrived at his apartment. It was evident that Tom was not home. *At least he's partying somewhere other than our apartment tonight,* Peter thought to himself. Picking up the receiver, Peter heard the familiar voice of his friend, Jerry Parker, on the other end of the line.

"Hey Peter, I need to ask you a question. I figure now that you're working with a big investment shop in Chicago—and you seem to know a lot about investments—have you ever heard of anything called a CBO before?"

Peter loved to be looked upon as an "expert" in finance. Although he wasn't quite sure what a CBO was, he knew where he could find the answer. "Just a minute," Peter replied. He ran quickly to the kitchen counter where he had left his briefcase. He paused for a moment before opening his briefcase, wondering if it was the right thing to do. Nonetheless, resolved to help his friend Jerry, he pulled out the econometer and punched in the letters "CBO."

The following definition scrolled across the screen of the econometer:

In finance, 'CBO' is an acronym that can either stand for 'Congressional Budget Office' or 'Collateralized Bond Obligation.'

Peter knew the Jerry wanted information on an investment vehicle, not a government office. He hurried back to the phone and responded. "I'm sorry. I had to take care of something in the kitchen. So, are you looking for information on a Collateralized Bond Obligation?"

"Yeah," Jerry replied. "That sounds right. I've been working with the investment folks the past couple of days, and I've found out that our company is a pretty big originator of CBOs."

Eager to show off his knowledge, Peter typed "define collateralized bond obligation." The econometer replied:

"A CBO is a structured finance product that typically securitizes a diversified pool of bonds. In other words, if an investor purchases a bond issued by General Motors, he is paid back by the cash flow generated by General Motors. If an investor purchases a CBO bond, he is paid back by the cash flow from the underlying pool of various corporate bonds."

The definition was a bit too difficult for Peter to grasp immediately. So he stalled for time.

"So you mean you're creating a structured finance product?" Peter asked, not fully understanding the concept.

"Yeah. Get this. Since Hoosier Insurance typically buys a certain percentage of high yield bonds for its own investment portfolio, all these investment banks started telling us that we ought to issue our own CBOs. I guess if you have a good track record of managing high yield bonds, investors will be interested in buying CBOs that you manage. It's kind of like managing a junk bond mutual fund. If you're a good portfolio manager, people will invest with you. Anyhow, I told the people here that I know someone who works at American Dinero, and now they're wondering if you would be interested in buying some of the lower-rated tranches, and possibly the equity, of our latest deal."

"I'm not sure, Jerry. I don't know if we've ever bought any CBOs before. I can ask the people I work with. I'll let you know. So—how are things going for you in Indianapolis?"

"It's great. I'm really learning a lot at work, and Indy is a fun town. Not only is Butler University here, but they also have IUPUI and the University of Indianapolis, and a couple of other smaller schools. Plus, a lot of IU and Purdue grads work here. So there's lots of young people and lots of neat things to do."

"Good for you. Are you planning any trips back to Michigan City soon?"

"Probably not this weekend. I actually have a date. Get this, we're going to go to the symphony. Do you believe that? Me? Going to the symphony? Anyhow, the company has great seats, and no one was using them this weekend. So I get to impress a babe, and it won't cost me a dime. Not bad, huh?"

"Yeah, but you better drink a couple cups of coffee before you go. Chances are you won't impress your date too much if you fall asleep in the middle of the performance."

"That's not going to happen, man. You 'region guys' just don't have the same class as we have down here in Indianapolis," Jerry joked. He was obviously enjoying some of the work perks being thrown his way. "You've got to realize that there's more to life than just rap and rock and roll music." Jerry added with a laugh.

Peter smiled as he hung up the phone with Jerry. He recalled Jerry's initial belief that all the folks who grew up in Long Beach, Indiana, were snobs. Three years later, Jerry's enjoying classical music at the symphony, while Tom's out partying in the streets of Chicago. The irony amused him.

Peter turned back to his research work on Consumer Media. Before long, he was again interrupted by the phone. This time it was Sarah on the other end. It was the first time they had spoken in a week.

"So, Peter, I don't know how you guys are doing at American Dinero, but Lakefront Fund Management just got a new $25 million dollar endowment client." Peter knew that Lakefront Fund Management was the official name of the money management unit at Michigan City National Bank. It was not uncommon for the investment area of a bank to adopt a separate name to give them the look and feel of a boutique money manager. Peter also knew that a $25 million account was a decent piece of business for a bank the size of Michigan City National.

"Wow! That's great, Sarah. How did you guys get that business? Does your dad know somebody on the Investment Committee of the endowment?"

"No," Sarah replied, offended by the suggestion. "In fact, this particular endowment just happens to be located in the state of Missouri. They knew nothing about us. We just happened to answer an RFP from their investment consultant. Their consultant was so impressed with our investment performance over the past five years that he asked Doug to visit with the Investment Committee to make a presentation. Anyhow, Doug let me go along with him on the presentation. We thought it went well, but we weren't sure. And then, we found out this afternoon that we won the business."

"So you went on a trip to Missouri with Doug?" Peter asked suspiciously.

Sensing the tone in Peter's voice, Sarah replied, "Peter, do I detect a note of jealousy in your voice?" She was happy to realize that Peter cared.

"I just don't see why you had to go. Did you guys spend the night?"

Sarah gritted her teeth, took a deep breath and paused to compose herself.

"Listen, Peter, Doug wants me to learn the business. You know that presentations are part of the business. It's no big deal."

"So when did you start calling him Doug?" Peter preferred Sarah referring to him as "Mister Keyster."

"Forget it, Peter. I'm sorry I wanted to share my good news with you. I didn't think this would turn into an interrogation of my personal life."

"So you're telling me that Doug Keyster is now a part of your personal life?"

Sarah was now fully annoyed at Peter's jealousy.

"Would you just listen to me for once? I obviously caught you at a bad time. There's nothing between me and Doug Keyster, okay?"

"You mean, other than the fact that you guys are going on trips to Missouri together?"

"Good-bye, Peter."

Peter slowly put the phone down, immediately sensing that this would be a conversation that he would later regret.

Frustrated, he tossed an empty Coke can across the room. He didn't trust Doug Keyster. What a rotten day this was turning out to be. First, he was worried about the return of the Sandman. Now he was worried about some hot-shot fund manager named Doug Keyster. He tried to refocus by continuing to research the Consumer Media bonds. "I've got to get back to work," he mumbled to himself. Taking a seat in front of the computer in the corner of his room, he quickly accessed the Internet to continue his research. He was soon distracted by the news reports detailing the damage caused by the earthquake that had occurred almost four weeks ago. The total death toll had now risen to 510, and thousands were still left homeless. Peter thought back on the tsunami-like event that had taken the life of residents of Michigan City three years ago. His thoughts eventually turned to his lost friend, Steve Shindler.

"Who am I kidding? I'm not going to get any work done tonight," he said out loud. He shut down his computer and took a deep breath before getting up. Retiring to his bedroom, Peter turned off the lights and flopped down on his bed. Looking up at his ceiling, Peter began to pray. "Dear Lord, please help all of those poor people who suffered as a result of the recent earthquake. And I continue to ask that you forgive me for allowing the 'inflation creation monster' to take the lives of Steve Shindler and the others in Michigan City. I ask that you let me know your will, so that I may know how to serve you better. And, although I realize this is a very selfish thought, I ask that you please—at least consider—allowing the relationship between me and Sarah to endure." Peter then rolled over onto his stomach, and pulling his pillow tight to his chest, drifted slowly off to sleep.

Two hours later, Peter was awakened by the sound of Tom Nelson puking in the bathroom. "Did you have a good time?" Peter asked in a half-sleep state.

"Oh, man," Tom groaned as he stumbled over to his bed. "Just be sure to wake me up in the morning. I have to get to work on time tomorrow. I heard that my new boss is going to be back." Peter heard Tom fall into his bed. Within a minute, the sound of Tom's snoring was dancing to the reverberation of the Chicago "EL."

CHAPTER ELEVEN

"So, Peter, did you finish my report on Consumer Media yet? What do you think? Should I buy the bonds or not?"

Peter winced at the sound of David Koslow coming up behind him. He was disappointed with himself for not getting more work done the previous evening. "I'm almost done with the report – not quite, I stayed up pretty late working on it last night."

"Dude, I don't need a written masterpiece from you. We know the bonds I'm interested in purchasing are rated B2. They're currently trading at a spread of 750 basis points over five-year treasuries. This means that if I want to buy a five-year bond right now, I can either buy five-year treasuries at a yield of 4.45%, or I can buy these beauties at a yield of 11.95%. Most five-year, B2-rated bonds currently trade at a spread of 575 basis points over treasuries. In fact, these bonds were trading at 600 basis points over treasuries just two weeks ago. Since then, the company has announced they're going to do an acquisition and a stock buyback that will increase their leverage. What I need to know from you is whether or not you think the credit will be downgraded, and what are its prospects for staying out of bankruptcy the next five years?"

Peter quickly looked over his notes and then reported to Koslow what he had found.

"Well, I know the company just announced they were selling their Education and Training unit for about $100 million. That business unit accounted for about 9 percent of their revenue, but only about 2 percent of their EBITDA." Peter had found out last night from his econometer that EBITDA stood for "earnings before interest payments, taxes, and depreciation expenses." He had learned that this was a very important number in determining the credit-worthiness of bonds because it helped the analyst determine how much cash was available to repay debt. In other words, interest payments on debt would be made prior to any payments for taxes or new equipment purchases.

"So, I figure that cash should give them a decent cushion to buy back their stock. In addition, selling the Education and Training unit shouldn't have a material effect on the cash flow they generate."

Peter looked up at David Koslow, who stared at him in silence. The silence gave Peter the feeling of a doctor painfully probing his body. Sensing that Koslow wanted more, Peter continued with his analysis.

"Uh..their pretax interest coverage has improved each quarter from 0.7 times last year, to a current 1.4 times. So they're clearly covering their debt interest obligations. And that number compares pretty well to similar B-rated companies. In addition, their total debt to capital has gone down from over 200 percent, to a current 155 percent. So the trends seem pretty positive."

Again, Peter glanced up to meet the stoic face of Mr. Koslow. Slowly, Koslow began to smile before he broke into a broad grin. Koslow slapped his large hands onto Peter's shoulders, tightening his grip so that Peter's body began to shake under the pressure. "Good for you, my boy. You convinced me. I'm going to go ahead and buy the bonds. If you come up with any other good ideas, let me know."

As Koslow walked away, Peter closed his eyes and whispered, "Please, God, don't let anything bad happen to Consumer Media before my summer internship is finished."

✳ ✳ ✳

Two blocks down the street, Tom Nelson was nursing a hangover at his empty cubicle when his phone rang.

"Hello."

"Can I speak to Tom Nelson, please?"

"This is Tom."

"Tom. My name is Doctor Cregar. I apologize that I haven't gotten in touch with you sooner. As you might have heard, my family was affected by the recent earthquake. And I had to take care of some personal matters. Nonetheless, it's been a few weeks now and it's time for me to get back to work."

Tom could hear the stress in Doctor Cregar's voice.

"Anyhow, while I was down in Missouri, I was introduced to an amazing discovery as a result of the earthquake, and I was wondering if you would be interested in helping me work on a potential blockbuster drug discovery."

The thought of working on something important grabbed Tom's full attention. He opened up a file drawer to the right hand side of his desk, and fumbled as he tried to open a bottle of aspirin.

"I'll work on whatever you want me to work on," he replied.

"Well, good. If you have a minute, why don't you come up to my office? I'm here on the 17th floor. Talk to the receptionist as you come off the elevator, and she can direct you to my office. I look forward to meeting you."

As Tom hung up the phone he imagined the stories he could tell his friends. They were always bragging about the important projects assigned to them at work. Here, at last, he would get an opportunity to work on something important. *This could change the world!* He grinned to himself as his imagination ran wild.

CHAPTER TWELVE

Upon entering Jonah Cregar's office, Tom observed the numerous plaques on the wall acknowledging Doctor Cregar's accomplishments. Doctor Cregar rose and extended his hand to Tom, saying, "Tom, it's good to finally meet you. I've never met your dad, but I hear he does a terrific job for the Company. Have a seat. Let's get to know each other."

Tom figured Jonah Cregar was in his early fifties. A little over six feet tall, Cregar was slightly overweight, with streaks of gray hair. The wrinkles and dark hues under his eyes were indicative of a man who had worked hard over a productive lifetime. Seating himself across the desk from Doctor Cregar, Tom noticed the family picture that hung above Cregar's computer monitor. It looked to be a picture taken a few years ago, perhaps on a family vacation at the beach. Doctor Cregar looked younger, thinner, and more vibrant in the picture, sporting a summer tan. Beside him were the images of a loving wife and two young daughters. Tom imagined that the recent stress of losing his family had contributed greatly to the dark circles that now weighed beneath his eyes.

"I heard what happened to your family, Doctor Cregar. I'm so sorry for your loss."

"Thank you, Tom. I noticed you were looking at the picture hanging on the wall. That was taken two years ago, during a family vacation in Florida. It's funny, my youngest daughter, Emily, was always apprehensive about swimming in the ocean. When she was a young girl, she once panicked when she got caught in a riptide. The current started pulling her out and she didn't think that she'd be able to swim back to the shore. I heard her screaming and I swam out to help her back in."

Tom saw the tears welling up in Cregar's eyes as he looked up at the picture. Tom sat patiently, wanting to hear more, but Cregar's thoughts were far away. He was reliving the past, two years ago on the beach. Cregar remembered that it was an extremely hot day, but the wind indicated an approaching storm. The waves were crashing on the beach. He could barely hear the faint cries of Emily calling for help. He vividly recalled each stroke he took, fighting through the water, the waves slapping at his face. He couldn't forget the joy of grabbing hold of his daughter. His job was complete. After a minute of silence, Cregar returned to the present. Tom was leaning forward, eager to hear more. Cregar felt compelled to oblige.

"It's one of those instances that a father always remembers. The water was the one thing in my life that made me a hero. In turn, it gave my daughter a sense of confidence. She had an unyielding faith that I would always be there to save her. The tragic thing is that when this earthquake struck, I wasn't there." Doctor Cregar's voice began to trail off as he looked down at the floor.

The silence was awkward, and Tom was at a loss for words.

"Anyhow, I guess there's nothing I can do for them now... other than pray and thank God for the wonderful memories. I know that they would want me to carry on with my life— and that's what I intend to do. Though I must admit, it's a bit awkward being around people again." He paused and took a deep breath. "So, tell me a little about yourself. I see here that you're from Michigan City. I didn't know that that's where your father lived."

"Yes sir—It's a good place to grow up. Not quite as high a cost of living as around here."

Creger smiled in acknowledgment.

"I'm going to be a senior in marketing at IU this year, and I'm hoping I can use my skills to help you this summer."

"I'm sure you will. Coming from Michigan City, how much do you know about the work they're doing at the Lake Michigan Research Institute?"

"To be honest, I don't know much about it. I know that it was great news when the government decided to build the facility in Michigan City. It's a great source of jobs. I guess the added benefit is that they'll clean up Lake Michigan, while trying to work on some kind of scientific discoveries."

"That's right. The research they're conducting at that facility could prove to be life-altering. Perhaps you've heard, Tom, one of my main responsibilities for Care4 is to work on similar types of research. My department works hard to discover promising drugs that our company can bring to market. Unfortunately, the vast majority of the drugs we work on never do make it to market. It takes years of testing not only the effectiveness of the drugs, but also ensuring that there are no negative side effects. As you can imagine, it's a very time-consuming and expensive process."

"Yeah, my dad tries to keep me informed of all the new products."

"As I said, most of the new drugs never make it to market. So, about a year ago, management at Care4 Pharmaceuticals started looking for ways to limit the risk associated with drug research. To put it bluntly, they became more interested in profits than in research. Personally, that's not the way that I, as a scientist, was brought up in this business. Company management informed me last year that they were contemplating exiting early-stage therapeutic research and the vaccine business. The new plan will be to focus efforts on in-licensing and merger and acquisition efforts. In other words, they're going to try to buy product with patent protection, rather than try to develop the products themselves. "

"Why? Are we having problems developing our own products?"

"It's not that we're having problems coming up with ideas. The problem is that companies don't believe they can earn a sufficient monetary return, researching products that might actually heal people. Instead, the pharmaceutical industry has decided it needs to focus on products that make them money. Research for research's sake is being pushed back to the universities that are not ruled by shareholders.

"Let me give you an example. Three years ago we developed a great vaccine that cured very specific types of lung cancer. It was the result of many years of research and considerable amounts of money. It worked perfectly. The only problem was that the estimated number of people that would benefit from the drug wasn't large enough to justify the research and development costs. We figured only one in ten million people would contract that type of cancer, and it generally occurs in much later years of life. Additionally, because our drug effectively cured the cancer, we only needed to sell the patient a month's supply and they were cancer-free. It was a great drug! A miracle drug! Unfortunately, because of the small sales potential, it wasn't considered a profitable drug. It cost us much more money to develop the drug and market it, than what we were going to earn selling it."

"So are you telling me that in order for drug companies to become profitable, they have to develop maintenance drugs that the consumer will have to take over a lifetime? I've heard my dad say the same thing. Is that true?" Tom was incredulous. "You can't make a profit on drugs that actually cure a disease?"

"It's not easily done, unless the government supports the research through significant amounts of grant money."

"I'm surprised the politicians aren't doing more to solve this problem," Tom mused. He could see his response had struck a nerve with Doctor Cregar.

"Now, don't get me wrong. There are exceptions to the money problem. In 1983, Congress adopted the Orphan Drug Act, which gave drug companies a seven-year monopoly for bringing a new treatment for a rare disease to market. The Act was the result of one person's crusade to change the law because her son suffered from a disease that only afflicts about 50,000 people a year. In this case the drug companies had stopped research on the drug because the disease didn't affect enough people. Anyhow, the new act adopted by Congress gives the drug company, in effect, the same market protection that a patent does, without requiring the company to go through the lengthy—and expensive—process of getting a patent.

"There are currently over 300 so-called orphan drugs on the market, and many more under development. Some of these orphan drugs have generated revenues of over $1 billion a year. But keep in mind, the only reason that these drugs are able to generate so much money is because they have patent protection that mandates no other company can make a similar drug that competes with their product. The patent protection allows them to charge whatever price they want to charge for the drug. Some of these drugs cost patients as much as $150,000 to $200,000 a year."

"That's ridiculous! No one can pay that much for their medicine!"

"Insurance used to pay it. They figured that since few people were affected by these rare diseases, they could pick up the cost of the medication and spread the costs over their total insured base. Unfortunately, as more orphan drugs got developed, and as costs continued to rise across a larger population, insurers found they could no longer afford to provide coverage."

"So what happens to the people? The drug doesn't do them any good if they can't afford it!"

"Well, this is how bureaucracies get started, Tom. You'll find that most governments and companies are slow to repeal their original actions due to unintended consequences. In this case, one of the consequences of the 1983 Act was the emergence of the biotech industry. If we repealed the Act, we would deal a significant blow to a growing industry. That's one of the reasons the government wrestles with any kind of tax reform. Could you imagine the number of accountants, financial-planners and estate-planners that would be put out of business if we made taxes clear-cut and simple? We've become a slave to our creations."

"I guess everyone's got their own interests," Tom mumbled.

"So, getting back to your question, the latest development to make the drugs more affordable is to have insurance companies fund charities that grant money to patients needing these drugs. Similar to the creation of the tax-advisor industry, and the creation of the biotech industry, a whole new industry has been developed as a result of an act of Congress.

"Do you understand the vicious cycle being created, Tom? In order to cope with rising medical costs, insurers are requiring patients to pay higher premiums and co-payments for drugs. Although the poor and uninsured can often get these drugs paid by Medicaid or Medicare, people with insurance are finding it difficult to make their co-payments. In response, drug companies are giving money to charities specifically set up to help patients cover their drug costs.

"These new charities solicit money from the drug companies and the insurance companies. The contributing companies get a tax break for their donations. The drug companies increase the price for the drug, and the insurance companies increase the co-payments. The charities help pay the co-payments. Everyone's a winner. With help from the charities, the patient can afford the drug. Meanwhile, in order to cover their tax-free donation, the drug companies charge high prices for the drug. Similarly, in order to cover their own tax-free donation, the insurance companies charge high co-payments on the drug."

Tom glanced at his watch. His head was beginning to ache. Nonetheless, he did not want to offend his boss. "Doctor Cregar, I've learned more in the past hour than I learned during a whole semester at school! Thanks for helping explain how all this works. The relationships among all of these companies are fascinating."

"If you found my history lesson fascinating, you're going to be even more fascinated by what I'm going to tell you next."

Tom leaned forward in his chair, waiting to hear what Doctor Cregar was preparing to tell him.

CHAPTER THIRTEEN

"**D**oug, we received another RFP in the mail today!" Sarah shouted excitedly, waving a document in her hand. She now understood that an RFP represented a potential client's request for a proposal of the investment services Lakefront Fund Management could provide, as well as the associated cost of the services.

"This one's huge! It's a $200 million mandate for a Large Cap equity and investment-grade fixed income manager. We could do that!"

Doug smiled to himself. "I appreciate your enthusiasm. Who sent the RFP?" He asked, not looking up from his desk.

"It doesn't say who the potential client is. The RFP is from some investment consulting firm, named 'CYA Consultants.' Have you ever heard of them?"

Doug's smile faded as he walked over to Sarah with a chagrined look. Pressing close against her, Doug peered over Sarah's shoulder to review the materials she held in her hands.

"CYA Consultants. Yeah, I know them. They've sent us stuff before. We're in their database. Our investment performance has consistently ranked us in the top ten percent of all investment managers, and so they feel obligated to ask us to complete these RFPs on their clients' behalf."

"Well, have you gotten much business from them?"

Again, Doug smiled and laughed. "Do you know what I think CYA stands for? It stands for 'cover your ass.' All investment consultants should be named CYA. That's the only reason the industry exists. Let me tell you something about the institutional money management business, Sarah. Investment committees manage their assets in a similar way that some businesses manage their operations. It's all about avoiding liability. That's why half of the foundation boards in this country are run by lawyers. Nobody wants to risk being sued. So they lay the risk on some third party. Endowments and pension funds form investment committees who are charged with the mandate of deciding how their funds should be invested. You'd think that in forming these committees, the boards would take care to select people who are knowledgeable about investments, and who are capable of making appropriate investment decisions. The problem is that nobody on these committees wants to assume the liability of having to make investment decisions on their own. So instead, they spend their foundation's money to hire investment consultants to pick 'appropriate' money managers. In effect, the committees choose to cover their asses and blame the consultants if any of the investment managers do poorly."

Sarah wasn't sure why Doug was so upset, and she questioned him on it.

"It seems to me that if they don't let the consultants make the decision, they might be accused of potential conflicts of interest." Sarah paused. "Don't you agree? I mean, they don't want to give the impression that they're just selecting their buddies. They do have a fiduciary duty."

"Sarah, do you honestly believe that the consultants don't have conflicts of interest? You don't think the consultants go to events sponsored by the large money managers? The consultants are just parrots hiding under the guise of *independent advisors*. Have you heard about their most recent 'great idea?' They're steering their clients toward commodities, like oil and agriculture. They are calling these commodities 'alternative asset classes.' These aren't investments that generate earnings! They're commodities that are driven by supply and demand. Prices go up when demand increases, and prices drop when supply adjusts. These are trading vehicles. They're not long term investments."

"I've been reading about this. My understanding is that it's good to have commodities in your investment portfolio to reduce the risk. In other words, commodities might go up in price when stocks and bonds are falling. Isn't this the whole concept behind diversifying your investment portfolio?"

Doug was speechless...but very impressed. Obviously Sarah was taking an interest in the business.

"Sarah, financial contracts, based on raw commodity prices, were created to hedge the risk for manufacturers who use those commodities as ingredients for their products. In other words, since manufacturer's can't change the price of their product each time raw material prices change, they can use commodity contracts to offset the risk. Likewise, the contracts were also designed to protect the farmers who sell to the manufacturers."

"Fine. Maybe that's why the products were originally created. But the financial markets seem to have found a new use for these products. Why can't they be used to hedge the risk of stock and bond investing?"

"Sarah, don't you get it? Wall Street loves to manufacture new products. That's how Wall Street makes money. Don't you find it odd that ever since Wall Street started designing new products the volatility and risk in investment returns have *increased*? The only entity that has benefitted from these new financial products is Wall Street, and maybe the consultants who have a new way to 'add value' to their clients."

It was evident the subject bothered Doug, and he was not going to let it drop. Sarah looked for a chair to sit down. Doug graciously offered his seat, and then continued with his tirade against the investment consultants.

"Keep in mind, Sarah, the consultants don't want to take on risk, either. So rather than recommend a money manager like us, with a verifiable good track record, they select the large money managers, like your boyfriend at American Dinero. The consultants figure that if everyone else has their money at American Dinero, they have a built-in excuse if the performance goes bad one year. They'll rationalize their decision by arguing *'How was I to know? Everyone was caught off guard by this unexpected event.'* On the other hand, if they advise their clients to trust their money with us, they'll have to defend their decision to stray from the crowd. The first year we have bad performance, the consultants will fire us quicker than a New York Yankee manager."

The look on Sarah's face showed that she didn't follow Doug's analogy. Still, she knew she had to get him back in the right frame of mind.

"Well then, don't give them the opportunity, Doug. Don't have a bad year. Obviously the big guys who get all of the recommendations don't have bad years."

"Bullshit, Sarah! The consultants just give the big guys more latitude. If they have one bad year, the consultants will stick with them to see if they don't turn around their performance in the next year or two. We have one bad year and we're toast."

"Wow, you sound kind of cynical, Doug. But tell me, why should the consultants put their necks on the line?"

"Because that's what they're paid to do! They're supposed to add value. Similarly, the investment committees should want to find new, undiscovered managers that might provide more personal attention than the big boys. For that matter, the committee members should want to talk to each of their investment managers at least annually. They shouldn't use the consultants as gatekeepers. The consultants are allowed to treat us like some helpless patient in an HMO plan with restricted access. How do you establish a relationship of trust with your business partner in that type of environment?"

Sarah opened her mouth to interject, but Doug was not about to stop. She actually enjoyed watching how wound up Doug was—in fact, she found it kind of cute. So she let Doug continue with his tirade.

"If investment committees want the same managers as everyone else, why should these committees spend their money on consultants in the first place? Why don't they just go to the big managers directly and save themselves some consultant fees?"

"Don't the consultants come up with new ideas, and compute the investment performance of all the various managers?" Sarah asked.

"No! The consultants get all of their information from the underlying money managers. We supply consultants with performance numbers and market intelligence. It's a big marketing scam. And guess what? No one even bothers to tell the investment committees that a master custodian will calculate the performance of each of the underlying managers as part of their service. Again, the consultants are not adding a whole lot of value. But it's a hell of an industry, isn't it? "

Sarah was clearly confused by Doug's rambling. She wasn't sure what a 'master custodian' was—but she was done with this lesson. Realizing she had to refocus him on the task at hand, she attempted to summarize the conversation.

"So...I don't get it. Are you angry at the investment committees—or the consultants?"

"I'm angry at both of them! Neither of them wants to take responsibility. The consultants are like the babysitter who pulls the infant from scalding water after filling the bathtub in the first place. The money manager is the only one who constantly adjusts the water and is held accountable!"

"Well, I guess that's why my dad pays you the big bucks, huh?" Sarah was trying to get Doug to smile. "So do you want to complete this RFP, or not?"

"Go ahead and give it to me. I'll complete it. Next time you talk to your father, why don't you request an expense budget, so that I can wine and dine the consultants. Maybe if I treat them to a steak dinner every week like the big boys do, they'll be willing to throw me a bone every once in a while."

"You poor, poor, boy." Sarah smiled, as she stood up and affectionately patted Doug on the back.

Doug responded by slowly brushing the side of Sarah's cheek with his hand. It was amazing how quickly he was able to calm down and display his charm.

"Thanks for letting me gripe."

Sarah bit her lip, momentarily losing her thoughts in Doug's deep blue eyes. Regaining her composure, she turned quickly and softly uttered, "Well, I've got to get back to work. Let me know if you need any help."

CHAPTER FOURTEEN

"So, Tom, you've been patiently listening to me drone on about all of the challenges of the pharmaceutical industry; are you ready to hear what's got me so excited from my recent trip?"

"I'm all ears," Tom replied.

"While I was down in Missouri, I got a call one night from a man who identified himself as Doctor Richard Lake. I had never heard of him before. He said he had been studying some of the work I had done at Care4, and he thought I might be interested in something he was working on as a result of the recent earthquake. As you can imagine, after my recent personal tragedy, I was in no mood to start discussing work. Nonetheless, his discovery did sound intriguing. He convinced me that his idea was worth exploring, if for no other reason than to take my mind off my own personal sorrow."

Just then, the phone in Doctor Cregar's office rang. Cregar apologized for the interruption, and picked up the phone.

"Hello? Oh, hello, Doctor Lake. We were just talking about you… Yes, I've got an intern in my office who is working with me this summer. I thought he might be able to assist us on some of the work we need to do for developing Rivermass this summer…Well, I think that maybe we should do more lab testing before we do any human trials…But, Doctor, I really don't think that's wise yet…Sure, I imagine that I could make a trip down there early next week…I look forward to it. I'll see you then. Goodbye."

Hanging up the phone, Doctor Cregar had the same pained look on his face as he did when first hearing the news of his wife and family.

"Is everything okay, Doctor Cregar?"

"Yes, Tom. It's just rather hard to believe how quickly Doctor Lake has synthesized his discovery. He's been working tirelessly over the past four weeks in his lab. He says that he's already tested Rivermass on monkey subjects, and he reports some pretty remarkable findings. He wants to start testing on human subjects."

Tom could see that Cregar was troubled by the thought.

"What exactly does Rivermass do?"

"Our tests indicate that it's a new type of living cell capable of fusing with human muscles to increase lean muscle, while burning fat. It's basically the miracle body-enhancement formula that people have long searched for. It's like a super vitamin. Doctor Lake is convinced that this is a safe alternative to any kind of surgery or dietary supplement currently used by people who suffer from obesity."

"So is this like some kind of steroid?"

"Not exactly." Cregar looked at Tom, as if trying to determine how much he should tell him.

"How much do you remember from your biology class, Tom?"

"I never really grasped biology." Tom was no longer shy about exposing his ignorance.

"Fair enough," Doctor Cregar replied with a smile.

"Let me refresh your memory with a very simple tutorial on how muscles work. Muscles are basically made up of cells called muscle fibers. These muscle fibers are much longer than the other cells in your body. Muscle fibers are also different from other cells in your body in that they are multi-nucleated, meaning that they have more than one nucleus. All of our genetic codes, or DNA, reside within the nucleus. While our genetic code determines the 'blueprint' for building a person, proteins pretty much do the rest. Proteins are the construction materials, the tools, the workers. They provide the architecture of cells. They make up the working machinery. Hormones, enzymes, and antibodies are all proteins. Since cells need to supply themselves with protein, and since muscle fibers are so huge, you can imagine that these cells need more nuclei to be able to make all the proteins they need."

Tom nodded his head, despite having no recollection of this discussion in biology class.

"Earlier you asked a good question, Tom."

"I did?"

"Yes. You asked whether this drug acted like steroids. Nobody fully understands exactly how steroids work in the body. They appear to increase protein production, and so increase the size and strength of the muscle. But it's also been found that this process can be reversed if the muscle isn't stimulated. That's why training is an important factor for bodybuilders who use steroids."

"But you say that this drug is different from steroids?"

"Yes. Steroids tend to attach themselves to different body cells, such as hair follicles or certain areas of the brain. This has resulted in potential long-term health problems, such as weight gain, acne, cataracts, deterioration of the bones, and diabetes. Additionally, the protein product of steroids is different enough from natural proteins that it's easily detected in drug testing of athletes."

Cregar could see that Tom's mind was beginning to wander. Recalling what it was like to sit through long college lectures, he decided to get directly to the point.

"Now let me tell you what we've discovered as a result of this recent earthquake. The earthquake effectively re-shaped the Mississippi River. The devastating aspect was that a large portion of the river flooded cities like Memphis. However, we also found areas that were previously underwater are now exposed for the first time in hundreds, maybe even thousands, of years.

"While examining the newly exposed area, Doctor Lake discovered a natural living cell among the algae mass. And he's been successful in getting this cell to reproduce within his lab. We're calling this cell 'Rivermass.' Doctor Lake has given a liquid form of this cell to various animal subjects, and he's had amazing results.

"It appears that this liquid form is somehow able to travel within the blood stream until it reaches the muscle fibers. These cells then fuse themselves with the muscle fiber, making the muscle fiber bulkier. They also seem to increase the blood supply, drawing more oxygen to the muscle cells, thus increasing energy and burning fat. In short, this seems to be the miracle drug we've always wanted. If we can confirm that there are no negative side effects to this drug, this could be a multi-billion dollar product. Tom, if you continue working on this with me, you could become a very rich man, at a very early age."

Tom thought about his friends, Peter Jangle and Jerry Parker. Peter was always talking about the piles of money he helped manage at American Dinero. Likewise, Jerry talked about the money he was helping to manage at the insurance company. Tom smiled. *I'm glad I have friends who know how to manage money*, he thought to himself, *because I'm going to have plenty to manage.*

CHAPTER FIFTEEN

"**K**athy ... would you please come in here?"

Kathy walked into the office of Tim Jones, one of the young associates at Singer, Roth & Kuhn, the law firm where she was interning for the summer. Kathy despised Tim Jones. He always wore stiff, white starched shirts to work, and he must have polished his black tasseled shoes on a weekly basis. Kathy always felt that if she were a boy, Tim Jones would be the one she would single out to bully. She viewed him as a spineless suck-up to the partners in the firm. She was certain he was cheating his clients.

"Ted Singer told me that you voiced a concern over some of the hours I was charging my clients. Tell me, Kathy, is that true?"

Kathy felt the glare in Tim's eyes like a punch in the stomach. She had feared this day would come. Over the past couple of weeks she had become increasingly concerned that some of the associates at the firm were over-charging their clients. It had gotten to the point that she had trouble sleeping at night. She was certain that Tim was one of the biggest offenders. On the other hand, she knew that she would risk her job, and perhaps her reputation, if she were to rat on her superiors. She had shared her dilemma with her mother, who had convinced her to do the right thing, even if it was difficult. Kathy's mom told her that ignoring the situation would continue to weigh on her conscience. Kathy was longing for a peaceful sleep. In the last week she had become increasingly depressed at the thought of going to work in the morning.

She trusted Ted Singer the most of all of the partners in the firm. Kathy's mother had taught Ted's children. Ted was the person responsible for hiring Kathy this summer. She hoped that Ted had not betrayed her trust.

Kathy mustered all of her courage to look Tim Jones in the eyes. "Tim, I know that there is no way you worked sixty hours on the Children's Bureau case. The Children's Bureau is a non-profit agency, Tim. They don't have the resources to pay unreasonable lawyer fees."

Tim just stared at Kathy in silence. Kathy could notice a large blood vessel protruding from his right temple. His eyes were devoid of sympathy or mercy. Still, Kathy hoped to avoid an ugly confrontation.

"Perhaps you made a mistake," Kathy continued. "I'm not necessarily saying that you didn't work the number of hours you stated; maybe you just billed the wrong client."

"You little bi-" Tim stopped himself before he said something he would later regret. "How dare you tell me that— 'perhaps I made a mistake!' You were hired here as a filing clerk, and that's all I expect you to do. For your information, I did talk to Mr. Singer about this. I explained to him that I had no problem with the number of hours I charged the Children's Bureau. And you know what? The Children's Bureau has no problem with the hours I charged them, either. So guess what your little story got you? Your buddy, Mr. Singer, said that I could handle this matter however I saw fit. And you know how I see fit? I see it fitting that you get your little butt out of this office. You're done! Finished!! Get your stuff, and get out of here. And if I were you, I'd start considering some career other than law for your future!"

Kathy looked at Tim Jones in stunned silence. Tears welled up in her eyes. She was determined not to let Mr. Jones see her cry. Kathy bit her lip, and without saying a word, she turned and walked out of Tim Jones' office. Her pace quickened as she walked through the lobby toward the main elevator. After the elevator door shut, Kathy looked around to ensure that she was alone. Assured, she slammed her fist into the wall and broke down in tears. She had never felt like this before. She couldn't even tell which emotion was stronger, between the hurt and the anger.

Later that evening, Kathy and her mother sat together on their porch, trying to cool down from the humid evening air. Lisa Cohen had her arm around her daughter, as they gently rocked on the steel glider that had occupied the porch ever since Kathy could remember.

"You know what, Kathy? Jobs come and go. Even if you lose your wealth, you really haven't lost that much. But if you lose your character, *then* you've lost everything."

"I know I did the right thing, Mom, but it still hurts."

Her mother flashed a proud smile at Kathy and asked, "You know what I do when I've had a bad day?"

Kathy knew the answer. Her mother had always told her that there was no emotional pain that a bowl of ice cream couldn't heal. She smiled in anticipation of her mother's answer.

"You're smiling. You know the answer, don't you? I think we're just going to have to get ourselves a double fudge sundae. Does that sound good to you?"

Kathy nodded in acknowledgment.

"After we pig out on ice cream, we can turn on a movie, and you can sleep in my bed tonight. I was the one who promised you would sleep better once you got this off your conscience. I want to ensure that you sleep well tonight."

✵ ✵ ✵

While Kathy and her mother were able to sleep peacefully, not everyone in Michigan City was so fortunate. The first week of July punished the Midwest with unbearable heat. The humid evenings brought little relief from the burden of the scorching daylight hours. A tiny spark ignited in the silence of the night. The flame quickly grew in intensity to a raging fire. A thick pall of smoke began to billow on the outskirts of town. The foundation of a small wooden church succumbed to the oppressive heat. Within minutes, the 150 year-old Saint Jude Church was reduced to a dismembered labyrinth of red hot embers.

✵ ✵ ✵

While the church was burning, Peter Jangle was tossing in his bed, trying to find a comfortable position. He kicked the covers from his feet in frustration; the bed sheets were damp with sweat. His digital clock read 4:46 a.m. He knew it would soon be time to get up for work. Still half-asleep, he noticed a mild burning smell as he stretched over his bed to turn the small knob on his clock before the alarm rang. Peter sat up in bed, his eyes wide open, and began sniffing the air. It smelled like an electrical fire. Jumping out of bed, Peter walked from the bedroom to the main entrance of his apartment. He smelled nothing. Walking into the kitchen, he took a deep breath through his nose, but still smelled nothing. The burning smell returned—and intensified—as he cautiously walked back toward his bedroom. Like a detective looking for clues, Peter crawled along his bedroom carpet, searching for the source of the smell. He quickly determined it was coming from under his bed. Lying flat on his stomach, Peter extended his arm underneath his bed until his hand found something to grab. It was his econometer! The econometer had no outward signs of burning and it was not hot to the touch. Peter pulled the econometer out from under the bed, and tested it by typing on the keyboard, "*define inflation.*" The screen remained dark. The odor emanating from the device smelled like slow-burning incense. Peter vigorously shook the econometer, hoping to bring it back to life.

Remembering the last time he had used the econometer, he typed "*define collateralized bond obligation.*" Once again there was no reply. Discouraged at the thought of losing his source of knowledge, Peter set the object on the floor. Out of the corner of his eye he saw two nearly imperceptible yellow lights. Hoping that the econometer was once again returning to power, Peter grabbed the device and stared at the screen. Suddenly, like an ember igniting into a flame, the lights intensified, causing Peter to flinch in fear. As Peter looked back at the screen he could swear that he saw the image of the Sandman. His piercing yellow eyes. His fully clothed body bedecked with the familiar dark fedora and dark black coat. Peter was convinced that the Sandman was sneering at him, before the image slowly faded away.

Not wanting to disturb Tom in the next room, Peter softly whispered, "The Sandman is back." Peter knew he somehow had to prepare himself for a hidden enemy. Seeing he had plenty of time before work, Peter quickly dressed in a T-shirt, shorts and sneakers and left the apartment for a vigorous run along the Lake Michigan shoreline. The sound of the waves pounding away at the shoreline reminded Peter of the destructive forces of the Sandman.

✳ ✳ ✳

Peter checked the econometer one last time before going to work at American Dinero. The screen was as dark as a starless night. Peter had a hard time concentrating on the research papers that covered his desk at work. David Koslow had purchased the bonds of Consumer Media based on Peter's recommendation the previous week. As a reward, Peter was now working with Terri Tanaka on two additional companies to research for possible purchase. Glancing at the calendar, he took comfort in the fact that today was Wednesday, July third. He had read an email this morning, from Fran Solli, stating that the financial markets were closing early as a result of the July fourth holiday. This meant that the American Dinero employees would be able to leave work around 2 p.m. Peter and Tom Nelson were both planning on taking the 3:30 train from Chicago to Michigan City. Since the fourth of July fell on a Thursday this year, both boys were allowed to take Friday off. Wondering whether Jerry Parker would be making the trip to Michigan City from Indianapolis, Peter decided to give him a call.

"Jerry, my friend, how are they treating you down there?"

"Things are going well. I'm learning some new things about the insurance industry, and they're allowing me to help research possible bond purchases for the CBO they're trying to market to outside investors. Speaking of which—have you asked the folks there whether they might be interested in buying the equity tranche of our CBO?"

"No. I'm sorry. I haven't talked to anyone about it yet. I will."

Peter quickly tried to change the subject.

"I called you because Tom and I are planning on going home this weekend for the Fourth of July. I was wondering if you're planning on going home?"

"Yeah, my boss said that I could take Friday off. I'm getting ready to leave in a few hours. I should be getting in around seven. I don't know if I'm going to be doing anything tonight though. The drive always burns me out, and I'd like to spend some time with my mom. She's never really been the same since my brother died."

Peter shuddered with thoughts of the Sandman whenever the subject of death surfaced. In an effort to break the prolonged silence, Jerry continued.

"Hey, maybe I can bring some marketing materials with me to explain the structure of our CBO deal. You can have a look at it and tell me what you think."

"Sure. That'll be fine."

Peter wondered whether he would be able to understand the complexities of the deal without the aid of the econometer.

"Okay. Why don't you give me a call tomorrow and we can plan to meet somewhere."

"That sounds good," Peter replied, still preoccupied with thoughts of the Sandman. "Hey... Jerry..."

"Yeah? What's wrong, Peter?"

"Nothing. Just drive safely, okay?"

"I always do, my friend. I always do."

CHAPTER SIXTEEN

Tom Nelson and Peter both left work early, stopped at the apartment to collect their things, and hustled through the Chicago streets to reach the train station in time. Sweaty and out of breath, they plopped down in their seats aboard the South Shore Railroad just in time. Within a minute, Tom had the victorious smile of someone who had just pinned his older brother in a wrestling match. He couldn't wait to tell Peter what he was working on. His first impulse was to question Peter.

"So how's work going for the high finance guy?"

"It's going all right." Peter took the bait. "How are things for you at Care4?"

Tom's smile grew even wider as he leaned toward Peter to share the news. Tom had always relied on others to help him in the past. His hope was that the Rivermass product being developed by Care4 would allow him the opportunity to repay the debt he felt to others.

"I told you that I met my new boss, Doctor Cregar, right? The guy is amazing! Even though he lost his whole family in the earthquake, he's now working non-stop trying to develop this new drug that will help people lose weight and gain muscle."

Peter smiled at Tom's obvious enthusiasm. "Hasn't the miracle weight-loss drug been marketed by other companies before?"

"This is different. Previous drugs have typically focused on increasing the body's resting metabolic rate. The downside to that solution is that it puts too much stress on the heart. Other drugs have been designed to switch off the brain receptors involved in food cravings. Those usually don't work because scientists lack a complete understanding of how the brain works. What Doctor Cregar and his partner, Doctor Lake, have discovered, is a living organism that complements and enhances the existing proteins in the human body. In other words, it's not some synthetic chemical, alien to the body. It's a natural protein that enhances the body. Dude, *this* is what you should be investing in!"

"Wow, I thought you were going to be a salesperson for Care4. I didn't know you were training to be a chemist. So tell me, doctor, exactly how does this drug work?"

Tom saw that Peter wasn't taking his news very seriously, but he wasn't going to be deterred.

"Okay. Here's a quick summary of what I learned from Doctor Cregar. As you may know, many of our physical and mental characteristics are pre-determined by our genes. Our genes contain the instructions for building particular proteins, much like a how-to manual. There are millions of different variations of proteins that our genes might design. This is really important, because ultimately, the way a protein functions is dictated almost entirely by its shape, and how it folds, or interacts with other proteins. If it doesn't interact correctly, it can have terrible consequences. Misfolded proteins, for example, are thought to be the cause of Alzheimer's disease."

Peter was impressed with Tom's knowledge, and was now interested to hear more about this new drug.

"So...your drug, Rivermass, is a perfectly folded protein?"

"Yeah, I think so. We're putting living cells in the body that somehow manage to attach themselves to the muscle cell. The resulting super muscle cells are then able to reproduce. In other words, unlike synthetic drugs or hormones that are injected in the body, Rivermass links to, and improves, the original DNA pattern. The most compelling aspect for athletes is that it's totally undetectable by any kind of drug testing."

"Wait a minute! Are you telling me that the purpose of this drug is to help athletes cheat?"

"No. I mean, it can help athletes ... but the real benefit is that it will help overweight, and obese people, live healthier and happier lives!"

"Well ... that's a much better marketing pitch. It sounds interesting. I hope it works out for you guys."

"Interesting?! Peter, this is a *world-changing drug*. This is the Holy Grail! It will make billions and billions of dollars!"

Peter smiled and turned his head to look out the train window. As Tom continued to gush about the wonders of his new miracle drug, Peter grew exhausted by the day's events. His eyelids grew heavy as the train slowly swayed, pausing at its scheduled stops in East Chicago, Gary, and Hammond, Indiana.

The voice of the conductor was barely audible over the old speaker system.

"Next stop, Ogden Dunes!"

In a dreamlike state, Peter slowly opened his eyes and looked out on the suddenly dark, rainy afternoon. As the cooler rain met the scorched pavement, an eerie steam forged a barrier between the ground and the sky. Commuters exiting the train ran to their cars using briefcases or folders to protect themselves from the unexpected downpour. One lone commuter stood on the platform, seemingly frozen in time. Peter first noticed the raindrops slowly dripping from the black fedora. The man was dressed in black from head to toe. He seemed to relish the rain as if it were oxygen itself. Peter tried to avoid peering at the man's face...but the temptation was too great. Peter's eyes were drawn to the mysterious man as if pulled by an inexorable force. Peter caught a brief glimpse of his face, just before the train pulled away from the station. The Sandman was back! Peter turned to his friend, Tom Nelson, for support, but Tom had talked himself into a heavy slumber. Peter knew that it was time to discuss his suspicions with his dad. His father would be his best ally against the Sandman.

On the third day of July, in the comfort of his home, Peter described the recent events with his father. David Jangle wasn't sure how to reply. He fully trusted Peter. Nonetheless, the story seemed so unbelievable.

"Peter, are you sure you aren't just imagining that this genie has re-appeared?"

"No, Dad. Think about it. The same things are happening this time as what happened last time. Think about how hot it's been lately. It was unseasonably hot the last time the genie was here."

"Yeah, but the last time we were entering the month of December. This time it's the start of July. It's supposed to be hot. What about any other signs? You don't know of anyone who's been killed yet, do you?"

"Not directly. But what about the earthquake? The last time the genie appeared, we experienced a tornado and a small tsunami. This time we had an even more devastating earthquake."

"Listen, Peter, you know that I'll do whatever I can to help you. We just need to be sure we don't blame a genie for every natural disaster that occurs. We've had disasters on this planet for centuries. It's a part of life that we need to accept. In the meantime, stay vigilant, and look for signs of trouble. Above all else, don't attempt to fight your battles alone. I'm your father. You need to remember that I'll always be at your side."

Peter gave his dad a hug in appreciation for his words. "Thanks, Dad. We beat the Sandman once. I know we can beat him again."

"Keep in mind, Peter, it was your love that beat the Sandman last time. We're mere mortals. We can only use the power that God gives us. Only by love can we conquer evil."

Peter smiled, unsurprised that his dad would use the opportunity to try to strengthen his faith, but the comfort was short-lived. Later that evening, despite his best efforts to relax, Peter tossed in his bed, listening to the sound of the occasional firecracker exploding in the sky. He flinched with each blast that echoed through the night. His mind raced as he contemplated the potential schemes the Sandman might employ in his return. Before finally falling asleep he thought to himself, *"What if the Sandman is seeking revenge against me?"*

CHAPTER SEVENTEEN

The dark clouds parted, and the sound of fireworks could be heard early on the fourth of July. Peter had planned to wake up early to get in a quick bike ride before meeting his friends at the beach. Dressed in a cut-off T-shirt, biking shorts, and sunglasses, Peter cruised down Lake Shore Drive at a speed averaging 17 miles per hour. Viewing Lake Michigan as he raced down the road, he thought about the inflation-creation monster. He desperately tried to convince himself that the monster was not his creation. He vividly recalled what the genie had said to him three years ago.

"What can I say, Peter? You are your own greatest enemy. Your actions have unleashed a monster. An inflation-creation monster. Have you ever known the undertow in the lake to be as strong as it is this year? The waves are pushing people toward the shore and then pulling them back. Or is it something else pulling people back?

Perhaps your friend Steve was right. Perhaps it was the inflation-creation monster pulling on him."

Peter shuddered and tried to concentrate on the road. Despite the early morning hour, the heat was already intense. Peter was dripping with sweat as he pedaled past the Washington Park Zoo. The squawks of the exotic birds in their cages seemed to mock Peter as he rode by. Peter had never liked those birds. He stopped briefly to look out toward the Michigan City Harbor.

Looking to the west, Peter gazed at the US Coast Guard jetty, which culminated at the Michigan City lighthouse. The jetty extended 200 yards out into the lake, serving as a breakwater for young swimmers. The concrete jetty had two flat walkways on each side for fishermen to cast their lines. In times of rough surf, there was an eight-foot high wall topped by another five-foot wide pathway that could safely guide pedestrians to the lighthouse. Peter remembered the seven fishermen who did not have time to climb to safety the day that the inflation-creation monster arrived in his city. Peter's anger began to intensify. He knew he had to find the Sandman to prevent him from doing any further harm. Peter concluded that his best chance to find the Sandman was to ride his bike out to Mount Baldy. But today would not be the day. He had already committed to meet his friends at the beach, and he would never forgive himself if something were to happen while he was away. Wiping the sweat from his brow, Peter jumped back on his bike and headed home.

Within two hours, Peter was on the beach with his friends. Resting on the sand with his eyes closed, he wondered whether he should have traveled on to Mount Baldy to seek out the genie.

"You seem kind of quiet today, Peter. Is there anything wrong?"

Peter squinted, shading his eyes from the sun. He looked to his right, where Sarah Banks lay next to him. The bike ride had taken a lot out of him. He was both physically and mentally exhausted. Peter took a deep breath, wondering whether or not he should share his suspicions of the Sandman's return with Sarah. Looking into Sarah's eyes, Peter decided she was someone he could trust.

"I don't know. I just have a lot on my mind lately." Peter then gently tugged at Sarah's arm and pulled her to her feet. "What do you say we go on a walk down the beach?"

Ten feet away, Tom Nelson had his arm around Jerry Parker's shoulder.

"I'm telling you, man, Rivermass is going to make you a star."

Jerry and Tom had been fierce competitors during their high school football days. While Tom played his first year at IU as a walk-on, Jerry was awarded a scholarship, and was slotted as the second-string halfback for the upcoming season. Tom was convinced Jerry would benefit from the Rivermass pills.

"Who knows, maybe you could even get drafted to the pros based on the strength these pills provide."

"I don't know, Tom. I think that my playing days will be over after this upcoming season. Things are going pretty well for me down in Indy this summer. Some people are hinting that I might even get a job offer with Hoosier Insurance when I graduate next year."

"Okay, dude. Let me be sure I've got this straight. You think a career in insurance might be more exciting than a career in professional football!? Come on! The only profession I could think more boring would be some kind of accountant."

"Hey man, it's not like I'm going to be calling you up and selling the stuff. I'm going to be on the money side, like Peter. And believe me, there's an awful lot of money in this business."

Suddenly, an intriguing thought popped into Tom's head. "Hey—you guys offer health insurance, don't you?"

"Yeah, we offer both life and health insurance."

"Well…think about it. Rivermass has potentially incredible health benefits!" Tom was drawing on every sales skill he had learned.

"You should ask the people you work with whether they would consider covering the cost for Rivermass customers. It's just like covering the cost of any other health medication."

"What are you talking about?"

"Think about it. Health insurance companies have to pay millions of dollars in claims each year because people suffer from diseases like diabetes, high blood pressure, and heart disease caused by obesity. Your insurance company would have less expensive claims for these life-threatening diseases if they would just be willing to pay for the cost of our Rivermass formula. It's called 'preventive' medicine."

Tom figured that if the insurance companies would pay for the cost of Rivermass, Care4 would be able to charge a higher price for it. Consumers would not hesitate to pay a higher price for Rivermass if they knew that the insurance companies would be the ones ultimately footing the bill.

"Why should insurance have to pay for it? If it's as good as you say it is, people will buy it on their own. Anyway, I don't think insurance pays for over-the-counter medications. You're going to have to get this stuff approved by the FDA, as a safe and effective medication. And then you're going to have to get doctors to prescribe it. You oughta know how the game works. Your dad deals with doctors all the time."

"Yeah, I know how it works. Reps like my dad pay the doctors off with lavish gifts to encourage them to prescribe our company's pills. I've never really understood that practice."

Fresh from a swim in the lake, Kathy Cohen bent forward and then whisked her wet hair back. Her body had developed well during her college days, but it was her confident smile that immediately grabbed Jerry's attention. The dry sand on the beach seemed to squeal in delight as she walked over to the two boys.

"What deep conversation are you guys engaged in over here?"

Wanting to avoid further pressure from Tom, Jerry was quick to change the subject.

"Hi, Kathy. You're looking good, as always. Did you have a refreshing swim?"

"As a matter of fact I did. Thanks for asking. But that's not what you guys were talking about, is it?"

"Tom and I were just trying to solve the country's health care problems. That's all."

"Well, isn't the problem caused by the big pharma companies charging too much for their drugs?"

Tom took offense at the blame being placed with the pharmaceutical companies.

"Kathy, that's not fair. We need to charge enough to recoup the millions of dollars we spend on researching and testing new drugs. Think about it. What if the government were responsible for doing drug research? First off, it would be a much more inefficient process, and the price of discovery would probably increase. Second, how would the government pay for the high cost of labs, and testing, and oversight? They'd have to raise taxes on the public. We all know the public would never approve tax hikes. As a result, we wouldn't have the advances in medicine that make this such a great country."

"Can't the research be done at universities?" Kathy asked.

"We're doing some of that." Tom replied. "But we still have a need for the pharmaceutical companies. The universities need the pharma companies to do the manufacturing and the marketing."

Kathy nodded thoughtfully and turned to Jerry. "He's got a point, Jerry. Maybe the problem lies with *you* guys in the insurance industry. Drug companies like Care4 are making all of these great medical advances, but nobody can afford the medication. We should be able to buy health insurance to pay for our medications, but you guys have made health insurance so expensive, nobody can afford the premiums."

"Kathy, you need to understand. The insurance companies need to make a profit, just like the drug companies. Pharmaceutical companies need to charge a high price to recoup the cost of developing drugs, and we need to charge a high premium to recoup the cost of high claims. Not only are the claims for prescription drugs going up, but so are the fees that doctors and hospitals charge for their services. You should be *thanking* the insurance companies. We're the ones trying to contain costs by limiting the amount that we reimburse the doctors and the hospitals. We typically only reimburse the doctors and hospital seventy percent of what they charge."

"So what are you saying, Jerry? Are you saying that the doctors and hospitals are charging too much?"

"I don't know. The doctors and hospitals will say that they are forced to charge high amounts to patients *with* insurance because they are obligated to treat people *without* insurance. They could lower the price of their services if they believed they would get paid by everyone, but the people without insurance have no way to pay their debts. The only way they can make up their losses on the uninsured is to charge excessive amounts to the people who do have insurance."

"Yeah, but the hospitals know that the insurance companies won't pay the full amount of the invoice. It's really a pretty silly game," Tom said.

Jerry agreed and commented, "I've also heard the doctors say that they need to charge high prices because of the high cost of their malpractice insurance. In other words, the doctors will blame the legal system. Every time they make one simple mistake, they face multi-million dollar lawsuits."

"One simple mistake!" Kathy interjected. "Do they realize that one simple mistake could totally destroy someone's life, as well as the lives of his or her family? Do you know how many horror stories I've heard due to 'mistakes' in the hospital?"

"I know, Kathy. And I guess I forgot that you're now planning on being a lawyer. But you need to realize that humans do make mistakes. Mistakes will happen as long as we live on this earth. It's inevitable. In addition, most of the money won in these lawsuits goes to the lawyers, not the victims. And I find that offensive."

Kathy looked Jerry in the eyes. She knew that he was truly concerned about finding an answer to these problems. He had grown up in a poor area of the state, and many of his childhood friends lacked the health care that they had been discussing. Kathy had not yet told anyone about what happened to her summer internship.

After a moment's thought, Kathy said, "I guess there's plenty of blame to go around. We're all trying to help the less fortunate. The problem is that each industry tries to defend itself by placing the blame elsewhere. All industries need to share the blame. No one industry should have to shoulder society's burden by itself."

"Of course not! That's why we have the government to pick up the pieces, right?" Tom replied sarcastically. "The government's the one with the broad shoulders. All they have to do is print more money."

"Well, at least the government will focus on the mission of affordable health care, rather than a mission to maximize profits," Kathy shot back.

"Let me give you a quick example of what I mean," she continued. "Has anyone noticed how many new hospitals are being built? Why do we need so many hospitals? All of these hospitals are trying to build more elaborate facilities to compete with other hospitals. Meanwhile, the building costs continue to go higher and higher, and we, the public, have to pay for it. What's up with that?"

Smiling, Jerry said, "You're right, Kathy! All of the health care problems are the fault of the hospitals. And as long as we're on the subject of ridiculous building costs, how are school administrators able to justify spending money on state-of the-art sports complexes, rather than paying their teachers a decent wage?" Jerry knew that comment would elicit a response from Kathy.

"God, I love you!" Kathy exclaimed as she wrapped her arms around Jerry.

Sensing agreement, Jerry stated, "I'm glad we solved some major problems today—what do you say we all jump into the lake to christen ourselves as the country's problem solvers." Jerry slapped Tom on the back and hugged Kathy. Pressing her body hard against Jerry and wrapping her arms around him was the most comforting feeling Kathy had felt in the past week. Looking him in the eyes, she said, "You know, you really understand a lot of society's problems. You ought to run for Congress some day and do something to change things."

Jerry merely smiled and repeated, "I said, we all need to get baptized!" Grabbing Tom with his right hand and holding Kathy with his left, Jerry led the group of young problem-solvers into the waves of Lake Michigan.

After they had walked in silence for a couple hundred yards, Sarah was the first to speak. "So, Peter, what's bothering you so much?"

Peter stopped and looked out over the water. The sound of the waves crashing onto the beach sent a shiver up his spine.

"I have no way of proving it...but I think the Sandman is back."

Peter looked back at Sarah to try to gauge her reaction. Sarah's first reaction was to grab Peter's arm and squeeze tightly. She thought carefully about her next comments, not certain that she wanted an answer.

"Why? What's happened? Has someone been hurt?"

"Well...obviously there was the earthquake in Missouri."

Sarah was relieved that there was nothing more.

"Peter, lots of things have happened in the last three years. We've had droughts; we've had floods; we've had tornadoes. You've never blamed any natural disasters on the Sandman before."

"I know, but...I'm pretty sure I've seen him. The econometer he gave me is no longer working, and I think I saw him at the South Shore train stop in Ogden Dunes."

"Are you sure it was him, Peter? Did he say anything?"

"No. I was thinking about riding my bike to Mount Baldy today to look for him. But it's getting late, and I wanted to talk with you first."

"Well, I'm glad you did. Peter, maybe there's nothing to see. Maybe the econometer just burns out naturally after a while. Think about it. You've had it for three years now. And maybe the guy you saw at the train station was just someone who looked like the Sandman. Lots of people dress in black. And you yourself said the Sandman can change appearances if he wants to. If he's around, he might look completely different today."

Peter realized he had no proof that the Sandman had returned. The two people he trusted most, his father and Sarah, remained skeptical. Peter suddenly felt like a warrior with no battle to fight. He realized he would have to be patient. Patience was not a strong character trait for Peter Jangle.

Trying to change the subject, Peter asked, "So what time do you want to go to the fireworks tonight?"

Sarah was unprepared for the question, and had to think before replying.

"I'm not sure that I'm going to the fireworks. My dad's family is in town. So he wants us all home for dinner. My grandfather isn't doing too well health-wise. He can hardly get out of bed any more. It's been very hard on my mom and dad to take care of him. They really think that his days are numbered. I hate to say it, Peter, but I often pray that God will just take him and end his suffering. It's hard on my parents, and it's hard on me, to see death so close by in our house."

Peter had always admired Sarah's exceptional compassion. He no longer wished to burden her with his groundless fears. Pulling her into his arms, Peter hugged Sarah tightly. As they embraced on the beach, their statue-like forms looked like a beacon of hope and comfort to the lost souls of the sea.

After two minutes of silence, Sarah whispered, "I'll come by your house after dinner and we can take a short walk through the golf course to the fireworks."

✫ ✫ ✫

As the day turned to dusk, Sarah Banks walked up and down the hills of Moore Road toward Peter's house. Earlier that evening, she had walked into her grandfather's room and stood by his bedside. Suddenly her grandfather opened his eyes. Looking up at Sarah, he asked nonchalantly, "Have you come for me, angel? I'm ready to go."

Sarah thought she had lost him as he faded back to sleep.

Peter was outside practicing his basketball shots when Sarah arrived. Wiping a small bead of sweat from his forehead, he called, "Come on, Sarah, hurry up! We need to get there early to stake out a good spot to watch the fireworks."

Peter Jangle's house was located on the seventh hole of the golf course. Each year the town of Long Beach put on a spectacular fireworks show on the first-hole fairway. Just before leaving the house, Peter ran into the garage and grabbed for something barely noticeable in the corner. "Wait, Sarah! Let me put some mosquito repellant on you before we leave. You don't want any mosquitoes nibbling on you, do you? You'll have enough to worry about with *my* nibbling."

Sarah smiled. "You better be careful that I don't swat you dead."

Peter and Sarah traversed the golf course in near silence. Sarah was thinking about her grandfather and Peter was thinking about the Sandman. A crowd had already gathered by the time they reached the first-hole fairway. Peter searched for the perfect spot to spread out a blanket and they both sat down and rested. Peter kept glancing at Sarah as the fireworks began. Her image looked angelic in the light of the red, white and blue hues bursting in the sky. Peter knew that Sarah was the perfect complement to his somewhat impetuous behavior. The fireworks show evoked feelings of both pride and gratitude within Peter. Peter put his arm around Sarah during the finale. While the rest of the crowd was preparing to leave, Peter took Sarah into his arms to deliver a deep, passionate kiss. The kiss was only partially returned. Sarah's thoughts were elsewhere.

"So what do you want to do tomorrow?" Peter asked.

"I told my dad that I was going to help him tomorrow. I promised that I would go in to work with him."

"What about tomorrow night?"

Sarah feared Peter would ask about Friday night. *What was she going to tell him?* She had forgotten that Peter was going to be home for the Fourth of July weekend. She remembered she had promised Doug Keyster that she would go to a Fourth of July party with *him* on Friday night. She had made the plans far in advance, when Doug was complaining about his woeful social life. At first she resisted Doug's invitation, telling him that she didn't feel comfortable going out with him. But Doug assured her it was not a date. He just wanted Sarah to meet some of his friends. Sarah was now confronted with the dilemma of explaining her intentions to Peter. She didn't want to hurt Peter's feelings. Nonetheless, part of her was excited about going to the party with Doug.

"I'm sorry, Peter. I can't do anything tomorrow night. Can we do something on Saturday?"

Sarah's inability to look Peter in the eye immediately aroused Peter's suspicions. Nonetheless, he chose to overlook Sarah's evasive behavior.

"Sure...are you doing something with your family tomorrow night?"

"Yeah. You know...we don't think my grandpa has much longer to live. My parents would like me to keep him company whenever possible."

"Well maybe I can come over and help you keep him company."

Growing increasingly frustrated with her own deceit, Sarah raised her voice, "No, Peter! I...I just want to be alone for a bit, okay?"

"Fine." Peter said. He remained suspicious, but figured he had already said enough to exacerbate any guilt that Sarah was harboring.

Peter walked Sarah back to her house. The humidity of the evening only seemed to aggravate the pressure building between them. Peter gave Sarah a curt goodnight kiss before turning to head home. As he walked down Lake Shore Drive, he couldn't help but be drawn to the sounds of the waves crashing on the beach. The whitecaps foamed like a shark's menacing teeth. Peter questioned whether or not he was overreacting to Sarah's behavior. One block from Sarah's house, he came upon a sign indicating Bus Stop 31. The location was furnished with two long wooden benches, resting on a weather-worn wooden deck. A rectangular sign in front of the shelter read "Private Beach. For Residents Only."

The time was approaching midnight, and Peter looked down toward the beach for any sign of campfires or other activity. The beach was vacant. Descending the wooden steps, Peter grew increasingly troubled by Sarah's mysterious behavior. Upon reaching the sandy beach, Peter slipped off his shoes and let his bare feet dig into the sand. Abruptly, he took off in a full sprint. Peter raced 100 yards in the soft, dry sand before stopping to catch his breath. Immediately he turned around and sprinted back to where he had started. Peter did six 100-yard sprints before finally collapsing in the sand. He struggled to catch his breath as perspiration poured from his body. Nonetheless, he felt somehow fulfilled. Slowly climbing the steps back to the road, Peter walked home alone.

CHAPTER EIGHTEEN

P eter woke the next morning and decided to surprise Sarah at the bank. Feeling guilty about the previous night, he figured that taking Sarah out to lunch would be the perfect way to make amends. After a brief shower, Peter slipped on a freshly starched shirt and left the house. Peter walked through the entrance to Michigan City National Bank just before noon.

Spotting Ms. Sanders at the reception desk, Peter walked up to ask where he could find Sarah. Caught in the middle of a particularly nasty coughing spell, Ms. Sanders struggled to describe how to get to the trust department, and directed Peter to the elevator. Peter kept looking back at Ms. Sanders, wondering if he should offer some assistance. However, as soon as the elevator doors opened, her coughing stopped, reassuring Peter that he could proceed. Upon reaching the fourth floor, the elevator doors slowly opened, and Peter immediately recognized the sweet sound of Sarah giggling. Peter always felt that her laughter could nurse a terminally ill patient back to health. Everything she did seemed to have a calming, soothing effect.

Following the laughter, Peter came upon Sarah. She was sitting at her desk with a sweeping grin across her face. Doug Keyster was standing close to her side. Each of his arms surrounded her, as if shielding her from any oncoming danger. Doug was peering down over Sarah's shoulder, and she was gazing back up at him. Her eyes were fixed on Doug, as they shared an obviously humorous story. It was not until Peter spoke up that they noticed his presence.

"Peter! What are you doing here?"

"I just thought I would come by to take you to lunch."

Nonchalantly, Doug Keyster extended his hand to Peter. "So...you're the stud money manager, huh? How are you doing? My name's Doug Keyster. I run this lowly little trust company here in Michigan City."

Peter's response was ice cold.

"Sarah's told me about you. She says you guys have put together some pretty good investment performance numbers." He paused. "Congratulations."

"Oh...you know what they say...better lucky than good. I've got to admit, we've been pretty fortunate to attract some good clients for a company our size. Here...let me show you around."

Peter resented Doug's smugness. Doug seemed innocent enough, but Peter could sense that Sarah was attracted to him physically, as well as by his care-free attitude.

Following Doug to his office, Peter asked, "So Doug, have you always wanted to be in the banking business?" Peter made a distinction between the banking business and the money management business, judging the banking business to be clearly inferior.

"No. Are you kidding?" Doug replied with a smile. "I would have loved to live the life of a rock star, or an artist. Unfortunately, I found that I just didn't have the talent. Investing just came naturally. I was always pretty good with numbers, and I do think there's a certain art to the investment process. Wouldn't you agree, Peter?"

Doug gave Peter an ingenuous smile and then continued with his tour.

"I've got to tell you, Peter, I've really enjoyed working with Sarah this summer. She has really been an inspiration to me when I'm feeling down. You're a lucky guy."

This time Doug waited for a reply.

"Yeah. Sarah's the best," Peter acknowledged, not really listening to Doug's words.

"I also appreciate you letting me take her to this party tonight. I think she felt sorry for me. I don't have time to date much and I just broke up with a short-term girlfriend. I caught her cheating on me. Do you believe that? Anyhow, my ex is going to be at this party with her new boyfriend. Have you ever had anyone cheat on you, Peter?"

Peter was speechless, trying to grasp whether he had heard Doug correctly. Getting no response, Doug continued talking.

"I wasn't even going to go until Sarah said that she would come along. Sarah always seems to save the day, huh, Peter?"

Peter was stunned. Sarah had lied to him, with a story that she was going to care for her sick grandfather. Though Doug continued talking, Peter was no longer listening. He was incensed. He felt a burning urge to break something. He started looking around Doug's office for something to throw.

His eyes then fixed on a large object sitting on the top of Doug's pre-fabricated bookshelf. It was a large hour glass. About fifteen inches in length, the glass was encased in a fine mahogany frame. It was beautiful. When Peter focused on the sand resting at the bottom of the hour glass, he immediately thought about the Sandman. *Was this a clue that the Sandman had been here? It must be a sign. How was the Sandman planning to hurt him this time? By stealing his girlfriend?*

Interrupting Doug's ramblings, Peter pointed to the hour glass and inquired, "Where did you get that?"

"This hour glass?" Doug picked up the hour glass from the bookshelf and lightly caressed its figure. "I forget where I picked this up." He then turned it over and set it on his desk. Both men watched the sand slowly trickle its way to the bottom.

"I love the beauty of it, don't you, Peter? The figure reminds me of a woman."

Peter tried to maintain his composure and abruptly announced, "I've got to go." Whisking past Sarah he said, "So, you've got to take care of your grandfather tonight, huh?"

Sarah knew right away her secret had been exposed. "Peter, wait!" she called, rushing after him to the elevator. "I was just trying to make him feel better. He was hurt from a recent break-up."

"I don't want to talk about it right now, Sarah. I don't really like the guy, and I'd prefer you don't go out with him tonight. But if you do...be careful! You have no idea who he might be!" The elevator door closed and Peter was gone.

✡ ✡ ✡

That evening Peter knew he had to do something to numb his wounded heart. He gave his friend, Tom Nelson, a call.

"Peter, I'll tell you what. I'll give Jerry and Kathy a call, and we can all get some beer and go down to the beach tonight. Maybe Kathy can tell us more about this Keyster guy."

Within two hours, the four friends were sitting around a campfire on the beach, with a case of beer. Kathy was the first to talk about her recent disappointment. She had decided to tell everyone what happened to her internship. In some way, she thought it might make Peter feel better.

"I can't believe I got fired. I was just trying to be honest."

"Just remember, Kathy, honesty is always the best policy. I know it hurts now, but I'm sure that, later in life, you'll look back and be proud of what you did. You should know that lawyers are not always the most virtuous folks. Sometimes I think it's harder to encourage honesty between two lawyers than it is to encourage cooperation between a snake and a rat."

"Wow, that's pretty blunt, Tom," Kathy said with a laugh.

Next, it was Jerry's turn to cheer her up.

"I agree with Tom, Kathy. Don't worry about it. You tried to do the right thing. I'm just amazed that you tried to defend the law profession during our conversation at the beach yesterday."

"Hey guys, don't start believing that my experience is a reflection of the whole profession. I'll still defend their role, Jerry. The law's an admirable profession. It's unfortunate that we have some sleazy professionals practicing. But I guess you could say that about any profession."

"Yeah. I guess the problem that I have with the law is that everything has to be black or white. If you admit guilt, even if it's a stupid mistake, you're likely to get punished like a villain. It dehumanizes us. Think about the medical profession. Doctors can't express their sorrow, or guilt, or even sympathy to patients when they make a mistake. They're trained that if they admit so much as a *possibility* that they made a mistake, it will be used against them in a lawsuit. So what do we do? We suppress our guilt until it simmers into self-hatred."

"Hate ever kills, love never dies. Such is the vast difference between the two."

All three of the others looked at Peter in stunned silence.

"What did you say Peter?"

"It's a quote by Gandhi. Haven't you ever heard it? Another quote I like is one by Ben Franklin, *'Beer is living proof that God loves us and wants us to be happy.'* Peter then guzzled the last quarter can of his beer and tossed it into the cooler. He was proud that he had remembered the Gandhi quote that his father had taught him. He was also happy to help himself to another can of beer.

"So how many beers have you had, Peter?"

"Don't worry about it, Kathy, it doesn't matter."

A silence fell over the group. No one knew exactly what to say to Peter. They all just listened to the crackle of the burning driftwood in the fire. Peter's temperament changed with each ounce of liquid anger that he imbibed. Finally he blurted out, "So, Kathy, has Sarah told you that she wants to leave me for this Doug Keyster guy?"

Tom had already told her what happened, so she was prepared to allay Peter's concern.

"Oh, don't worry about Doug, Peter. He's harmless. He's a ladies man. Sarah knows that. And for some reason, she still prefers you."

"Ladies man or not, I think he's evil."

No one knew what to say.

Trying to start a new conversation, Jerry asked, "Hey, Peter, not to change the subject, but have you had a chance to review that material I gave you the other day regarding our CBO?"

"No. I'm sorry. I'll look at it tomorrow. I think I'll head back to Chicago in the morning. That way I can focus on it over the weekend and call you if I have any questions. Then I'll talk to someone at work about it, and let you know what they say. I'm sure I'll be able to get them to purchase a small amount of the deal."

The four friends laughed and shared various stories about their summer internships until 2 a.m. Then they gathered their trash and went home to sleep.

The next day, Peter's dad tried to convince him to stay in Michigan City one more evening.

"Peter, are you sure you want to go back to Chicago today? Why don't you at least give Sarah a call and make sure that nothing bad happened to her last night. I know you're worried about her."

"I told you, Dad. I had Jerry Parker call her first thing this morning. He told me that she was fine. Nothing happened."

"So...I'm not exactly sure what your concern is... Do you still think that this guy Doug Keyster is the same genie you dealt with years ago?"

Peter was growing increasingly frustrated.

"No, Dad. I never said he was a genie. People have known him for years. I just think he might be using the genie's powers, just like I did three years ago. The genie gave me a coin that could influence the thoughts of others. What if he gave Doug Keyster the same coin? Think about it. He's doing great in his job. His investment returns are spectacular. And I think…I think he's starting to have an influence over Sarah. Doesn't that sound familiar? When I met the genie, my grades dramatically improved, we won the state football championship, and that was the first time that I ever made an impression on Sarah. The genie's getting his revenge against me for betraying him. He's empowering someone else to humiliate me in both my career and my relationship with Sarah."

"You know what, Peter? When I was young, my father used to tell me this story of a basketball player named Jude Scetairo."

Peter braced himself for another story from his father. He always thought his father would have made a good preacher. Peter listened as David Jangle continued with his story.

"Jude was a pretty good ball player, but never quite the natural athlete, like some of the other kids. He practiced as hard as he could, but he always got down on himself when he couldn't do as well as the others. He had a good coach, who noticed how hard he was working at practice. As a reward, the coach bought Jude a new pair of the most stylish red gym shoes he had ever seen. Jude loved the shoes. He felt special in the shoes. He worked even harder, practicing every day in his shoes for hours. The work started paying off. Jude earned a spot in the starting line-up, and often led the team in scoring. He became an inspiration to the other players on the team. Soon, the whole team was working harder. The coach thought it was only fair to start rewarding the other players. One by one, after a particularly well-played game, the coach would reward another player with a pair of these red gym shoes. Before long, the team was unbeatable. As the team started advancing through the state playoffs, and the competition got tougher and tougher, Jude was getting less and less playing time. Rather than celebrating the fact that his team was winning, Jude started dwelling on the fact that he wasn't getting as much playing time. The shoes were no longer special for him, and he was burning with jealousy because all the other kids had the same shoes. The night before the state championship game, Jude went through the locker room and stole everyone's red shoes. As you can imagine, the team got distracted on game day, and they got crushed by their opponent."

Peter looked at his dad in silence. "I'm not jealous, okay, Dad?"

"I just think it would be a good idea to give Sarah a call when you get to Chicago."

"Thanks, Dad. I'll think about it."

Peter embraced his father and then climbed out of their blue Ford Escort and walked into the train station.

The train ride back to Chicago was uneventful. Upon arriving at Randolph Street, Peter walked briskly to his apartment. Closing the door behind him, he stopped in the middle of the family room and looked toward the bedroom. He swallowed hard as his saliva strained against the growing tightness in his throat. Walking slowly toward the bedroom, he pondered whether or not the econometer would once again serve as a resource of knowledge. He got down on his knees, wondering whether it was appropriate to pray for it to work. Reaching under the bed, he pulled out the econometer. He turned it on, but the screen was dark. *What does this mean? Is the Sandman taking all of his gifts away from me—including Sarah?*

Peter looked out the window of his apartment. Seven pigeons were resting on the building ledge across the street. Suddenly three pigeons swooped down toward his window. Whisking by his window, they soared back into the sky. In the sunlight they looked as white as doves. *The Father, the Son, and the Holy Spirit,* Peter thought to himself. Perhaps it was a sign of a new beginning.

Wishing to put the past behind him, Peter grabbed the econometer, walked out into the hallway, and dumped it in the trash chute. "I think I'll research Jerry's CBO the old-fashioned way," Peter said with renewed purpose.

✵ ✵ ✵

Back in Michigan City, Sarah was wondering if she had done the right thing. She had also heard, from Jerry, what had happened to Kathy this summer. She needed to call Kathy.

"Hello, Kathy? It's Sarah. I spoke with Jerry Parker this morning, and he told me the news about your summer job. I'm so sorry. I can't believe it! Are you okay?"

"Yeah. It's okay. I'm sorry I didn't tell you first. I wanted to… but since you went out with Doug Keyster last night… and I was out with the other guys…Well, one thing led to another and I told them what happened. Anyhow, enough about that. How was your date?"

"Kathy, it wasn't a date. I just told him that I would go along with him this one time. I don't know why you can't accept the fact that I love Peter. Jerry was asking me the same questions this morning. He said that Peter actually was afraid Doug was going to hurt me."

"Well...that's Peter. Always there to save the day. This Doug guy didn't do anything to hurt you, did he?"

"No, just the opposite. He was really wonderful." Sarah's voice began to fade. "He treats me differently than the way Peter treats me."

"Okay, Sarah, now you've got my interest. What are you talking about?"

"You have to promise not to say anything to anyone."

"You know I won't. I'm your best friend. So tell me what happened. Did he kiss you?"

"I don't know how to explain it, Kathy. It was fun. It was different. Everyone there was older than me, but it didn't seem to matter. Doug introduced me to all his friends and they were all very nice. It was just so much more grown-up than the college parties we attend."

"Sarah, you're holding out on me. Did you kiss him?"

"Yeah...I did." Sarah spoke slowly, as she recalled the events of the evening. "It's weird, Kathy. I don't know how to explain it. I still love Peter. He needs me to take care of him. But Doug's different. He makes me feel like we're in an equal relationship with one another. Do you know what I mean? Peter's great. And he says all of the right things. But Peter always thinks he's right. He doesn't give me credit for the things I do to help him. Doug, on the other hand, encourages me to stand up for myself and not let other people walk all over me. He actually admires me, and thanks me for the help I provide him."

Kathy was taken aback by Sarah's honesty, and didn't know exactly how to respond. She cared deeply for Sarah.

She had always thought it was her job to encourage Sarah's self-confidence. She wasn't happy at the thought of someone else assuming her role. She chose her next words carefully.

"Are you sure you don't just have a crush on Doug, the same way that we all had crushes on certain teachers while growing up?"

"I don't know, Kathy," Sarah replied, with frustration evident in her voice.

Kathy could tell that her friend was confused; despite her frequent disagreements with Peter's opinions, Kathy knew that Peter cared deeply for her friend. Though certain of Peter's devotion to Sarah, she was not yet sure about Doug. Peter's warning about Doug the other night resonated within her. She decided she would have to have a talk with Doug Keyster.

CHAPTER NINETEEN

Peter spent most of Sunday evening researching the structured note product that Jerry had recommended to him. He was feeling relatively comfortable with his new knowledge. He had learned that CBOs were basically a structured combination of individual bonds. His finance classes— as well as his lessons with the genie— had taught him that bonds were simply IOUs that corporations issued investors. The evolution of finance continued to intrigue Peter.

Following the Great Depression, most people placed their savings in a bank, earning a nominal return. People were relatively comfortable with certificates of deposit issued by banks because, even if the bank were to fail, the federal government would insure the investment, up to a certain amount. Bank deposits were thus considered a very safe investment. The banking industry used the cash from its consumer savings deposits to invest in higher yielding instruments. The investments that banks funded ranged from loans to consumers, loans to corporations, or investments in publicly-traded bonds. Because there was more risk involved with loaning to consumers or corporations, the investment in these entities carried a higher return.

During the latter part of the twentieth century, mutual funds emerged as a more attractive long-term savings vehicle for consumers. Mutual funds and retirement plans offered higher potential returns than bank deposits. In addition, the government offered tax incentives to invest in these retirement vehicles.

Peter knew that most investors today are aware of the ability to invest in a diversified portfolio of equities or corporate bonds, through mutual funds. Corporate bonds are paid back from the issuing corporation in the same manner as an issuing bank repays its certificates of deposits (CDs). The difference between a bond and a CD is mainly an issue of credit quality. Since the government doesn't insure corporate bonds, if the company goes bankrupt, the investors lose their money. By contrast, if the issuing bank of a CD goes bankrupt, the federal government will ensure that investors are paid from a government insurance fund. As the financial markets have evolved, consumers may now purchase individual bonds directly through a broker, or they may purchase a diversified portfolio of bonds through a mutual fund.

Peter also learned that corporations are not the only entities that issue bonds. The U.S. government issues bonds to investors in the form of treasury securities. The government became further involved in the fixed income market through its desire to make home ownership possible for all Americans. One of the early creations of Congress, following the Great Depression, was the Federal Housing Administration (FHA). The FHA helped to standardize mortgage terms, so that a mortgage loan made by a bank in one part of the country would have similar legal repayment terms as a mortgage loan granted by a bank in a different part of the country. In addition, the FHA stated that if a mortgage loan met certain criteria regarding the amount borrowed, the value of the property, and the income of the applicant, the government would guarantee repayment of the mortgage loan. The government insurance reduced the risk for the banks and opened up the loan market to other investors, such as insurance companies.

Nonetheless, the demand from people applying for a mortgage to buy a home still exceeded what banks were willing and able to lend. The only way to increase the incentive to lend money was by developing a strong secondary market for mortgages. In other words, the government needed to create a market where investors could purchase mortgage loans, similar to the way they purchased corporate bonds. By attracting more investors to the mortgage loan market, more money would be available to fund the mortgages of people who wanted to buy homes.

While the FHA helped ensure the safety of some mortgage loans, it was not sufficient to create a secondary market for mortgages. As a result, Congress created another government-sponsored agency, the Federal National Mortgage Association (FNMA). Fannie Mae was originally created by the government of Franklin D. Roosevelt, as part of his New Deal in 1938. Its purpose was to create liquidity and provide funding for homeownership. For about three decades, FNMA was the only game in town, insuring the majority of mortgages originated in this country. But once its balance sheet grew too large, the federal government worried that it was guaranteeing too much consumer debt.

In 1968, Congress divided FNMA into two organizations: the existing FNMA, and a new Government National Mortgage Association, popularly known as GNMA, or Ginnie Mae. This new entity was a true government agency created to provide the "full faith and credit of the US government" to support the FHA and Veterans Administration mortgage market.

By contrast, FNMA was a now a public company, created by the government. When FNMA was spun-off as a public company, it stopped guaranteeing government-issued mortgages—instead, it guaranteed mortgages issued by private banks.

Realizing that FNMA was a virtual monopoly in the private mortgage market, Congress chartered a competitor in 1970, called the Federal Home Loan Mortgage Corp., known as FHLMC, or Freddie Mac. The creation of a competitor to FNMA was deemed necessary at a time when the American economy was strained by the Vietnam War. As often happens in the private sector, both FNMA and FHLMC competed for growth. As their balance sheets began to grow dramatically, their complexity grew. As public companies, these two new entities aimed to provide the greatest return for their shareholders, while attempting to stay within the guidelines of the federal regulators.

Due to the increased availability of credit, the mortgage banking industry looked for new ways to issue home loans to consumers. Mortgage banks were created. Unlike traditional thrifts and commercial banks, mortgage banks did not have depositors. They were in the business of borrowing funds from sources other than deposits, and then lending money to the home buyer. However, rather than keep those loans on their balance sheet, they sold the mortgage loans to either banks, insurance companies, or the new entities called FNMA and FHLMC. Mortgage banks further enabled growth in the secondary market for mortgage loans. These bankers earned money from servicing the loans they originated, plus they received cash from originating the mortgage and selling the mortgage.

Growth in the mortgage market exploded. FNMA and FHLMC were able to borrow at extremely low interest rates, providing cash to purchase loans from banks. Having an outlet to sell their existing loans, banks were able to originate an increasing amount of new mortgage loans. Meanwhile, FNMA and FHLMC pooled together the loans that they purchased from the banks to diversify their holdings among different borrower types and different geographical areas. In other words, by combining hundreds of different thirty-year mortgage loans, these agencies were able to sell to investors a diversified investment product backed by the loan pool. The bond-rating agencies considered this a high-quality investment because it wasn't overly reliant on any one borrower or one geographic area. The risk was diversified. As a result of these creations, almost anyone who held a job or could prove some source of repayment, was able to obtain a mortgage loan. Before the creation of this secondary market, that was not always the case.

As the financial markets evolved, Wall Street continued to find ways to make credit available to borrowers other than home buyers. Companies that were previously seen as too great a credit risk by most financial institutions were now able to access credit. Insurance companies and mutual funds that were looking for higher yielding investments began purchasing the debt of higher-risk companies. Insurance companies kept these bonds in their investment portfolio, while mutual funds allowed the general public to share in the return on these investments, through the purchase of high-yield mutual fund shares. The goal of the financial community was to develop a secondary market for these high-risk companies, similar to the secondary market for home loans. By providing financing to some of these higher-risk companies, the country was better able to promote entrepreneurial business activity.

Soon, the insurance companies and the mutual funds started buying the bonds of these high-risk companies and pooling them together, similar to what FNMA and FHLMC did with home loans. Investors could then buy this pool of loans, which was more diversified, resulting in less risk. Knowing that some investors were willing to take on more risk to get a higher return, the creators of Collateralized Bond Obligations (CBOs) sliced the total loan pool into different risk classes, or tranches. The higher-risk class would absorb the first possible loan defaults in the pool. To compensate these investors for the additional risk, they were offered a much greater potential return if the companies in the pool did not default. This highest-risk tranche was called the "equity" class due to its high risk/return profile; it was often the most difficult part of the deal to sell. Most investors in the equity class made their purchase decision based on their faith in the investment ability of the managers originating the investment pool. In order for Peter to sell this class to the portfolio managers at American Dinero, he would have to convince them that the Hoosier Insurance portfolio managers were smart investors.

Peter also realized that the CBO market eventually evolved into the Collateralized Debt Obligation (CDO) market. Just as the CBO market provided easy financing for high-risk companies, the CDO market provided easy financing for sub-prime mortgage loans. Peter knew that the portfolio managers at American Dinero were not fans of the sub-prime loan market.

Peter reviewed the historical investment performance of Hoosier Insurance's high-yield bond team. They ranked among the top high-yield managers in the country. Additionally, Peter looked at the potential return that the equity portion of the Hoosier Insurance deal offered, and it was much greater than alternative investment options. Peter felt he knew enough about the deal to make a proposal to management. Armed with a full day's analysis of investment performance charts, historical default rates, personal biographies, and the investment process and methodology employed by Hoosier Insurance, Peter opened the door to American Dinero and walked toward his cubicle.

"Who was the freakin' moron who authorized the purchase of these Consumer Media Bonds?!"

Peter did not have to look up. He recognized the condescending voice of Tony Salami. Tony bellowed his question throughout the floor, as if daring anyone to confront him. Peter stood up in his cubicle and peered over the wall in the direction of the large trading desk. He was careful not to let anyone see him. He wanted to find out why Tony had an issue with the Consumer Media bonds—and see if anyone would point an accusatory finger his way. David Koslow rose to answer Tony's challenge.

"I had one of the other traders buy the bonds last week, Tony. You must have been in the can. We couldn't find you. What do you have against my bonds?"

"Koslow, don't you know that company is in play?"

"I knew they recently repurchased some of their stock. I figured they were purchasing their stock to *prevent* someone else from trying to purchase them. Why—what have you heard?"

"There's no official news yet, but I've heard rumors on the street. Management is talking to some private equity firms. Investment consultants have convinced pension and endowment funds to place their cash with private equity players, rather than traditional stock and bond managers. Now the private equity guys are looking to do deals with all of their new cash. Anyhow, the news isn't widely known, so Consumer Media bonds haven't gotten hit yet. I think we need to unload these bonds before the company does some kind of leveraged buyout."

"What do you mean they haven't gotten hit yet? The bonds are incredibly cheap."

"Dude, they're cheap for a *reason*. Believe me, they're going to get cheaper."

"Why? Because there's a rumor on the street? There are always rumors on the street! What makes you think this one has any credibility?"

Tony stood up from his seat and rolled his sleeves half way up his arms. Planting his hands squarely on his desk, he flexed his forearm muscles and stared coldly at David Koslow. "Let's just say I know it, okay?"

The two men stared at each other for what seemed like an eternity, neither saying a word. Finally Koslow said, "Fine.

Go ahead and sell the bonds. But you better find me a good replacement."

Peter watched David Koslow retreat to his office. He could sense that Koslow believed that Tony knew something. Nonetheless, Koslow did not want to ask Tony the source of his information. Tony continued to stare as Koslow recoiled. It was as if he were daring the portfolio manager to second-guess him. Once Koslow was gone, Tony looked around the trading area for anyone else foolish enough to challenge him. He then pumped out his chest and walked toward the aquarium set against the wall. Scooping a gold-fish out of the aquarium, he promptly fed it to the piranhas. Tony then walked over to the whiteboard fastened to the wall and began to write in bold red letters:

"ANALYSTS CAN DO THEIR BEST, AND STILL LOSE MONEY. ALL ANALYSTS ARE TO RUN THEIR IDEAS BY THE TRADERS BEFORE TALKING TO PORTFOLIO MANAGERS."

This was the third commandment that Peter had seen Tony put on the whiteboard. This commandment was especially offensive to Peter. He muttered in a low voice low so as not to be heard, "That guy must really think he's some kind of god."

He then sat back down at his desk and breathed a sigh of relief. David Koslow had not blamed him for recommending the purchase of the bonds. Terri Tanaka's voice suddenly startled him.

"What's all the commotion about, Peter?"

Turning around, he was glad to see a friendly face. Peter fidgeted with his pencil, not sure if he wanted to divulge the reason for Tony's sudden outburst. He remembered Terri had seen him researching the Consumer Media bonds. He worried that if he lost credibility with Terri, he would certainly be dismissed as a useless intern at American Dinero.

"I'm not exactly sure what Tony was upset about." Peter replied sheepishly. "I guess I didn't want to go and find out."

Terri gave Peter an understanding smile. She could tell Peter didn't want to discuss the matter.

"Don't worry about it, Peter. We have another task at hand. We've been asked to look for some attractive equity names in the health care sector. Got any ideas?"

Drawing on his familiarity with the industry, Peter suggested, "Well, I guess we can either look at the big pharmaceutical names like Pfizer, Lilly, Bristol-Myers and Merck, or we can look at the generic drug makers, like Teva."

"Why limit ourselves there? What about the hospital supply companies, like Abbott and Baxter, or the pharmacy benefit companies?"

Peter could feel his adrenaline pumping at the prospect of a new challenge, a new shot at redemption.

"Yeah, I guess those are possible, too. Which portfolio manager asked for our help? Is there a certain minimum market capitalization he needs? And do you know whether he's looking for a growth stock, or a value stock?"

"Now you're talking, Peter! Let's jump back on the horse and ride her again." Terri then placed her hand on Peter's shoulder and said in a hushed tone, "Don't worry about Tony. No one could have known that Consumer Media was planning any kind of leveraged buyout. In fact, who knows, Tony might end up being wrong on this."

Peter was embarrassed that Terri had caught him in a lie. She knew why Tony was angry. Peter looked down in shame before smiling at Terri and nodding his head. He was grateful for Terri's kind words and determined to impress her with his work on this new assignment.

That evening, while Peter was researching his list of health care stocks, Tom Nelson was preparing for an adventure. He had agreed to get in the car, first thing Tuesday morning, and visit Doctor Cregar.

On a hot and humid Tuesday morning, Tom Nelson traveled south down Interstate 55. Doctor Cregar had told Tom he would get the opportunity to meet Doctor Lake at the Rivermass lab, in Cape Girardeau, Missouri. Cape Girardeau was located 120 miles south of St. Louis, 53 miles north of New Madrid, and 170 miles north of Memphis. It was known in the region as "the place where the river turns a thousand tales." The city was situated between Interstate 55 and an almost unnatural westward bend of the Mississippi River. The farther south Tom drove, the more evident was the devastation caused by the recent earthquake. Almost two months had passed since the quake, and this main interstate highway was still mired in the process of reconstruction. Tom had been driving for eight hours, having passed St. Louis about an hour ago. It was 2 p.m. His eyes weighed heavy and his clothes were spotted with sweat, even though the car's air conditioner was set to high cool. Most of the highway traffic consisted of construction crews and large semis carrying pre-fab houses to those left homeless. Tom was growing frustrated with the many detours he needed to take because some interstate overpasses were deemed too dangerous. He concentrated to keep his focus on the road which had become one continuous construction area. He decided he had better grab a cup of coffee at any roadside gas station that was still intact. He was worried that the farther south he traveled, the more difficult it would be to find an open gas station.

Relieved to see someone pumping gas at a station on the side of the road, Tom turned to fill up his car. Pulling up to the gas pump, he was outraged to see they were charging $5.20 a gallon of gas. *Another case of price-gouging*, he thought to himself. He had last filled his gas tank just south of Chicago for $3.10 a gallon. *I'm at the mercy of the market*, he thought. Nonetheless, the station had both coffee and gas—two things he desperately needed. He wasn't willing to risk delaying his trip over a couple of dollars. After filling up the gas tank and purchasing a fresh cup of coffee, he returned to his car to continue the journey.

Tom wondered whether this trip was just another empty dream, as he inserted his key in the ignition. Looking down to secure his coffee cup, he felt a sudden jolt rock the car, causing him to spill some of the hot liquid onto his hand. Startled, Tom gazed at an obviously delirious old man who had appeared out of nowhere, and was now resting the upper half of his body across Tom's car. The man looked as if he had been wearing the same tattered clothing for over a week. His scraggly beard and shoulder-length hair indicated that it had been days since he had showered.

The owner of the desolate service station stuck his head out the door and yelled. "Hey, Clem—get off that boy's car!"

Tom stared in disbelief as the old man raised his head and lifted himself off the car. The man walked slowly toward the gas station owner, as Tom backed his car out to pull away. Before leaving the pumping station, he noticed that the old man had picked up a sign off the ground, and was waving it in Tom's direction. The sign was made from the side of a brown cardboard box and scribbled in dark black marker were the words: "The End is Near."

Tom thought about the old man as he continued down the highway. What if the end really was near? How would he be remembered? Tom hoped that Rivermass would be an opportunity for him to leave a legacy. He finally arrived in Cape Girardeau at 7 p.m. He had been driving through a maze of detours for the last three hours. The sun was just beginning its descent and the temperature outside was still a humid 96 degrees. Tom exited on Nash Road and drove past the regional airport, to what looked like an abandoned industrial park. The dust from the dry, rocky road billowed into the sky as Tom searched for any sign of an industrial lab. Arriving at the address he was given, Tom stopped the car and stepped out. A thin layer of the red clay soil covered the car.

"Tom Nelson! I'm so glad you could make it down here. I wouldn't ordinarily ask anyone to make such a long trip, but I really think this is going to be worth your while."

Tom looked back in the direction of the voice. Although the voice was definitely that of Dr. Cregar, the figure approaching him looked much different than the Dr. Cregar Tom had seen two weeks earlier. The man approaching him looked ten years younger. The paunch around the middle of Dr. Cregar's waistline had vanished. His chest muscles and biceps seemed to stretch the limits of the blue T-shirt he was wearing. Sensing Tom's confusion, Dr. Cregar smiled and stretched out his arms as if to embrace Tom. Stopping short of an embrace, Dr. Cregar looked down at his toes and admired his body, as if seeing it for the first time.

"Well, what do you think, Tom? This is after just two weeks of using Rivermass. I'm telling you…I feel stronger… faster…I have more energy…. The results are amazing."

Tom looked at Dr. Cregar in stunned silence. He was mentally and physically exhausted after the long drive. The transformation in Dr. Cregar seemed almost surreal.

"You look good," was the only response Tom could muster.

"How selfish of me. I know you must be tired. Are you hungry? Come on, let's get out of this heat. Doctor Lake isn't here right now, but you can meet him tomorrow. You'll be amazed at the progress he's made. He's already figured out a way to turn the liquid form of Rivermass into a capsule, without diluting the efficacy."

CHAPTER TWENTY

I t had been three days since Peter last walked toward the trading area. He was still not sure if Tony Salami suspected his input on the Consumer Media bonds. Nonetheless, he had promised that he would give Jerry an answer regarding his CBO deal by the end of the week.

Jerry had provided Peter with his investment team's performance record, as well as a list of potential high-yield bonds they intended to purchase. Peter knew that Hoosier Insurance planned on purchasing a portfolio of bonds, and then segregating them in a separate legal entity called a special purpose vehicle (SPV). The sole purpose of the SPV was to collect funds from potential investors, purchase high-yield bonds with the funds, and then pass on the cash flows from the bonds to the investors. In effect, the SPV structure ensured that the high-yield bonds did not show up on Hoosier Insurance's balance sheet. The SPV operated similar to the way that individuals might set up a trust to keep their assets from being taxed. The SPV investors who were willing to take the most risk (i.e. assume the first losses on any bonds that defaulted) would realize the greatest potential gain if the portfolio experienced fewer losses than expected. Peter was going to try to see if Tony would consider investing in the portion of the Hoosier Insurance's CBO that carried the greatest level of risk, referred to as the "equity tranche."

"Hey, Tony."

"Yeah, what can I do for you, intern?"

"I was wondering if American Dinero has ever invested in any CBOs."

"CBOs, huh? I call those 'Catastrophes Bought by the Oblivious.' They're the ultimate dirty bomb."

"So I take it you don't like them?"

"I don't like them. But they do serve a need for some clients. For instance, our insurance company clients are forced by their regulators to set aside more capital if they purchase lower- rated investments in their portfolios. Investment bankers have somehow convinced Moody's and S&P, the two main rating agencies, to assign higher ratings to some parts of a CBO deal. You *do* know the majority of the underlying bonds in these CBOs are all rated below investment-grade, right?"

"Yeah, I know," Peter replied.

"Since these bonds have more risk they're called 'junk bonds,' right?"

"Yeah, I know, Tony, but we buy junk bonds, don't we?"

"Only because we have smart guys doing the buying," Tony haughtily replied.

"Right! So if you buy smart you can get very high returns, correct?"

David Koslow came out of his office to join the conversation. "Peter, are you trying to talk our Salami man into buying some high-yield bonds?"

"He was asking about CBOs," Tony replied without acknowledging Koslow's fun with his name. "I was explaining to our intern here that because of current low interest rates, insurance companies are having a hard time getting high yields if their investment policy limits them to higher-rated bonds. So Wall Street, in all its wisdom, found a way around this conundrum. They decided they could reduce the risk, and get a higher rating, if they created a diversified pool of junk bonds, with different levels of risk."

Tony walked up to the white board next to his desk, and began drawing.

"Think of a CBO as a four-layer wedding cake, all right?"

Tony seemed to be enjoying his teaching role. He carefully drew a four-layer cake on the board. The round bottom layer was the biggest layer, followed by a smaller layer placed on top of the bottom layer, and two incrementally smaller layers on top of the second.

"Each of these layers in a CBO is called a 'tranche,'" Tony explained; "And each tranche has a specific type of investor, with a specific risk/return profile."

Peter was actually beginning to appreciate Tony's knowledge.

Suddenly Tony got right in Peter's face and raised his voice, saying, "Now flip that cake upside down and you've got yourself a picture of a CBO. It's not too stable, is it?" Tony brushed Peter aside and plopped back down in his chair.

This guy's just like the Sandman—a teacher one moment and a jerk the next, Peter thought to himself.

"Allow me to add a little explanation to Tony's cake example," David Koslow offered. "For simplicity's sake, let's assume that the assets in this cake consist of $100 million in bonds. The cake's creator—in other words, the investment bankers selling the CBO—will try to find four specific types of investors in the deal as follows."

David began illustrating on the whiteboard as he continued talking.

"First we have to carve out the riskiest part of the deal, the 'equity tranche.' This would be the small top layer of the cake, which has now been flipped to the bottom. Let's say it's 10 percent of the total deal. The investment bankers will need to find one, two, or three buyers willing to invest an aggregate amount of 10 million dollars to buy this tranche. If none of the bonds in the underlying portfolio default—and remember, the underlying portfolio represents the *whole* cake—the equity investors can realize returns of up to 45% on the money they invest. However, if 10% of the bonds in the cake default, these investors will lose everything. The equity tranche investors need to make assumptions regarding default risk of the *entire* pool. They assume the realized return on their tranche will probably be somewhere between 45% and 0%, depending on interest rate movements and how many bonds default. The reason this investment class is called the "equity tranche" is because the rating agencies won't even assign a bond rating to this class of investments—it's considered very high risk. Thus, an insurance company that needs to disclose the ratings of its holdings to the insurance regulators, typically won't invest in this tranche. The investors in this tranche need to be more interested in potential gains, and less concerned with ratings.

"Let's assume the next layer of our upside-down cake represents 12 percent of the deal. The "equity tranche" mentioned earlier is subordinate in claims to this 12 percent tranche. Since the equity tranche represents 10 percent of the deal, its subordinated status means that it will absorb all losses on the portfolio up to 10%. In other words, if 8% of the bonds in the *total* cake go belly up, the "equity tranche" absorbs *all* of those losses, and the 12 percent tranche is unaffected. Because of the protection this higher-quality tranche is given, the rating agencies most likely will assign a 'BB' rating to this tranche. A 'BB' rating is still below investment-grade. This means there's still a large percentage of the investing public that is precluded, by their investment policy, from purchasing this investment. However, this tranche offers a much higher yield, or potential return, than other similarly rated bonds for investors interested in 'BB-rated' bonds.

"The next highest-quality investment class, representing 18 percent of the deal, has the two riskier classes protecting it from losses. In other words, 22 percent of the bonds in the portfolio will have to default before this class of investors is at risk. Because of the 22 percent subordination, the rating agencies will often assign a rating as high as A- to this tranche. This means investment-grade buyers can purchase this tranche, and quite possibly realize much greater returns than other investment grade options available to them.

"Finally, the largest 60 percent base of the cake—the part that's now at the top of our structure—is the easiest to sell. Because of the 40 percent subordination under this tranche, the rating agencies will often assign a 'AA' rating. The high rating entices a lot of insurance companies, which are looking for high yields and high ratings, to be interested in this tranche."

Peter was grateful for David's explanation. It reinforced his earlier conclusion that CBO deals were very similar to the mortgage-backed deals offered by FNMA and FHLMC. In both cases, the originator of the deal was pooling together a number of different bonds or loans, and then parceling out the interest and principal payments generated by the pool to specific types of investors. Different investors were willing to assume varying degrees of risk to achieve their desired investment returns. It was really not much different than the choice facing an investor who must decide between highly volatile stocks (often referred to as high-beta stocks), and less volatile, or low-beta stocks. The higher the volatility investors were willing to accept, the higher the potential return they could possibly achieve over a long timeframe. Feeling naturally curious, Peter questioned David.

"Since the 'AA-rated' tranche gets so much default protection from the lower-rated tranches, why does it offer such a higher potential return than other 'AA-rated' corporate bonds?"

"Because once you buy these things, you're pretty much stuck with them until they mature. They're hard to sell. In other words, they lack liquidity. With a corporate bond, it's easy to judge the quality of the repayment source—it's the individual company borrowing the money. Investors prefer buying things they understand. Corporate bonds will trade higher, or lower, based on interest rates and news events affecting that company. With a CBO, investors put their faith in the investment abilities of some other portfolio manager. After you buy the deal, it becomes very difficult to get information on how the deal is performing. In addition, if you want to sell your portion of the deal, you'll need to explain the story to a potential buyer. Because, guess what?

Wall Street's not real interested in explaining the story once they've got it off their books. It's much easier to sell a well-researched company than it is to sell a story. Stories make buyers nervous."

Based on David's explanation—as well as the fact that Tony was now ignoring them—Peter was pretty certain that Tony would not be interested in buying the equity tranche of the Hoosier Insurance deal. Nonetheless, out of a duty to his friend, he felt compelled to raise the subject.

"So...would you guys ever consider buying the equity tranche in a deal?"

Tony could no longer ignore the conversation without chiming in.

"Dude. The only people who consistently make money on those deals are the lawyers who structure them, and the underlying managers that manage the CBO. 'Catastrophes Bought by the Oblivious,' remember?"

Peter felt sufficiently humiliated as he turned and began to walk away.

"Just a minute, I'm not done with today's lesson." Tony called Peter back.

"Remember a few years ago when interest rates were held low for a ridiculously long period of time?"

Peter immediately became apprehensive, knowing that he and the genie had been the culprits behind the low-interest rate environment. He simply nodded his head in reply to Tony's question.

"Let me give you a brief history lesson on how those low interest rates affected the financial markets. Initially we were worried that the low interest rates would cause inflation to soar. After all, banks had a lot of incentive to make loans since their borrowing costs were low."

"But inflation never really got as high as people worried it would," Peter interrupted defensively.

"It didn't get high," Tony answered, "because the Fed finally came to its senses and raised interest rates to slow the economy."

Peter knew the inflation rate had not accelerated out of control because he had effectively killed the inflation monster, and he resented the fact that Tony was bringing up a history he wanted to forget. Nonetheless, he continued to listen to Tony's history lesson.

"Although inflation didn't become the problem that people anticipated, the low interest rate environment caused a huge wave of people to refinance their mortgage loans. In addition, because rates were so low, people started borrowing on the equity of their homes. As the competition to make loans intensified, credit standards deteriorated. Some banks didn't even require their borrowers to show any proof that they could make payments on their loans. Instead, the banks were lending based on the appraised value of the home, which was a bogus number. Do you know why this madness was all able to take place, Peter?"

How much does Tony know? Peter thought to himself. *It's almost as if he's blaming me.*

"No, but I'm sure you're going to tell me." Peter replied.

"Yeah, I'll tell you. It's because the banks, and other mortgage brokers, were able to sell the mortgage loans off via the CDO market. I call CDOs, 'Contagious Disease Opportunities.' Get it? They'll be the death of you."

Tony had to stop to laugh at his own humor before continuing. "The banks essentially were able to sell off all of their risk through the CDO market. Why not continue to lend if there's no risk involved? In addition, Fannie Mae and

Freddie Mac began to take on lower quality mortgages, and to trade derivatives against their portfolio of loans to control the risk. Eventually, these guys didn't even know if they were making money or losing it.

"And it hasn't changed. Mark my words, Peter, there's still lots of investors who have no idea of the potential time bombs in their portfolios. When this starts blowing up— and by the way, it *always* blows up—people won't know what hit them. Investment funds will blow up, banks will blow up, and ultimately the consumer is going to have to pay their loans off, or lose their home. You might get to witness the next Great Depression. That would be a hell of a mess, wouldn't it, Petey?"

Peter was speechless. No one, other than the Sandman, had ever called him "Petey." He cringed at the sound of the name. Peter remembered Sarah's warning that the Sandman might appear different this time. Peter's mind was engulfed with a sudden wave of thoughts. *Did Tony know that he was the one who had caused the low interest rate environment? Could Tony be the Sandman?* Shaking his head, Peter tried to dispel the thought. Nonetheless, if Tony's forecast proved correct, Peter would never be able to live with the consequences of his actions. He had already caused so much damage. Could a depression be on the horizon? Peter already felt about as depressed as he could feel.

Peter had to ask one last question. "Okay, Tony. I understand that you don't like these CDO's, but I know you buy mortgage-backed bonds, bundled by Fannie Mae and Freddie Mac. How are these so different?"

"Petey, the government can't let Fannie Mae and Freddie Mac fail. That would be disastrous." The sly smile on Tony's face gave Peter an uneasy feeling.

"I guess we better pray this doesn't end as abruptly as you're describing," Peter mumbled as he turned to walk away.

As an afterthought, Tony called out, "Oh, by the way, Peter, Terri and I got together and decided we're going to buy Crytonics as the health care company we needed. You don't need to work on finding any new names in the health care sector."

Peter looked back at Tony in amazement. He wanted to ask why they would buy Crytonics. It didn't seem to fit the parameters of the type of company they were looking for. Still, he could tell by the look in Tony's eyes that the decision was made.

Peter went back to his desk and wondered whether or not he belonged in the money management business. His first bond recommendation had been blasted by Tony, and sold. Initially, he was encouraged that he was given another assignment, working on analyzing a health care stock with Terri. However, it was now apparent that his input was no longer desired. It had been a week since he had talked with Sarah, and he wasn't sure that she even wanted to speak to him. To top it all off, now he had to worry about a coming economic depression. His life seemed to be taking a downward spiral.

Nonetheless, he couldn't just sit in his cubicle and dwell on how unfair life was to him. He needed to take action. He decided he would confront Terri Tanaka about the decision to purchase the Crytonics stock. As he walked across the floor, he struggled for the right words. He didn't want to destroy his relationship with Terri. She was the only confidante he had at work.

"Hi, Terri."

"Hey, what's up, Peter?"

"I don't know. Tony told me that you and he decided to buy Crytonics stock. Does that mean you don't want me to do any more research on health care companies?"

"Oh geez, I'm sorry, Peter. I meant to tell you myself. The Crytonics decision was pretty much Tony's call."

"But why Crytonics? It has no earnings. It's basically just a research company, isn't it? I don't even think they have any drugs close to FDA approval, do they?"

"They have a couple of promising drugs. Tony can tell you all about them."

Terri clearly did not want to go into great detail about the company, or the decision to buy the stock. Nonetheless, Peter was determined to learn the rationale behind the decision.

"Terri, I always thought you were more of a value-type analyst. No matter how you measure this company, whether by earnings, revenues, book value, asset value, or cash flow, I don't see anything compelling. Are you expecting one of these measures to suddenly show some kind of large future growth?"

"The market thinks so. Have you noticed that the stock is up over 15 percent in the past month?"

"All the more reason to worry about buying it now!" Peter replied.

"Listen, Peter, inherently, I think you're right. When I look to buy a house, I look for value. When I look to buy a car, I look for value. By nature, we're trained to buy things for fifty to seventy–five cents on the dollar. But stocks are a bit different. Most things we purchase, we plan on owning for a long time. You can't always take that approach when you're investing in the stock market. The stock market measures your performance on a daily, weekly, or monthly basis. Unfortunately, value investing is one of the worst timing indicators. A stock that appears cheap today might stay cheap for months, and maybe even a year, before the rest of the market recognizes the value. In the meantime, investors chase stocks that continue to rise on price momentum. It's the American dream, to get rich quick and easy. Analysts sell the belief that the companies they like will develop some new product, or new management will make changes that cause earnings to grow well into the future. Some investors are willing to bet on promises that might never come to fruition. However, as long as there are people continuing to buy the stock, the momentum investors will continue to make money. And they'll continue to make value investors like us look stupid. Tony's a trader—he's not an investor. He's buying a lottery ticket to make a quick buck. If Crytonics stock starts going bad, he'll get rid of it and move on."

"It sounds like multi-level marketing to me. As long as you can keep signing up people to buy into the story, you make a bunch of money."

"Well...let's not get carried away, Peter. Most investors are much smarter than the people who buy into the multi-level marketing game. Multi-level marketing involves selling someone a dream. Multi-level marketing dismisses the economic principle of supply and demand. It assumes that unlimited supply will be met with unlimited demand."

"Well isn't that what momentum investing is? You drive the stock price up to a point where there's no way the company can grow its earnings consistent with the growth assumption built into the stock price?"

"Yes. But if you buy the stock at a price that underestimates the growth of the company's earnings, and you sell it before it becomes too overvalued, you make a lot of money, don't you?"

"Yeah, and if you get into a multi-level marketing scheme early, and you get out early, you also make a lot of money."

Terri was growing frustrated at Peter's stubbornness.

"Multi-level marketing doesn't have assets, Peter! *Companies* have real assets that generate real earnings!"

Peter knew it was time to change the subject.

"So we're expecting great earnings growth from Crytonics?"

"That's Tony's call. I wash my hands of it. Here, let me show you something."

Terri grabbed Peter by the hand and led him toward the trading area. Her quickened pace and her tight grip signaled a sense of frustration. Silently, Terri pointed to Tony's whiteboard, and Peter read the following new proclamation:

"IF YOU QUESTION THE CONSENSUS, YOU WILL BE RIDICULED AND GAIN NEW ENEMIES"

"That was Tony's response to me questioning the purchase of Crytonics. He says that he knows something that we don't know about the company."

This was the second time that Tony had overruled the analysts on supposedly secret information. Peter was intent on finding out whether or not the genie was helping Tony succeed. He continued to question Terri.

"Does he do this a lot? I mean…does he know some kind of inside information about these companies that no one else knows?"

"I don't know. I brought it up with Fran Solli the other day, and he said he would look into it. You know…the thing is…I really don't want to know what Tony knows. I just want to be able to do my job."

Terri walked back toward her cubicle. Peter was growing increasingly frustrated. There were so many battles that he wanted to fight, but he didn't know where to start. He wasn't even sure he recognized the enemy.

After work, Peter returned to an empty apartment. Tom Nelson was still down in Missouri, working with Doctor Cregar. Peter paced from one end of his apartment to the other, not knowing what to do. Looking at the clock, he figured Sarah would be home. She was the only one who could understand his concerns. He took a deep breath and tried to rehearse the correct words to make up for his past miscues, while still voicing his suspicions regarding Doug Keyster. He slowly dialed the number. Peter could feel a knot in his stomach as the phone began to ring. He listened to the phone ring thirteen times before he finally hung up. Peter was alone. Seeking some form of escape, Peter changed into a T-shirt and running shorts, and headed out the door for a run.

Peter dodged the continuous stream of pedestrians filing out of their workplaces. The looks of fatigue on their faces convinced him he was not alone in his battles. The stress of work, combined with the 90-degree heat, exacerbated the pain with each stride that Peter took. Finally catching his breath, he looked beyond the speeding cars on Lake Shore Drive, and sprinted toward the beach of Lake Michigan.

CHAPTER TWENTY ONE

"Sarah, are you okay? I noticed you weren't at work yesterday, and you seem awfully quiet today." Sarah looked up from her desk to see Doug Keyster standing in front of her. She stood up to address him, with her eyes looking away.

"I'm sorry, Doug. I should have called in yesterday. I didn't even think about it. I was pretty upset. My grandfather died early yesterday morning."

Sarah's voice began to crack and tears welled up in her eyes as she said, "When I woke up, he was dead."

"I'm so sorry, Sarah. I'm really sorry to hear that."

Doug held out his arms, offering Sarah an embrace that she gratefully accepted.

"I take it you were pretty close to your grandfather?"

Struggling to regain her composure, Sarah replied, "Yes, I was. He's been living at our house the past six years. He was such a great guy. He was always trying to help others. This past year, though, he really couldn't do much on his own."

"That's got to be tough. My grandparents lived in a different state, and I only saw them once or twice a year. And despite relatively infrequent contact, I really loved them. It hurt when they died. I can't imagine what it would be like to have lived with, and cared for, your grandfather for so long... it must be difficult to let him go."

Sarah finally broke her long embrace with Doug. She looked him in the eye, almost in disbelief that he seemed to know exactly how she felt.

"I honestly feel like a part of me has died."

"I'm sorry. So, when is the funeral? Do you have a lot of family coming in to town?"

"The wake's tonight and then the funeral is this Saturday."

"Why did you even come in today? You shouldn't even be here."

"I know. But my dad came in for some meetings today, and I thought it would be nice to drive in with him. To be honest, our house feels kind of empty with my grandpa gone."

"Listen, I want you to take the rest of the week off. There really aren't any pressing issues that we need to address this week. However, next week I have something that we can start working on. Remember that RFP we received from CYA Consultants?"

Sarah looked up at Doug and nodded.

"Guess what? We're one of four finalists! We've been asked to make a formal presentation a couple of weeks from now. The client is an organization called 'World Hunger.' It would be a great client for us."

Doug looked at Sarah, not knowing what type of reaction to expect. She immediately gave Doug a hug and broke out in a smile.

"I'm so proud of you. I knew you could do it."

Doug held Sarah tightly, appreciating her praise. "Well, we'll worry about the presentation next week. You go home and help out the family, okay?"

"Thanks, Doug," Sarah said, wiping a tear from her cheek.

Doug watched Sarah as she walked toward the elevator. After the elevator doors closed, Doug called the florist and ordered some lavender orchids and lilacs to be sent to Sarah's home.

Far away, in Missouri, Tom Nelson woke up in a strange bed, still groggy from the long drive the day before. The room where he rested was sterile in appearance, with few amenities. It looked like a dorm room, long after all students had left for the summer. Dressed in the T-shirt and shorts in which he had slept, Tom walked out of his room in search of Doctor Cregar. Finding no one inside the home, he stepped outside. It was a humid, grey, overcast day. The air smelled of an impending storm.

Looking out among the cluster of warehouses, Tom spotted Doctor Cregar sitting on one of the small strips of grass, sandwiched between pavement and warehouses. He was tossing small pebbles toward one of the warehouses.

"Doctor Cregar. How are you doing today?"

"Good morning, Tom. I trust you had a good night's sleep?"

"Yeah, thanks. I slept great. So what would you like me to do for you today?"

Tom looked down at Doctor Cregar sitting on the ground. The gain in muscle mass for Doctor Cregar was amazing. He looked like he had followed a regimen of daily workouts for the past year. Doctor Cregar rose to his feet. The expression on his face did not exude the same enthusiasm that he had shown the previous evening.

"There's really not that much left to do, Tom. Let me take you over to the warehouse where we're currently manufacturing and storing the Rivermass. I think we'll be ready to sell it soon."

Sensing Doctor Cregar's sudden apathy, Tom questioned, "Are you all right, sir?"

"Yeah. I was just sitting here, thinking of my family. I miss them, Tom. This old industrial park gives me a place to think in solitude. Doctor Lake told me that he bought this whole park out of bankruptcy. You know this area of the country experienced a pretty significant economic downturn a few years ago. And the recent earthquake certainly didn't help things. Anyhow, Doctor Lake built the house that you slept in last night. He says he was undecided on what to do with the rest of this property. However, after discovering Rivermass, he thinks the whole complex can eventually be the campus where the drug is manufactured. It still amazes me how far he's come in developing this drug in such a short time."

"Yeah. I guess that I'm kind of surprised you said you've used some of the Rivermass already. Don't you think it still needs more testing?"

Doctor Cregar turned suddenly and glared at Tom as if he had just asked for his first-born. "What the hell do you know about medicine! I'm tired of listening to ignorant people telling me about all the testing that needs to be done. Do have any idea how drugs are made these days, Tom?"

Seeing that Doctor Cregar was visibly shaking, Tom replied, "No. I'll admit it. I don't know what I'm talking about. I'm sorry."

Regaining his composure, Cregar replied more calmly, "I'm sorry for snapping at you, Tom. It's just that ...thinking about my family...and thinking about some of the frustrations of marketing Rivermass...I don't know. What was I saying?"

"You were asking if I knew how drugs were made these days."

"Oh, yes. Well, I'm sure you've heard that penicillin was discovered, by accident, from a mold to kill bacteria. And do you know how the current drugs we use to control cholesterol were discovered?"

Tom shook his head.

"They were also discovered by a mold sample. Most early drug discoveries were the result of things found in nature. However, it seems that now most pharmaceutical companies have abandoned even entertaining the thought of drug development from natural elements. In fact, as I told you earlier, many pharmaceutical companies are abandoning new research and development altogether. Instead, companies have latched onto trendy areas such as synthesizing and testing thousands of artificial chemicals unknown in nature. They basically mix all of these synthesized chemicals in a batter together, and examine the output. It's like baking a cake—only you don't know what kind of cake you'll end up with."

Tom was encouraged that Cregar was starting to sound like a scientist again, rather than a madman.

"It's amazing, Tom. Did you know that some of the most promising drugs being developed today come from compounds found naturally in sea squirts, Gila monsters, and vampire bats? How about that for irony? Vampire bats might actually represent hope, rather than danger."

"Pretty cool," Tom replied, unsure what to say.

"With Rivermass, I believe that nature has once again provided us with an amazing discovery. And I'm not going to let a bunch of bureaucrats keep us from the fruits of our labor. Where is Doctor Lake? He can tell you. He shares my passion. We're not going to let the pharmaceutical companies, or the FDA, or anyone, stifle us again. I'm sick and tired of people! I hate people!"

Tom watched with trepidation as Jonah Cregar, once again, went on a rampage. And then, as if a switch in his brain had turned off, Tom heard Cregar whisper softly, "I lost the only people I ever loved." Jonah Cregar walked away in a manner suggesting he wanted solitude. As Tom watched the muscular figure depart, he couldn't help but think that despite Doctor Cregar's enhanced physical strength, he was still a broken man.

Late Friday afternoon, Tom Nelson returned to his Chicago apartment. He still had many unanswered questions. One undeniable fact, however, was that Rivermass seemed to produce amazing results. Although the manufacturing facilities appeared limited, he remembered seeing numerous cases of the completed product in a storage room in Cape Girardeau. Tom was excited to show his friends the physical evidence of the miracle drug he had been promoting. In the trunk of his car were three boxes, filled with finished product of Rivermass. Each box contained 100 capsules. By the time Peter arrived home from work, Tom was waiting, with a beer in his hand, and a smile on his face.

"Hurry up, Peter. I want to try to catch the 5:30 train back to Michigan City."

"Yeah, buddy. It's nice to see you, too. So...how was your trip to Missouri?"

"I'll tell you on the train. Are you all packed?"

"Tom, I don't even know if I want to go to Michigan City this weekend. I've had a lousy week. I've been kind of a jerk with Sarah. She called a couple of times, and I haven't even bothered to return her phone calls. I don't know what to say to her. Then I called Jerry the other day, and I told him that we wouldn't be able to invest in his CBO deal, so I think he's mad at me. Meanwhile, everyone at work seems to think I'm just a stupid idealist..."

"Enough already, Peter! You're not the kind of guy who's ever been a whiner. Please don't start now. Remember when we used to play football together? When the game got tough, you got tough. And as far as being a stupid idealist...Well, you may be an idealist, but you're certainly not stupid. Now quit feeling sorry for yourself, and let's go."

Tom flashed his infectious smile at Peter, and Peter couldn't help but respond with a grin. "Come on and get your stuff. We have a train to catch. I can't wait to tell you about some of the things I discovered in Missouri."

Peter and Tom left their apartment and hurriedly shuffled toward Randolph Street. The loud thunder of the Chicago "L" rumbled over their heads. Within ten minutes they were in their seats on the South Shore Railway. As the train started rolling down the tracks, Tom took a deep breath and placed his back pack on his lap, examining his surroundings before slowly opening his belongings. Shoving his hand into the open back pack, he pulled out a clear sandwich bag that contained approximately 50 capsules.

He glanced around the train one more time and then looked Peter directly in the eye. "This is it," he said softly. "This is the Rivermass."

"Whoa, you mean to tell me you already have this in pill form? I thought you just discovered the stuff."

"Not only are the pills already made, Doctor Cregar has actually started taking the stuff. You should see him! It's amazing. He looks like Arnold Schwarzenegger. This stuff works."

"Are you sure it's safe?"

"He seems to think it's safe. When I was down in Missouri, he showed me how they're manufacturing the stuff. They have only six guys that work there. But they have an incredible amount of supply. They've figured out a way to regenerate these cells. And the cells regenerate incredibly fast. They have huge vats of this stuff. And then they just pour the liquid into these capsules and you have instant muscle mass and instant weight loss."

"Where did you say they're doing this?"

"It's right outside Cape Girardeau, Missouri. The Mississippi River used to jut out to the downtown of Cape Girardeau. But after the earthquake, the whole path of the river has been altered. The river now takes a more eastern path, down toward the Gulf of Mexico. That's why Memphis was so devastated by the flooding. Anyhow, now there's only a small portion of the river that ends at Cape Girardeau. Much of the land that used to be underwater is exposed for the first time. That's how they discovered all of these new Rivermass cells."

"Have you taken any of these pills yet?"

"Not yet. But I'm certainly thinking about it. Doctor Cregar asked me to show them to my dad. He figures that maybe my dad can convince some of the doctors he knows to recommend Rivermass to patients who suffer from obesity."

Peter just shook his head in disbelief. "Well, at least it sounds like you're contributing to your work. I'm not so sure about myself."

Tom couldn't believe that he finally had something exciting to share—but Peter was in no mood to listen. It took every ounce of patience he had to keep from shaking the self-pity out of Peter.

Barely concealing his disinterest, Peter sighed, "Well, I hope your dad's able to help you guys sell this. It sounds great."

Then, wanting to change the subject, Peter asked, "Do you know if Jerry's coming home this weekend? He'll probably be interested in hearing about these pills."

"Last time I talked to him, he said he was going to try to come up."

"Great," Peter replied sullenly. "I think I'll try to get some rest before meeting up with everyone this weekend. Chances are I'll have to be on the defensive."

Peter rested his head against the window of the train, and surveyed the landscape as the train made its scheduled stops at the Hegewisch, Hammond, and East Chicago stations. At each stop, Peter looked up and down the platform for any sign of the Sandman. By the time they reached the Dune Park station, Peter's body was numb from the constant jostling of the train. His eyes were heavy, and he was uncertain whether he even cared to look out the window.

"Dune's station," was the call from the conductor. As the train slowed to a stop, Peter searched among the people lining the platform—men in loosely hanging ties, and women in their business suits, moving like zombies after a hard week of work. The Sandman was nowhere to be seen. Looking over at Tom, he asked, "How are you getting home from the train station?"

"My dad said he would come by and pick me up. Do you need a ride home?"

"Yes. Thank you."

✵ ✵ ✵

The car ride home was relatively quiet. Most of the questions from Tom's dad were directed toward Peter and his work this summer. Peter wanted to bring up the subject of the Rivermass pills, so he kept looking at Tom, trying to prod him to open his back pack. Peter desperately wanted to hear Mr. Nelson's reaction. By the time the car turned off Highway 12 and rolled across the railroad tracks marking the entrance to Long Beach, Peter realized the subject would not be discussed while he was in the car. As the car pulled into the Jangle driveway, Peter got out and said, "Thanks for the ride, Mr. Nelson."

"No problem, Peter. Tell your parents hello for me."

"Tom, I'll give you a call tomorrow and we can plan on going to the beach, okay?"

"Sounds good. I'll see ya."

The car door closed and Tom immediately looked at his father and asked, "So how was your work this week?"

"It was all right. Busy."

"Did you visit with a bunch of doctors this week?"

"I visit with doctors every week. That's what I do for a living. I try to compete with all of the other pharma reps out there, scrambling to get one or two minutes of quality time with the doctors. Most won't even let me in the door unless

I promise to get them tickets to a sporting event, or take them out to lunch."

Tom could sense the frustration in his father's voice. He knew his father had lost his love for his job. In fact, he couldn't think of many people who *did* love their job. Still, he tried to encourage his dad to keep plugging away. He remembered Peter telling him about the toll that Mr. Jangle's unemployment had taken on their family.

"Well, as long as you get to expense the cost of the lunch with them, it doesn't sound like that bad a job."

"No. I guess not. How are things going for you at Care4? Your mother tells me you were traveling out of town this week."

"Yeah. I went down to Cape Girardeau, Missouri."

"Isn't most of that area still damaged by the earthquake?"

"Yeah. With all the road construction, it seemed like it took forever to get down there. It was worthwhile, though. I've been working with one of the chemists at Care4…Doctor Cregar."

"How's he doing? I heard he lost his family in the earthquake. People say that he's become a bit of a recluse since then. I can't even imagine the effect that a tragedy like that would have on a person. A loss like that would be tough for anyone to endure."

"He's an interesting guy. I mean…he's nice enough to me. You can tell that he's still pretty bitter over his loss. Of course, sometimes it seems that he's just as angry at some of the folks at Care4 as he is about losing his family."

"These are tough times, Tom. Unfortunately, Care4 has been forced to cut back on much of its research and development department. I'm sure many of management's decisions don't sit well with Doctor Cregar."

"Yeah. I think that's putting it mildly. But Doctor Cregar's been working on some really neat things. As a matter of fact, I've got something to show you." Tom reached into his pocket to pull out a handful of the Rivermass pills.

✫ ✫ ✫

While Tom was revealing his secret, Peter and his family were gathering around the dinner table. David Jangle led them in prayer.

"Thank you, Father, for the many blessings you bestow upon our family. Thank you for a good job, good food, good friends, and good health. In gratitude we ask that you guide us to do your will here on earth. In the name of the Father, the Son, and the Holy Spirit."

The whole family answered in unison, "Amen."

David Jangle's prayers always included thanks to God for his current job. He had just completed his third year of employment with Bruce Shindler's Company. Mr. Jangle's previous period of unemployment played a large role in Peter's initial encounter with the Sandman. Peter's silent prayer was to avoid another confrontation with his nemesis.

✫ ✫ ✫

Ten miles from Long Beach, in a more modest area of Michigan City, Jerry Parker sat at the dinner table across from his mom. It had been three years since his older brother was gunned down on the streets of his hometown, Gary, Indiana. With his father in jail for a prior offense, Jerry realized he was now responsible for his mother's welfare.

"How are you doing, Momma?"

"I'm doing fine, Jerry. Don't you worry yourself about me. I have a good job down at the bank. The people I work with are wonderful."

"Are you still visiting dad at the prison?"

"I visit your father occasionally. But don't count on any kind of a future between your dad and me. We've grown apart over the years. I did tell him about your college and your job this summer. He was so proud. We are both incredibly proud of you, Jerry. How are things going in Indianapolis?"

"It's going great. There's more opportunities in Indy than I'd ever have here. Plus, I enjoy what I'm doing."

"Are they giving you an opportunity to prove yourself?"

"Yeah. Don't worry, Momma. They're not making me do all of the grunt work." Jerry flashed a smile of amusement at his mother's question. His mother was always looking out for him.

"Well, I'm just saying...you need to stand up for yourself. You've got to realize that we don't always get the opportunities that some of your friends have."

"Mom, believe it or not, things are getting better. We've made some progress over the past thirty years. If I do a good job, I'll get better opportunities. It's just like football. If you train, and if you perform, you get rewarded, regardless of your race."

"I hope you're right, son. Just keep in mind that you're being watched. And you're being judged. People in this world tend to define people by their sex, or their nationality, or by the color of their skin. If you mess up at Hoosier Insurance, those folks are going to think twice before hiring another young black student from Indiana University. I'm talking about responsibility, son."

Jerry reached across the dinner table and took hold of his mother's hands. With a gentle squeeze, he looked into her concerned eyes, "Listen, Momma, I'm not going to let you down like the other men in your life, okay? I'm better than that. I can't promise you that I'll never screw up...you know me too well...but I *can* promise you that I won't give up. I'm focused, Momma. I'm going to be a success. Okay?"

Jerry's mom smiled. She knew she could trust her son. She would do anything she could to protect him.

"I know you're going to be a success, Jerry. You don't need to prove anything to me."

As if to reaffirm her point, Jerry's mom changed the subject from his work life to his personal life.

"So...how's your social life? Have you found any girlfriends in Indy?"

Jerry laughed. "Don't even go there, Momma. I don't have time for that right now."

"I just want you to be happy."

"I know, Momma. That's the same thing I want for you."

CHAPTER TWENTY TWO

Peter looked at the alarm clock. It read 9:33 a.m. He had tossed all night, wondering whether or not he should call Sarah. Rising out of bed, he walked over to the window. There wasn't a cloud in the sky. A perfect day for the beach. He dropped to the floor, did 20 quick push-ups, and then went downstairs for breakfast. Reading through the business section of the newspaper, he searched for any news forewarning of an economic depression. Everything seemed fine. Putting aside his worries, he reached for the phone to call Tom Nelson.

"So, Tom, are you still up for the beach today?"

"Sure. I told you I would."

"Great...uh... do you think you could give Jerry a call? I think he's still mad at me."

"Sure. I'll give him a call. Are you going to call Sarah or Kathy?"

"Well...I figure we'll be in front of Sarah's house. She'll probably see us down there. If not, we can walk up and see what they're doing."

"Whatever, dude. You're going to have to talk to her some time. We'll meet you down there around 11:30, okay?"

"Cool. I'll see you there."

Peter arrived at stop 31, on Lake Shore Drive, at noon. The temperature was already 88 degrees, and the lake was barely moving under the heat of the sun. Peter sat on a bench to take his shoes off before walking down the stairway to the beach. Reaching the beach, he let his feet sink into the sand. He stood for a few minutes, staring at the lake. He watched as parents playfully splashed with their young children in the water. He saw a group of kids who looked to be high school age, lined across the beach on their towels. It reminded him of his own high school days. He figured that perhaps things hadn't changed much over the past three years. Reassured, he trudged toward stop 36 to meet Tom and Jerry.

"What's up, guys?"

"Not much," Jerry replied. "Tom was just telling me about this miracle pill that he and the folks at Care4 have discovered."

"Our own little mad scientist. Did you ask your dad about the pills?"

"Yes. He thinks Doctor Cregar is a little crazy. But I've seen what these pills have done to his body. It's amazing. I know they work."

"So is your dad going to try to get the docs to prescribe them?"

"The doctors won't prescribe anything that isn't FDA-approved. My dad said that it would take years for this stuff to go through FDA testing. That's the same thing Doctor Cregar told me. I don't think he's willing to wait that long."

"So what are you going to do?"

"I don't know. I suppose that's up to Doctor Cregar. I told Jerry that he ought to try them. They would help him have a Heisman-type year in football."

"Jerry, be careful. You don't want to put something in your body that might do damage to you later."

"Oh, so now you're looking out for me, Peter? It would've been nice if you'd shown the same concern for me when selling our CBO to your folks at American Dinero."

There was definite sarcasm in Jerry's voice.

"Come on, Jerry, that's not fair. I tried. You don't understand this guy I work with. He can be a complete asshole. If I say black, he says white. He's a freakin' pig."

"Whatever, Dude." Jerry looked away, unconvinced.

Feeling he had let Jerry down, Peter withdrew into the water. The cool lake was a refreshing respite from the hot sun.

It was now 2:15, and neither Sarah nor Kathy had come down to the beach. Unable to contain himself any longer, Peter asked, "Has anyone heard from Sarah or Kathy lately?"

"No, Dude. She's your girlfriend—you should know what she's doing."

"We had a bit of a fight over that Keyster guy. I don't trust him. I mean…he's ten years older than her."

Jerry laughed. "Oh, man. Peter's trying to protect his little girl."

"What the hell, Parker? You should be trying to protect her, too. She's your friend, too, isn't she?"

Tom interrupted. "Cool it, guys. Her house is right above us. Let's just walk up and see how she's doing. Is that all right with you, Peter?"

Peter hesitated, not sure what he wanted. Finally he relented. "Okay, let's go up and see them."

The three boys walked up the dune that led to Lake Shore Drive. Across the street were approximately 30 steps that led up to Sarah Banks' house. As the boys climbed the steps they could hear many voices coming from the top of the hill.

"It sounds like they're having a party," Tom remarked.

Reaching the top of the stairs, the boys noticed a large number of people, dressed in suits and skirts, both inside and outside the house.

"Hey guys, I don't think we should go up there in our wet shorts. It looks like Sarah's parents are having a party."

Unsure whether or not to turn back, Peter peered into the glass-enclosed porch that led out to the Banks' back yard. He spotted Sarah, talking to Doug Keyster. Peter was temporarily frozen when Sarah's eyes fell upon him.

"Come on, let's go," he said, as he turned back towards the stairs.

It was too late. Sarah came out through the sliding glass door and called "Peter, wait!"

Peter didn't stop until Sarah ran to the top of the stairs and cried out, "Why are you leaving?"

Peter then turned and replied, "Because I obviously don't belong here."

Before Sarah could say another word, Peter continued.

"*Now* do you understand why I didn't want to call you? I know what's going on between you and that Keyster guy. Are you going to give me another excuse that you need to stay home and watch your grandfather?"

Sarah stood in stunned silence.

"What's wrong, Sarah? Are you afraid to tell me that you don't want to see me anymore? I mean, come on, Sarah, don't sneak around behind my back. Tell me to my face."

Sarah could not contain herself any longer. Her eyes began to well up and a tear ran down her cheek. Wiping the tear away, she softly said, "My grandfather died, okay? Everyone here just came back from the funeral. A funeral that you didn't even bother to attend, Peter."

Sarah's tears streamed down her face as she turned and ran back to the house. Having witnessed the whole incident, Doug came out to meet her. Peter stood halfway down the stairs, shocked and shamed into silence.

Tom walked over to Peter. "Peter, man, it's time to step up. You've got to go talk to her."

"I can't talk to anyone right now, guys. I've got to get out of here. I'll see you later."

Peter raced down the steps and continued running down Lake Shore Drive toward his home. The hurt was building up inside him. The hurt gradually gave way to anger. Unfortunately, he didn't know where to direct his anger. Was he mad at himself? Was he angry with Doug Keyster? He just kept running, past Stop 31, and up Moore Road. Up one hill and down the next, his mind was spinning like a tornado. He was bent on destruction, with a singular destination in mind.

Reaching his house, he went straight to the garage and grabbed his bicycle. He pedaled quickly over the hills of Moore Road and back to Lake Shore Drive. Completing a left hand turn, he darted down Lake Shore Drive toward Washington Park. Cars tagged with Illinois license plates lined the houses along the street. Peter desperately wished he could regain the power that he had previously obtained from the genie. Pumping his legs faster, he closed his eyes. He shook his head back and forth with each rotation of the bike pedals. The wind in his hair and the sweat on his forehead provided a temporary distraction from his heartache. Within twenty minutes he had reached his destination. He stood at the foot of Mount Baldy.

Drenched with sweat, Peter could feel the adrenaline flowing through every vein in his body. He charged up the side of the dune, passing other beach-goers along the way. After reaching the top, he stopped to survey his surroundings. The clear blue lake reflected the sunlight onto the old steel stacks of the lifeless mills in East Chicago and Burns Harbor. Looking to the east, he gazed over the prison walls of the Indiana State Prison. He thought about the fact that Jerry Parker's father was still locked behind those walls, and could only imagine the heavy burden that must place on Jerry and his mother. Finally, he fell to his knees, oblivious to those around him. Assuming a sitting position, he placed his elbows on his knees, and buried his head in the palms of his hands.

"Dear Lord, please help me. I don't know what to do. I'm so filled with anger—and I have no explanation or remedy for it. My only remedy can be with you. Please rid my heart of its hatred and relieve me of my pain. What do you want me to do, Lord? What is my calling?"

"Why, Peter, your calling was to be Chairman of the Federal Reserve...President of the United States...I handed you everything you wanted. What more can you want from your Lord?"

Peter immediately recognized the voice. He had no need to lift his head out of his hands. Still, he could not resist the temptation to look. Peering up into the glare of the sun, he could barely discern the genie that had tested his morality three years ago. Shielding the sun with his hand, he looked at the figure that had not aged over the past three years. Dressed in a charcoal black suit and topped with a black fedora, the genie did not break a sweat despite the intense heat. Looking around, Peter saw no one. The once-crowded beach was now deserted.

"I knew you were back."

"Of course you knew I was back, Peter. I'm not one to make subtle appearances. What did you think of the earthquake? Was it a little much?"

"What do you want from me?"

"Oh…nothing much…just your soul." The Sandman chuckled at his own wicked humor. "But you refuse to give that to me, don't you, Peter? You want me to do things for you, but you're unwilling to reciprocate. I guess I'll just have to extract payment from everyone else."

"Is that what this is about? Are you trying to take Sarah away from me? Did Doug Keyster sell you his soul? Did you arrange it so that he'd become a great investor and steal my girlfriend?"

The Sandman offered a sinister smile.

"Once bitten by a snake, Peter, you are now frightened by every rope that resembles a snake. I have nothing to do with that. Your own paranoia is pushing your girlfriend away from you."

"What about the hourglass in Doug Keyster's office? The sand in the hourglass represents you, doesn't it? Are you magically putting him in positions of power? Are you using him the same way you used me three years ago?"

"Peter, I don't need to use magic anymore. My job has become much easier over the years. I merely plant seeds of hope."

"The only seeds you plant are seeds of greed, selfishness, and deceit."

"And why did you come here, Peter? Wasn't it for your own selfish purposes? You wanted to know whether or not I was taking away your girlfriend. You can accept the fact that I exist, as long as I don't affect your life. Am I right? You haven't even shown any concern about all those poor souls who lost their lives in the earthquake. I don't hear you praying for them. Instead, it's all about you."

"That's not true! I hate you for saying that!"

"That's right, Peter, go ahead and hate me. Let your anger rage out of control and soon you'll be coming home to me."

"That's not true! I'm going to fight you."

"Fight on, Petey."

Peter closed his eyes and clenched his fists so hard that his fingernails were piercing his skin, and then he cried out, "Oh, God...Help me!"

Suddenly he heard the playful sounds of people frolicking in the water. Opening his eyes, he saw the familiar crowds of people enjoying themselves, sprinting up and down the sand dune. He rose quickly to his feet and looked around for any sign of the genie. The Sandman was gone.

CHAPTER TWENTY THREE

Although Sarah was trying her best to forget the incident that had just occurred at her house, Kathy Cohen knew she had to step forward. At the first opportunity she pulled Doug Keyster outside, away from the crowd at the Banks' house.

"Listen, Doug, I need to know your intentions regarding my friend Sarah."

Doug was a bit taken aback by Kathy's direct approach.

"I'm sorry. Who are you again?"

"You know who I am. I'm Sarah's friend. My best friend is hurting because she doesn't know who she can trust anymore. She's been a caregiver her whole life. Now she has to deal with her grandfather's death, and at the same time she's questioning the future with her boyfriend of the past five years. I want to be sure that if she leaves her boyfriend, you're not going to be the next one to break her heart."

"Break her heart?! Listen, I like Sarah. I like Sarah a lot. But I don't think I've ever led her to believe that I was interested in a relationship with her. I will certainly apologize if I misled her in any way."

"Doug! You asked her out to one of your friend's parties. You comforted her, and held her when her grandfather died. You sent her flowers! You kissed her! Why wouldn't she think you were interested in her?"

"Listen, Kathy. I'm like that with everyone. I'm a naturally affectionate man. I like to shower women with hugs and kisses. I'll admit it...I like women...and Sarah is a special girl. Believe it or not, I don't have many male friends. Sarah has been someone who I can talk to at work. I'll admit, I am attracted to her. It's as if she's able to fill a certain emptiness in me. But I would never let it go any further than that. I have too much respect for her, and for her father."

Doug's childlike blue eyes were now betraying a vulnerability that Kathy had not seen before. She believed Doug. She knew she could communicate with him in a non-threatening tone.

"You guys are all alike. But at least you're being honest with me. Will you promise me that you'll be honest with Sarah?"

"Kathy, believe it or not, I'm not an evil guy. I would never do anything to hurt Sarah, okay?"

Kathy was satisfied.

✵ ✵ ✵

Later that evening, Peter fidgeted at the dinner table, silently pushing the food around on his plate. His thoughts spewed an endless array of questions regarding the genie's intentions. After taking a few bites of his food, Peter asked to be excused from the table and retreated to his bedroom.

Claire Jangle looked at her husband, David, with concern. "Is there something wrong with Peter?"

"I don't know. I think he's having a hard time at work."

"Well… are you going to go up and talk with him, or shall I?"

David smiled at his wife. She would never accept uncertainty. Claire was a woman of action. She was the force that kept him focused.

"I'll go up and talk to him."

David Jangle was unsure how to console his son. He knew that Peter had been obsessing about something that David did not fully understand. He sometimes wondered if Peter needed professional counseling. David didn't want to do anything that might make the situation worse. Nonetheless, he believed in his son. It was a fact that people had died in Lake Michigan three years ago. It was also a fact that he had been on the verge of taking his own life three years ago. Due to David's strong belief in God, he realized he needed to accept the likelihood that evil exists in the world.

Knocking on the bedroom door, he asked for Peter's permission to enter the room.

"So, Peter, you were pretty quiet at dinner tonight. Is there something on your mind?"

"Dad, I know you think I'm crazy, but the Sandman is back."

"Peter, I don't think you're crazy. I love you and I want to help you. How do you know he's back?"

"I saw him. I rode my bike to Mount Baldy today and I saw him."

Peter's dad sat down on the bed next to his son.

"Well, I guess that answers that question. Why did you go to Mount Baldy? Were you looking for him?"

"I don't know...I was angry. Sarah's grandfather passed away this week and I didn't even know it. I barged in on a reception they were having after the funeral and I made a fool of myself."

"So...do you think the genie had something to do with Sarah's grandfather dying?"

"I don't know. I doubt it. Sarah's grandfather has been ill for some time. It was expected."

"Well, what did the genie say to you?"

Peter tried to recall the events. "He didn't say much of anything to me. He mocked me." Peter looked down at the ground in silence. Then, as if the thought suddenly popped into his head, Peter looked into his dad's eyes and added, "I think he might have caused the earthquake."

"Did he say that?"

"Not directly. But he seemed to gloat about it. And then he said that I didn't care about the people who lost their lives. That's not true, Dad."

"Of course it's not true. Listen, Peter, I know you're concerned about those people who lost their lives. The words seem so simple, but the practicality of it all is so incredibly difficult. There are so many people in need. It's overwhelming. So we do what we can. We care for those who are close to us. We pray that if everyone in the world cares for a few people who are close to them, somehow, some way, everyone will be cared for. But when something like a natural disaster happens, there's not much we can do. I guess we can try to raise money for the victims. But other than that, we can't save the world single-handed."

"But if he caused the event...maybe I can stop him."

"And prevent natural disasters from occurring? Are you also going to stop people from oppressing others? Are you going to stamp out world hunger? Peter, these events are outside our control. This is not Eden. Remember the story of Adam and Eve, Peter? I actually believe that God originally offered us a perfect world. Unfortunately he loved us so much that he also gave us free will. And guess what, Peter? We rejected Eden. We were too concerned about our own personal gain. First we took the forbidden fruit because we wanted more knowledge, then Cain killed his brother Abel out of jealousy. That's our history, Peter!"

"So what are you saying, Dad? Are you saying that we should just accept that bad things will happen? Are you saying we shouldn't fight?"

"Peter, I don't know the answers. But I do believe that you need to look inward first. The first step is to be self-aware. If the genie is your demon, yes, you should fight. In the Bible, the Lord said to Cain, *'Why are you so resentful and crestfallen? If you do well, you can hold up your head; but if not, sin is a demon lurking at the door—yet you can be his master.'* We all have demons, Peter. Our first priority needs to be mastering our own demons. Only then can we help others conquer theirs."

"Do you think I created this demon?"

"No. But he obviously has a connection to you."

"So how do you defeat a demon?"

"How did you defeat him last time?"

"Don't you remember, Dad? Last time I had his bottle. He can't survive water in his bottle. Whenever I put the lake water in his bottle he started to drown. That was the leverage I had over him last time. That's how I defeated him. I don't have that leverage this time. I have no idea where his bottle is hidden."

"I don't know, Peter. I may be naïve, but I'm not sure it was the water that defeated him last time. You asked me how to defeat a demon? I think love is the answer. Love defeats evil. Evil offers us power. The power often corrupts. By contrast, love offers us peace and happiness. Evil entraps mankind, love sets people free. Remember how entrapped I felt when I got laid off a couple of years ago? Your mom's love set me free."

Peter gave his dad a long embrace. "Thanks, Dad. I'm still not sure how I'm going to defeat this genie, but I know I love you."

"I love you too, Peter…and that's how we'll defeat this genie."

For the first time in a week, Peter slept in peace.

CHAPTER TWENTY FOUR

The next morning Peter went to Sunday mass with his family. Looking around the congregation, he spotted a young mother holding her new-born infant tight to her bosom. He observed a nine-year old boy teasing and pushing his younger brother. He watched an embarrassed father, quietly scolding his toddler son for pulling the liturgy books out of the church pews and throwing them to the floor. In a world filled with distractions, Peter knew he had to stay focused. Seated between his mother and father, he squeezed his father's hand with his right hand and his mother's hand with his left. He flashed them both a smile, knowing full well that his strength grew through their bond.

After the service, Peter worked up the courage to call Sarah Banks.

"Hi, Sarah. I just wanted to call you to apologize. I'm so sorry about your grandfather and I'm sorry about the way

I've been acting. I've been a total jerk. I don't know what's wrong with me." Peter did not think this was a good time to mention the Sandman to Sarah.

Sarah was quiet on the other end of the phone. Although she saw incredible potential in Peter, at times she wondered whether she was fooling herself. She feared that Peter's jealousy, if not controlled, could eventually suffocate her.

"Listen, Peter. I realize you couldn't have known anything about my grandfather. But the reason you didn't know was because you didn't call."

"I did try to call you. I could never get an answer." Peter could not admit that he was too proud to call.

"Well, you should have left a message. Obviously I was busy with all of the funeral arrangements." She paused and took a deep breath. "But I thank you for your thoughts."

"Can I see you some time today before I go back to Chicago?"

Sarah hesitated, before relenting. "Fine. Why don't you come by in an hour? My parents will be happy to see you." Sarah concluded coldly.

Peter hung up the phone, contemplating Sarah's last reply. His hope was that Sarah, as well as her parents, would be happy to see him.

After an hour, Peter borrowed his dad's car and drove toward Sarah's home. Turning off Lakeshore Drive at the sign marking bus stop 36, Peter drove up a hill and turned right into a heavily wooded area where the road ended. The driveway leading to the Banks' house was on the right. The house stood high on a hill of grass. Peter drove up the driveway, away from the dense forest of trees that hid the entrance to the house. It was a long ranch-style home with a full basement. In total, the house had approximately 5,000 square feet of living space, a generous amount for a family of three. Peter walked up the steps to the front door. Peter had always thought that he had to move out of Michigan City to find a place he would like to live. But surveying his current surroundings—a view of the forest in front, and a view overlooking Lake Michigan at the back, he wondered whether he had a distorted view of luxurious living. Perhaps an expensive condo on Lake Shore Drive in Chicago wasn't necessary.

Peter rang the doorbell and waited for someone to answer. He resisted the urge to invite himself in. Peter didn't know what to say when Sarah answered the door. He smiled sheepishly to break the ice, but she turned quickly and led him inside. They walked back to the family room, overlooking the lake, where Peter greeted Sarah's father.

"I'm sorry to hear about the loss of your father, Mr. Banks."

"Thank you, Peter. He was a good man. He led a good life. In some ways though, I suppose it was a blessing. He was basically confined to his bed these last couple of months. He wanted to be free." Mr. Banks paused to control his emotion, and changed the subject. So, tell me, how are things with your job in Chicago this summer?"

"It's going well. It's different, you know, trying to learn all of the different personalities. But I'm learning a lot."

"Well, good. That's important."

"And how are things at the bank?"

"Things are going well. The economy's doing much better, and it's had a great impact on our financial results. The Lake Michigan Research Institute has already created over 200 well-paying jobs in the area, and we expect more to come. One benefit of the new jobs is that home building in this area is taking off nicely. We've seen many homes appreciate

30 percent in value over the last three years. That's led to lots of demand for home-equity loans at our bank."

"So wealth is being created in Michigan City?" Peter asked hopefully. Advancing Michigan City's economy was one of the promised results the Sandman had offered when he gave Peter the power to lower interest rates.

"I would say that some of our citizens have done very well due to home appreciation." Mr. Banks answered.

"In fact, more and more of the newly wealthy from Chicago are buying homes in the beach area, at inflated prices, and razing the house to build newer, larger homes. In effect, they're buying very expensive dirt. The benefit of increased home building is that it translates into jobs in the construction industry and increased sales for landscapers, appliance retailers, and furniture retailers. The housing sector is having a tremendous effect on our overall economy. "

Peter was pleased to hear that the local economy was doing well, but he still resented that his home town was being invaded by out-of-state residents. It left the same repugnant sense that he felt when losing a big football game to a rival team. Deep down he knew he would always be loyal to his home town.

"What do the people who sell their homes do?" he asked.

Steve Banks could sense Peter's concern.

"You have to understand that many people view their home as an investment. They're willing to sell and move on if they're able to realize a good return on their investment. Meanwhile our bank benefits from a growing deposit base, and we still have strong demand for home loans and home equity loans. The local economy is as good as it's been in the past ten years. Even our trust department has done extremely well in the past couple of years. Sarah has attracted a couple of big clients to LakeShore Funds this summer, haven't you, Sarah?"

Peter could hear the pride in Steve Banks' voice, as he turned to look at his daughter.

"I was talking with Doug Keyster at the funeral reception yesterday, and he told me you were recently invited as a finalist to possibly manage money for the World Hunger Foundation. Doug also told me that you were instrumental in filling out the RFP. It sounds like you're doing a great job, princess."

Sarah blushed, not wanting to make Peter feel inadequate in front of her father. She was still inexplicably attracted to him—despite her lingering feelings of frustration and anger. Although she was also attracted to Doug, she knew that she loved Peter.

"Well...Peter's doing pretty well also, Dad. They manage a lot more money at American Dinero than we do."

"Listen, Peter, we may not compare to the size and prestige of American Dinero, but Doug Keyster has done a great job for me over the past five years. I think his investment record would be competitive with any large money manager. Despite our good investment performance, we've always had a difficult time attracting money, due to our smaller size. However, now that we have a strong five year investment record, we seem to be included in many more investment searches. You might want to consider looking for a job with us when you graduate next year. We would certainly be happy to have you."

Sarah was happy her dad offered Peter a job, but she knew Peter resented the accolades being bestowed on Doug Keyster. She knew it was very unlikely that he would ever agree to report to Doug.

"Dad, don't try recruiting Peter yet. He's going to have all kinds of job opportunities to consider next year. You guys are going to have to offer a lot of money if you want him. Right, Peter?" Sarah winked and smiled. Peter smiled back.

"Well, I just want to make sure that he doesn't try to take my baby girl too far away from me," Steve Banks replied.

"Believe it or not, Daddy, Michigan City is not the center of the universe. Who knows where I might decide to live after school? And it's not necessarily going to be Peter's decision." Peter's smile faded.

"No, you're right, dear, I used to think New Madrid, Missouri was near the center of America, too."

"What are you driving at?" Sarah asked.

"My point being that the center of activity is not always the best place to plant your roots. You've got to realize that sometimes true happiness might be found a bit off center."

Sarah rose from the couch and gave her dad a quick hug. "Well, it's a good thing I have a full year to think about where my center might be."

Then, taking Peter by the hand, she led him outside to the back yard.

From high above Lake Shore Drive, Peter and Sarah stared out across Lake Michigan. Peter didn't want to upset Sarah, but he needed to know the status of their relationship.

"So, you told your dad that you might explore the country without me. Does that mean that I've lost you, Sarah?"

Sarah was not ready to engage in a long, serious conversation about their future.

"Peter, who knows where we'll be a year from now? Let's just enjoy the present. We can worry about the future later."

"That's fine, Sarah, but I don't think my future will be complete without you."

Sarah smiled. Looking back at Peter, she couldn't resist giving him a quick hug. Then, pulling away from Peter's grasp, she waved her index finger in front of his face and warned, "Peter Jangle, you better never pull that jealous crap again, got it?"

Feeling reassured that he had not destroyed his relationship with Sarah, Peter replied, "I promise."

"So, when are you heading back to Chicago?"

"I told my dad I was going to try to catch the 2:15 train. He agreed to give me a ride to the train station."

"I'll tell you what. I'll follow you home and I'll drop you off at the station. How's that sound?"

Peter smiled. "It sounds like I have an angel looking out for me."

After dropping off his father's car at the house and grabbing his essentials for the upcoming week, Peter jumped into the passenger seat of Sarah's car. He studied Sarah's face as they drove in silence toward the South Shore station.

"Why are you staring at me?"

"I don't know. You're beautiful. You know that?" Sarah blushed and gazed at Peter briefly before returning her focus to the road ahead.

Peter continued, "A lot has happened to us in the last four years, Sarah. A lot has happened to this city. It sounds like your dad's bank is doing much better. The economy has improved. The Lake Michigan Research Institute actually seems to be a pretty good thing. I mean, despite all of the trouble the Sandman brought into our lives, things seem to be improving."

"But at what price, Peter? Think about the people who died. Think about Steve Shindler. Sure, we go on with our lives. We're the lucky ones. What gives us the right to life over someone else? Think about it, Peter—which alternative is better...all of us struggling together, or only some of us benefiting at the expense of others?"

Peter knew Sarah was right. He turned to look out the passenger window with feelings of guilt. He then looked back to Sarah.

"Do you blame me for Steve Shindler's death?"

"Of course I don't blame you, Peter. You know that. You had no way of knowing the Sandman's plans. I'm just saying that we can't forget. Even if the Sandman helped you to create the Lake Michigan Research Institute, he did more harm than good. The things that have improved are things that we could have eventually improved through our own hard work. The end doesn't justify the means."

The car pulled in front of the train station. Peter and Sarah looked at each other in awkward silence. Peter's face suddenly turned white as a ghost.

"What's wrong, Peter?"

Peter stared at the car radio and slowly turned up the volume. Metallica's classic rock anthem, *Enter Sandman*, was playing on the radio. Peter knew he had to share his discovery with Sarah.

"The Sandman is back."

Sarah's jaw dropped.

"You're kidding, right?"

Peter's silence told Sarah that this was not a joke.

"Peter, how can you be sure of that?"

"I saw him."

"Where?"

"After the reception for your grandfather. I rode my bike to Mount Baldy and I saw him."

"Peter, you were angry that day. Are you sure it was him?"

"I know it was him."

"What did he say?"

"I don't know. I asked him if he was trying to take you away from me. I thought that maybe he had made a deal with Doug Keyster."

"Oh, Peter. Don't tell me you still believe that, do you?"

"I don't know. I don't know what to believe. I don't know why he keeps appearing to me. I've got to believe that he comes into other people's lives besides mine. Why would he choose to haunt me?"

Peter did not want to believe his dad's suggestion that perhaps the genie had formed a special bond unique to him. He was determined to prove that the Sandman was working through someone else this time, just as he had worked through Peter three years ago. He wanted to prove to Sarah that Doug Keyster would be nothing without the Sandman's help. Peter realized he was succumbing to jealousy.

"Peter, you're scaring me."

"You don't need to be scared, Sarah. You always do the right thing. I'm the one who always seems to find a way to screw up. I just have this feeling that something bad is going to happen. And I don't know how to stop it. I'm worried that I'm going to be put to the test again. And I might make the wrong decision, again. The main thing is that I want *you* to be careful. I'm probably overreacting, but I don't trust Doug Keyster."

Peter hugged Sarah with all his might. "I don't want to lose you, okay?"

Sarah bit her lip, trying to hold back her tears. He had won her over again. Despite all his faults, she really did love him.

"Don't worry, Peter. I'm not going anywhere. But you need to stop jumping to dumb conclusions."

Seeing the disappointment in Peter's face, Sarah assured him, "I will always be here to help you fight your demons...I love you, Peter."

Sarah kissed Peter on the cheek.

"Try to get the genie out of your thoughts, but if you do see him again...let me know. Our relationship will go nowhere if you can't confide in me."

Peter smiled. He was slowly learning that he needed to depend on others. Despite his tendency toward self-reliance, he knew that this battle could not be fought alone.

"Thank you for sharing your fears with me, Peter. Let me know if you see him again. I'll come to Chicago and stand by your side."

"I know you will. I can always count on you, Sarah."

Peter cupped Sarah's head in his hands and gave her a deep kiss. He then opened the passenger door and left to catch his train.

As the South Shore train rumbled past the city of Gary, Indiana, Peter noticed an old long-forgotten sign welcoming people to "The Magic City." Gary had earned this moniker due to its origin as a city that sprang from the ground out of nothing. In 1906, Judge Elbert H. Gary, then chairman of U.S. Steel Corporation, acquired 12,000 acres along Lake Michigan to build a $100,000 steel mill. The lure of jobs turned the area into an ethnic melting pot, and Gary grew from 16,800 people in 1910, to 100,000 by 1930. But Gary suffered from a downturn in the manufacturing industry in the late 1970s and early 1980s. By the end of the century the city was making headlines for averaging more homicides per capita than any other major urban area in the nation.

Peter wondered whether the genie had been at work even then, giving people false hopes of salvation, only to squash those hopes as the companies that they served and the city where they resided crumbled to decay. As he pondered the future of the communities surrounding New Madrid, Missouri, the thought occurred to Peter: *How many times throughout history had the genie repeated this cruel cycle of events?*

CHAPTER TWENTY FIVE

It was late Sunday evening, and much of downtown Chicago had retired for the night. An uncharacteristic silence enveloped the city. Peter Jangle tossed restlessly in his bed, unable to sleep. The events of the weekend kept repeating in his thoughts. He was still in a dream-like state when his alarm clock sounded on Monday morning. Unconsciously flailing at the off button, he rolled over and went back to sleep. He didn't get into work until 9:30 a.m. It was the first time all summer that he had been late for work.

"Peter, where have you been? Tony's been looking for you."

Of all people, Peter did not want Tony to know that he had overslept. *Damn, the Sandman got me again*, he thought to himself.

"I'm sorry, Terri, I didn't hear my alarm clock go off. Why is Tony looking for me? Am I in trouble again?"

"Don't worry. He's actually in a pretty good mood today. He wants you to help out on a proposal for a potential client."

"You're telling me that he trusts me to work on this proposal alone?"

"Well, actually, he wanted me to work with the marketing folks on the proposal. I suggested that this would be a great learning experience for you. So now he wants to be the one to give you the good news." Terri took satisfaction in reassuring Peter that she was on his side.

"Gee, Terri, I'm not sure whether I should thank you, or curse you."

"Just go see him. We need to get the document from him so we can get started. The response to the client is due next week."

Walking up to the trading desk, Peter overheard Tony talking on the phone to one of the brokers who covered American Dinero.

"Listen, dude, everyone and their mother has shown me those bonds. If I wanted them, I could certainly get them cheaper than you're offering. Tell your trader that if he really wants to sell the bonds, he better at least know the appropriate level to price them. If you hope to sell them at the level you quoted me, you'll have to start calling your retail clients. Don't call me unless you've got something that will actually add value to our accounts." Tony slammed the phone down.

Noting Peter's arrival, Tony flashed a big smile and asked, "Where have you been, Petey?"

Peter cringed at the name, and then recovered with an appropriate response.

"I had some work I had to complete at home this morning. I'm sorry. Terri told me that you were looking for me."

"Did she tell you why I wanted you?"

Recalling Terri's statement that Tony wanted to be the one to deliver the news, Peter replied simply, "No, she just mentioned that you wanted to see me. Can I help you with something?"

"Well, it just so happens that you *can* help me. And guess what, Peter? If you do this well, you just might have a future in this business. You see…the people who are truly successful in the money management business are the ones who are able to bring money in the door. It's just like any other business. Sell the product, and you'll be able to make a very nice living for yourself and your family"

"So what do you want me to sell?"

"I want you to sell my expertise, of course! It really shouldn't be that hard."

Peter just stood there, not knowing how to respond to Tony. He decided that Tony was the most egotistical person he had ever met. But then he remembered that there were probably some folks who would accuse him of being just as egotistical.

"Listen, Peter, we've been selected as a finalist to present to a foundation called the 'World Hunger Foundation.' Dave Koslow is going to represent the Portfolio Management Group, Terri Tanaka is going to represent the Analyst Group, and I'm going to represent the Traders. I thought that maybe it would be a good idea for you to be involved in the RFP process. I thought it would be a good learning experience for you."

Tony was puzzled by the smile on Peter's face.

"What's so funny? Did Tanaka tell you that this was her idea?"

"No. It's not that. It's just that a friend of mine who works for Lakeshore Fund Management in Michigan City was also invited as a finalist.

"Lakeshore Fund Management? Who are they? I've never heard of them."

"They're the investment arm of Michigan City National Bank. It's a small bank in my home town. Supposedly the investment guy there has put together a good performance record over the past five years. I guess they're getting more and more attention from the consultant community now."

"Oh, yeah? Well these guys are our consultants. They've been feeding us business for years. I'm not about to let some little Podunk bank get its foot in the door. Do you think you can get me some literature on these guys? I like to know my competition."

"I guess I could get you some info. From what I understand, the consultants, CYA, are looking for different managers for each asset class. I think that Lakeshore Funds are only going after the 60 percent of the funds allocated to equities. Maybe we should go after the 40 percent allocated to bonds."

"Why, Peter? Don't you think we can beat your hometown boys in equity management?"

"No, it's not that. I just think that if the consultants want various managers, we ought to lead with our strongest asset class. We're one of the best bond managers in the world. What's wrong with sharing the account with another manager? The consultants might appreciate the fact that we followed their instructions by only pursuing one asset class. We might have a better chance of winning if we don't go after the whole pot."

Tony was unreceptive to Peter's idea. He clenched his teeth, casting a cold stare in Peter's direction.

"Dude, I already told you that these consultants are my guys. They'll support us, okay? You better decide what team you want to be on. We only hire winners here. I don't need any of your hometown bleeding heart, and I don't give a damn what the consultants say they're searching for. It's our job to convince these guys that we should manage all of the money, not just a portion of the funds. Don't worry, I know how to butter the consultant's bread."

Tony jumped up from his seat, and with one quick motion, grabbed a goldfish with his bare hand. Shaking the fish in his hand, he abruptly threw the fish to the piranhas.

Tony looked to Peter for a reaction, but found nothing.

Still trying to intimidate Peter, Tony walked over to his whiteboard and wrote in dark blue marker, "**THE GOOD YOU DO TODAY WILL CERTAINLY BE FORGOT-TEN TOMORROW**"

Peter stood aghast, as his eyes darted between the words on the whiteboard and the piranhas devouring the goldfish. This was the fourth commandment that he had seen Tony write on the whiteboard since the beginning of his internship. He had seen enough. He could no longer contain his anger.

"I used to be like you, Tony! I used to think it was all about me, and my interests. Don't you realize there's more to life than your own selfish needs? What about your moral compass?"

Tony flashed Peter a disdainful look.

"Moral compass?! Petey, my boy...puh-leez!! What's gotten into you? You're not on the beach in Michigan City any more. This is the big city. This is real business. I have a job to do. American Dinero pays me well to help them prosper. Don't try to preach your moral standards to me!"

Hearing Tony's words, Peter realized the difference between Tony and Doug Keyster. Doug enjoyed life. His enjoyment of life carried over to his job—and Doug's job enriched his life. By contrast, Tony was consumed by his job. His job seemed to define his life. Without success in his job, Tony would find no success in life. Peter began to think that perhaps Tony was more influenced by the Sandman than Doug. Perhaps Tony was the bigger threat. *Was it the Sandman's intent for Peter to suspect everyone?* He shook the thought out of his head. He felt compelled to confront Tony.

"There's a difference between being prosperous and being greedy. You can be profitable without being immoral."

The sound of Tony's laughter was hauntingly familiar.

"Peter, why did you want to work for us this summer? Why didn't you go work with your homeboys in Michigan City? Wasn't that greed? Wasn't that spurred by a pretense of ambition?"

"What's going on out here?"

Peter and Tony both turned to see the imposing figure of Fran Solli walking out to the trading desk.

"Oh, hi, Fran. It seems that our intern here is not so sure that we should compete with his pals in Michigan City on this RFP for the World Hunger Foundation."

"Is that true, Peter? I'll tell you, business is just like any other sport. It's all about winning."

"I know. You're right. I don't know what got into me. I apologize."

Tony wasn't about to let Peter off the hook that easily.

"So—are you going to get me that information on this Lakeshore Funds outfit?" Tony demanded.

Peter looked to Fran Solli to see if he would intervene on his behalf. Fran recognized Peter's look, and realized this could be a good coaching moment.

"Peter, you told me that you played football in high school, right?"

Peter nodded.

"Well, getting information on the competition is like watching game film on your opponent before a big game. It's an accepted and necessary part of preparation."

Peter again nodded his head in affirmation.

"Come on into my office, Peter. Let's have a talk."

Peter glanced at the aquarium as he was leaving. A faint hue of bloody water was all that remained of the goldfish. The piranhas appeared to have a grin on their faces.

Fran Solli closed the door to his office and leaned back in his leather chair. Peter pulled up a small chair and took a seat across from Mr. Solli's desk.

"Would you like something to drink, Peter?"

"No, thank you."

Fran took a deep breath, looked around, and then leaned forward to talk to Peter in a confidential tone.

"Listen, Peter, I know that Tony can be intimidating at times. But he plays a very important role in this firm. The only way we succeed in this business is by differentiating ourselves from the other money managers out there. Nine out of ten money managers adopt some type of investment style to appease the consultant community. Whether they call themselves Large Cap Managers or Small Cap Managers, Value Managers or Growth Managers....they select the benchmark that they want to be compared against, and then they fill their investment portfolios with most of the same names that comprise the benchmark. In essence, they elect to avoid risk...and in the process...they lose the ability to differentiate themselves. We'll never be a leader in this business by avoiding risk. Rather, we need to manage risk. Tony is innovative. He comes up with new ideas. He introduces risky strategies that have the potential to generate enormous returns for our clients. However, it's up to Terri, and me, and the others, including you... to manage that risk.

"I like the way that you stood up to Tony. Not many kids your age would have the guts to do that. I hope your resolve never falters. I don't want you to be exactly like him. But I also don't want you, or any one else, to take us in the opposite direction. I don't want to be like all the other money managers. Do you get what I'm saying?"

"Yes. I understand what you're saying. But does that mean that we have to spy on our competition and deride our fellow teammates?"

"Remember, Peter—this is a game. Life is a game. Things happen. One of the things that makes man so unique is the fact that the same, exact occurrence in life can be perceived in a thousand different ways, by a thousand different people. We perceive things differently based on our own independent feelings, wishes, hopes, and fears. What you perceive as spying, others perceive as market intelligence. What you perceive as deriding, others perceive as motivating. All men, and all businesses, are driven to survive based on their individual perceptions of what is necessary to survive."

Although Peter did not understand half of what Fran was saying, he felt it important to continue the conversation.

"But there has to be rules governing what is universally acceptable. In a football game, the refs enforce the rules to keep things from getting out of hand." Peter hoped this would return Fran's focus to the sports analogy.

"Exactly, Peter, but it's extremely important that the refs stay independent. They can't be affiliated with any particular team. That's the role of government in our society. The government represents the referees in society who balance individual rights with corporate rights. The government needs to be sure that corporations don't violate the law. However, as long as corporations act legally, government needs to stay out of the way. We want minimal government interference in our economy."

"I don't understand how government interference relates to the issue of Tony suggesting that we spy on our competition."

"Well, it sounds to me like you want some kind of referee, like the government, to support your moral objections. You can't have that wish. Our system of government is predicated on the separation of church and state. Governments based on moral or religious rationales have a history of killing innocent people. Similarly, governments based on 'social equality' have a history of stifling innovation. It's only through capitalism, with minimal government interference, that countries can advance their standard of living."

Fran Solli noticed the bewildered look on Peter's face. "I'm sorry, Peter. Did I go off on a tangent there? Sometimes I find it hard to suppress my Ayn Rand philosophy of life."

Peter smiled. He remembered Mr. Solli's initial representation of himself as Old Major in *Animal Farm*. Peter found himself both inspired and amused by Fran Solli's vision.

"Mr. Solli…if you want to set yourself apart from the competition, why don't you set up some hedge fund strategies? Market yourselves as a hedge fund that can operate without restrictions."

"Because then the consultants win. Don't you get it, Peter? Many hedge funds today have the same innovative talent that mutual funds used to have before the investment consultants constrained them with style boxes. While mutual funds never shorted stocks, they were free to invest in Value Stocks, Growth Stocks, Small Caps or Large Caps, depending on what names they felt offered the best risk/

return trade-off. The consultants have stifled these innovative managers by mandating that they stick to one strategy, regardless of whether they think that particular strategy offers the best risk/return profile in the current economic environment."

Fran Solli pounded the table. "I will not be constrained!!"

Peter was fairly certain that Mr. Solli had long forgotten why he had invited Peter into his office. Trying to reassure Mr. Solli that something productive had been accomplished, Peter summed up their brief meeting, "So you want me to be innovative, independent, and motivated, is that it?"

"Absolutely! You're a smart young man, Peter!"

"Thank you, Mr. Solli."

"Call me Fran."

As Peter walked out the door of Mr. Solli's office, he quickly glanced at the trading desk, where Tony Salami sat munching on a bag of potato chips. The white board above the trading desk had a new phrase in bold letters.

"WHAT YOU SPEND YEARS BUILDING, SOME UPSTART COULD DESTROY OVERNIGHT"

✿ ✿ ✿

The outside temperature was well in the 90s when Peter left work for the day. Walking south down Dearborn Street, he could still hear the words of Tony Salami and Fran Solli resonating in his head. Rather than going straight home, he detoured east on Van Buren Street, toward the Harold Washington Library Center on State Street. Peter could feel the moisture of his perspiration accumulating underneath his suit coat. The air conditioning in the old library building offered a cool respite.

Peter walked up to the computer terminal to search the library catalogue. He quickly found the book he was looking for: *Animal Farm* by George Orwell. Peter smiled in anticipation of flipping through the pages. He hoped that somehow the novel would reveal how his summer internship at American Dinero would end. He thumbed through the paperback novel until he came to a page describing a manifesto that Old Major was delivering to the other animals:

"Your resolution must never falter. No argument must lead you astray. Never listen when they tell you that Man and the animals have a common interest....we must not come to resemble him...No animal must ever live in a house or sleep in a bed, or wear clothes, or drink alcohol, or smoke tobacco, or touch money, or engage in trade."

Peter smiled.

CHAPTER TWENTY SIX

Jerry Parker sat motionless in his apartment, contemplating the advice his mother had given him the past weekend. Perhaps she was right. Maybe he did need to devote more time to his social life. He looked at the contacts in his cell phone, and quickly made a selection before he could convince himself otherwise.

"Hello, Kathy? It's Jerry Parker. How are you doing?"

"Jerry! What a nice surprise! To what do I owe this pleasure?"

"Well, I was thinking about driving up to Michigan City to visit my mom this weekend, and I just wanted to see if you'd be interested in going out to dinner or a movie on Saturday night?"

Kathy Cohen responded by mimicking her best southern accent—it sounded more like southern *Indiana.*

"Why, Jerry Parker! I do declare! Are you askin' me out on a date?"

Jerry realized that this was not as uncomfortable as he'd originally worried.

"Well...yeah. After all, you fell down on your job this summer...and, of course, I'm making the big bucks down here in Indy. I thought it was the least I could do. You know, help out those less fortunate than me."

Jerry hoped Kathy wouldn't mind his poking fun about her job.

"Well, I think that's very sweet. Are you sure your mom's not going to mind you going out with a white girl?"

"Well, you always have such a nice tan in the summer... I'm hoping my mama won't be able to tell what you are," Jerry said with a laugh.

"Well, as you've already pointed out, since I'm out of work, I guess I'll have plenty of extra time to work on my tan before the weekend."

"Good. It's a date then."

"Hey, Jerry?"

"Yeah?"

"Thanks."

"No problem, Kathy. I'm really looking forward to it."

Jerry had a flood of emotions spinning through his mind as he hung up the phone. He hadn't felt this excited—and this nervous—about a date since high school. He had never gone out with a white girl before. *Would it be different? Why should it be different? We've been friends for five years now. This is nothing more than two friends going out together.* He tried to convince himself that the social barriers to inter-racial dating were history. This would be no different than any other date.

Jerry paced back and forth across his apartment floor and then quickly punched in another contact on his cell phone.

"Hello, Tom?"

"Jerry! What's up, my man?"

"You won't believe what I just did! I think I just asked Kathy Cohen out on a date this weekend."

"Okay...so?"

"Well... I wanted to know whether you and Peter were cool with that."

"Dude, what do you care what I think? Of course I'm cool with it. I'll tell you what... Maybe five years ago I would have kicked your ass. But those days are gone. You're my friend. I know you. I trust you...and I'm happy for you."

"Do you think Peter will feel the same way?"

"Of course he will. In fact, he just called to tell me that he's at the library. Do you believe that? We have our own apartment here in Chicago, and Peter's at the library. I'm telling you...the guy has been a basket case lately."

"Yeah. It sounds like he's been working with some interesting characters up there. I tried to get them to buy this CBO investment we're working on, but it sounds like they shot him down...hard. By the way, speaking of buying things, are you guys selling your Rivermass pills yet?"

"Awww...Jerry wants to look like a stud for his big date, does he?"

"It's not that. It's just that if you honestly think you could kick my ass—and if you've been taking these pills—the pills must be distorting your reality."

"Hey. You know that I was just kidding, don't you?"

"Yeah, I know. So—have you taken any of these pills?"

"Not yet...but I know Doctor Cregar has."

"These things are safe, aren't they?"

"Well, Cregar certainly thinks so. He's eager to start selling them. I've got some samples I can give you. I'll stop by your house with them this weekend. Hey—maybe I can chaperone you and Kathy on your date?"

"Yeah, right. I'll see you some time this weekend. By the way...tell Peter that our Chief Investment Officer down here just announced he's leaving. I'm not sure if they're going to replace the position in-house or not. But if he knows of anyone in Chicago who might be interested in the job, I can tell him who to contact."

"Fine. I'll pass the word on to Peter, and I'll see you this weekend. I'll talk to you later, Jerry."

A strong breeze from an open window caused the apartment curtains to flail wildly. Tom hung up the phone and looked outside to survey the city. The smell of rain was in the air.

The first rumble of thunder greeted Peter as he prepared to leave the library. The wind was now violently blowing the trash through the streets. Peter quickened his pace to get to his apartment before the onslaught of the impending storm. It was too late. The skies opened and unleashed a downpour on Peter, causing him to sprint toward safety. *Geez, I can't get a break today*, he thought to himself. After reaching his apartment complex and shaking himself dry, Peter opened the door to his apartment.

"Now, don't tell me that you were actually at the library!" Tom exclaimed. "Or is that just some kind of euphemism for the bars? Heck, I don't even know where the library is located in this city. Please, Peter, tell me you were at a bar."

"No can do. But I *can* tell you the location of the library, and it's NOT located close enough to our apartment. I got soaked on the way home."

Peter walked to his bedroom to grab a towel, and put on a dry set of clothes. Returning in a dry T-shirt and shorts, Peter headed straight to the refrigerator for a beer. Finally, he was ready to speak.

"Today was a brutal day at work. I had to go somewhere quiet to unwind. I forgot how peaceful the library can be. Enough said." He paused. "So what's on your schedule tonight?"

"I don't have anything planned. I'd be happy to chill with you. We can have a couple of beers and watch the Cubs game. They're in San Francisco tonight. The game doesn't start until 9:30, but that's all right. It'll be a good way to get your mind off your problems. After all, the Cubs have a lot more problems than we ever will."

It was at times like this that Peter needed a friend like Tom.

"You know, beer and baseball actually sound like the perfect combination tonight."

✲ ✲ ✲

It was 11:23 p.m., the Cubs were down by six runs, and Tom and Peter had each downed four beers. Tom started flicking through the television channels to find something more uplifting. His eyes were drawn to a curvaceous young woman reaching out to him from the television screen. Scrolling along the bottom of the screen were the words "SIX MINUTES LEFT TO ORDER YOUR FREE TWO-WEEK SUPPLY OF RIVERMASS!"

A middle-aged male and young female, both with ripped muscles and tight-fitting gym clothing, were preaching the benefits of Rivermass as they took turns showcasing their beautiful bodies.

"*Today, there's now a safe, all-natural, bio-active weight loss compound, so powerful, so effective, so relentless in its awesome attack on bulging, fatty deposits that it has virtually eliminated the need to diet.*"

"*But that's not all, Debbie! Not only did I lose my hard-to-fight love handles, but I also added two inches of muscle to my chest and arms.*" The older man began to flex like a bodybuilder. His younger counterpart beamed approvingly.

"*I was just going to comment on your wonderful physique, Don. And the women out there should know that Rivermass has worked wonders for my buns and thigh areas. Perhaps the best news is that Rivermass is an 'all-natural product' designed to attract and absorb excess calories and convert them to natural muscle. It will literally sculpt your body into shape. In fact, the more you eat, the more muscle you can add.*"

"*That's right, Debbie! And it's made right here in the good old U.S. of A. So be sure to call right now and get your free two-week supply of Rivermass. If you don't agree that this is the best body sculpting pill you've ever experienced, we promise to give you your money back. No questions asked!*"

"*We've spent the last 20 minutes talking about the external physical benefits of Rivermass, Don. But let's not forget the tremendous internal health benefits. The American Obesity Association recently released a report stating that 64.5% of the American adult population is now overweight. Of a total 127 million overweight folks, 60 million are obese and 9 million are severely obese. In fact, the AOA says that obesity is now the second leading cause of unnecessary deaths in the U.S., accounting for $100 billion in additional health care costs.*"

"*That's right, Debbie! Obesity can increase a person's risk for developing many illnesses, including high blood pressure, type 2 diabetes, heart disease, stroke, gallbladder disease, and breast cancer.*"

Like I said before, my previous lifestyle had put me on the fast-track for many of these complications. However, since I started using Rivermass, I have more energy and feel better than ever."

"I would have no problem dating a man your age, the way you look now, Don. So guys out there, give your body a second chance!"

"And ladies, just take a look at Debbie. The results are indisputable! Order Rivermass now!"

Peter and Tom both stared at the screen until Peter finally asked, "Isn't Rivermass the pill that you're developing?"

"Yeah. That's got to be it! I haven't spoken with Doctor Cregar in a while. He assigned me to work with someone else marketing a different Care4 product for the rest of the summer. I wonder why he didn't tell me that they were marketing Rivermass?"

"Did you tell him you wanted to stay involved?"

"I thought I made it clear. I've got to talk to him. Look at that babe on TV! This is going to make me rich!"

The infomercial was over and Tom once again began flipping through the channels until they came upon the Headline News. "Another strong aftershock shook the New Madrid area this afternoon. This is the fourth strong aftershock the area has experienced since the original quake almost two months ago."

Despite Tom's good fortune with the Rivermass pills, Peter was reminded that the Sandman was not done with his work. Peter had to figure out the Sandman's plan. He could not let down his guard.

CHAPTER TWENTY SEVEN

Two weeks had passed since the first airing of the infomercial for Rivermass. Two weeks remained before school resumed for each of the young friends from Michigan City. Tom had sent four email messages to Doctor Cregar, without any reply. Doctor Cregar's secretary explained he was on vacation. Tom was eager to know how the Rivermass sales were progressing.

Since Jerry Parker's summer internship at Hoosier Insurance was nearing an end, two of the investment team members allowed him to accompany them, and two New York investment bankers, on a sales pitch for their newly structured CBO. The five men would meet with a large money manager in Evansville, Indiana—a city located in the southwestern tip of Indiana, along the banks of the Ohio River. Jerry was told that Heritage Advisors managed approximately $2 billion in fixed income assets. Due to its southwestern location,

Evansville was one of the Indiana cities most affected by the New Madrid quake.

After their presentation, Jerry listened to the two investment bankers from McHugh, McCullen & Magnanimous, as they exited the late 19th century Commerce Building overlooking the Ohio River. The two bankers looked like the comedy duo of Laurel and Hardy. The one resembling Stan Laurel did most of the talking during the presentation. He was still in his fast-talking mode as they left the building.

"Listen, I think you guys did a fantastic job explaining your expertise in front of those folks. Your investment performance speaks for itself. Assuming we can get them on board to take down a couple million of the equity tranche, the deal is done. We have all the investors in place and we'll be able to launch the deal—and hopefully price it—next week. What do you say we get something to eat? Is there anywhere in this town where we can treat you guys to a good steak dinner?"

"Absolutely! No fast food joint for me. We earned a nice, big steak after this," Hardy confirmed.

Suddenly the ground began to rumble. The five-story building they had just left started swaying as if being shaken from its foundation. Hardy stumbled and fell to the ground in panic. Jerry knew they had to flee the area quickly.

"Hurry! We've got to get away from this building!" Jerry yelled, pulling Hardy up from the ground, before quickly ushering the rest of the group away from the unstable structure. They rushed for the doorway of a more recently constructed building.

Within 30 seconds, glass from the buildings that lined the street began to break and cascade down. Jerry was now physically shielding the other members of his group from the downpour of debris. Out of the corner of his eye, Jerry spotted two young children and their mother, running out of a nearby department store. The brick façade on top of the store was beginning to crumble. Like a flash, Jerry sprang to his feet and hurdled over a car to grab the young family and pull them to safety.

Suddenly they heard a loud crash. Looking back, they saw that the brick wall from the Commerce Building had crumbled to the ground. Smoke and dust billowed upward, casting a dark cloud across the afternoon sky. Seconds later, the earth's motion came to a halt. There was an initial eerie silence followed by muffled screams for help from underneath the debris.

Once again, Jerry reacted selflessly. Without a word, he ran toward an open stairway in the building and began calling for anyone who needed aid. Jerry led a team of reserves for two hours, casting aside bricks and debris in an attempt to uncover any buried victims. Once his associates from Hoosier Insurance had recovered from their initial shock, they assisted Jerry in the rescue efforts. The two investment bankers were on their phones, letting their families in New York know what had happened.

It was on this warm August afternoon that Jerry Parker was elevated to the status of hero. The severe aftershock had claimed the lives of two people in the collapsed building. Jerry was credited with saving twelve others. The local news media spread the story of Jerry's heroics across the state of Indiana. It was not until 5:30 in the evening, when Jerry had finished his last media interview, that the five men departed Evansville. They sat in silence, listening to the radio, as they drove the three-hour stretch back to Indianapolis. The only evidence of normalcy was the five-foot high corn stalks, reaching for the sky along the newly constructed interstate 69.

It was just past 10 p.m. when the car pulled up in front of the hotel where the two investment bankers were spending the night. Jerry was half asleep when Hardy firmly gripped his shoulder to get his attention.

"Jerry, you were a hero out there today. You were super-human. It was a real pleasure to get to know you. If the strength and quickness that you showed today is any indication of what you can do on the football field, I look for great things from IU football this year. I hope I get to talk to you again before you go back to school."

The next day for Jerry was as surreal as the previous day. His colleagues at work went out of their way to greet him. The Indianapolis media were hounding him for interviews. The executives at Hoosier Insurance were trying to determine an appropriate award they could present to him. But Jerry had grown tired of the attention and was looking forward to spending the night alone in his apartment. Upon returning to his apartment, he immediately took the land line phone off the hook, and turned off his cell phone. He didn't want to be disturbed. Mistakenly thinking that the attention would subside, he placed the phone back online around 9 p.m., and it rang immediately. Glancing down at the caller ID, he smiled as he answered the phone.

"Hi, Momma. How are you doing?"

"How am I doing?! I've been trying to call you since 6 p.m. Where have you been? Is my boy out saving more lives?" The pride in her voice was apparent.

"Oh noooo...I guess that you've heard, huh?" Jerry was starting to become genuinely embarrassed by all the attention.

"Jerry, *everybody* has heard. They had a big story about your heroics in the Michigan City News-Dispatch this evening. I even had reporters calling to interview me. You must have put on some kind of show down there."

"It was weird, Mom. The adrenaline in my veins just took control of my body. I actually leaped over the hood of a car. Do you believe that?" Jerry's voice then began to taper off a bit. In his mind he visualized the state championship football game during his senior year in high school. He winced as he visualized his whole body, flipping end over end, in an attempt to block a potentially winning kick. He remembered waking up in a hospital bed, his home for the next two weeks. He recalled the doctors telling him how close he had come to breaking his neck. He tried to shake the image from his thoughts.

"Well, I'm just glad you're okay. I'm really proud of you."

"You know, Mom...I think I had a reason to be there. I think I've finally gotten over my football injury. In some weird way, I think this was my destiny."

"What football injury? Did you hurt yourself again?"

"No, I'm talking about my high school injury."

"Jerry! That happened years ago. You've been playing football at IU the past couple of years. You've earned yourself a scholarship. I thought you got over that injury a long time ago."

"I don't think so, Mom. I've been playing the game at IU, but I haven't been playing the way I used to play. I've been holding back. I've been playing like an Indy race car on rocky terrain. I've been too apprehensive to go all out."

"Well, if you felt like a slow race car, maybe this was the pit stop you needed, Jerry."

"I think so. But enough about me—how are you doing, Momma?"

"I'm doing fine. I sometimes entertain the idea of retiring from my job at the bank when you get out of school, but I don't know what I'd do with myself. I'm in my mid-fifties. I'm only half way through my life cycle."

"That's right, Momma. You haven't even begun to ripen."

"I love you, honey. You take care of yourself."

"Love you too, Momma."

Jerry hung up the phone and thought about his mother sitting alone in her house. He thought about his deceased brother, shot down on the tough city streets of Gary. His mother had carried her burden well over the past 50 years. He wished there was more he could do for her. Jerry stared at the floor, wondering how things might have been different if his brother were still alive. He then walked over to the kitchen and reached for a small container of pills. He poured two pills into the palm of his hand, swallowed them, and washed them down with a glass of water. He placed the container back on the kitchen counter. The words Rivermass were scrawled, in pen, on a piece of adhesive tape attached to the container. Jerry wondered whether the pills could really be producing results this quickly. He then turned off the lights and retired for the evening.

CHAPTER TWENTY EIGHT

"Peter, wake up!"

"Tom, it's Saturday. Why are you up so early?"

"Let's drive down to Cape Girardeau."

"What! Are you kidding? That's an eight hour drive on a good day. They're still having aftershocks down there. Why do you want to do that?"

"I've got to see if Doctor Cregar is down there. Nobody in the office seems to know where he is. He's got to be down at the Rivermass plant."

"Can't you try calling him?"

"I tried that. I called information and asked for the number of a Rivermass plant in Missouri. There's no listing. I don't even know what the company is called. I can't get any information on it. Come on...please...do this as a friend."

"What time is it?"

"It's six in the morning. If we leave now, we can get there in plenty of time. We can find out what they're doing, and then get back here by Sunday evening."

"Fine. But you're driving the first few hours. I need a couple more hours of sleep."

Peter closed his eyes, trying to get some additional sleep, as the two friends drove south down highway 55. His mind was preoccupied by the knowledge that their presentation to the World Hunger Foundation account was scheduled for this Tuesday. Although he was not going along on the presentation, he knew that Sarah would be accompanying Doug Keyster, representing Lakeshore Fund Management. He had mixed emotions concerning the outcome. Gazing out the window, he pitied the cows on the Illinois farmland, seemingly oblivious to their ultimate fate in life. He was consumed with guilt about the information he had passed on to Tony regarding Sarah's investment team. He had provided Tony with Lakeshore's historic performance record and the typical composition of their equity portfolios. He had even told Tony personal information about Sarah Banks and Doug Keyster.

It was 10 a.m. when Peter reached for his cell phone to call Sarah.

"Hello, Sarah. How are you doing this morning?"

"Peter! What's up?"

"I don't know...I thought that I should talk to you. Are you ready for your big presentation to the World Hunger Foundation this week?"

"Yeah, we're pumped. It'd be a great account for us to get. I know you told me that American Dinero is also competing for some of the money. Hopefully we both can get a portion. Are you going on the presentation?"

"No. It's just our head trader, the portfolio manager, and our head analyst."

"Wow! I wish we had that many people. That's one of the things that make it difficult for us to compete. You guys have such a deep staff."

"Sarah. I...I just want you to know that the people who are presenting from American Dinero have a lot of market intelligence on Lakeshore Funds. They know how you structure your portfolios, and they might try to discredit your style during their presentation."

"What are you talking about, Peter? How would they know how we structure our portfolios?"

Peter was dreading that question.

"I told them the way you do things," he answered sheepishly.

"Peter! You *what?* Why would you do that! Do you hate Doug Keyster that much? You're not hurting Doug. You're hurting my dad's bank!"

"Sarah, I'm sorry. They made me give information. That's why I'm calling. I want to level the playing field. I'll give you whatever information you want, other than fees. I told my guys I didn't know what fees you would charge. However, since they know your style, I'll tell you our style. That way it's fair and, hopefully, the best presentation will win."

"Peter, I can't believe you would do this. What's gotten into you? This is crazy."

"It *is* crazy, Sarah. But this is how the game is played."

Peter spent the next ten minutes going into detail on the history of American Dinero, its investment philosophy, and how it structured its portfolios. He even provided Sarah with personal information on Dave Koslow, Terri Tanaka, and Tony Salami.

"Oh, by the way, you'll never guess where we are. Tom and I are just outside St. Louis, on our way to Cape Girardeau."

"Why in the world are you guys going down there? Isn't that close to the earthquake zone?"

"We're on a mission to find Tom's boss down there."

"Well, you guys be careful. And…listen, Peter…I don't know if I'm going to use this information or not. It sounds like the people you work with are pretty intense. I feel uncomfortable competing with you. Like I said before, I hope we both get some money."

"Me too, Sarah. But I'm telling you, these guys will be playing for it all. One of Tony's commandments is 'Thou shall not share with others,' and believe me, he doesn't intend to share."

"Tony sounds like an ass."

"He is. I love you, Sarah."

"I love you too. Have a safe trip."

Tom waited a moment before saying anything. Without taking his eyes off the road, he remarked, "That almost sounded like a confession."

"Maybe it was."

"You know, the last time I drove down here, it was right after the earthquake hit. The place was still under lots of construction. And of the few people that were around, there was this guy who was holding a sign that read, 'The end is near.' He came right up on me. It kind of creeped me out."

Peter was silent. Tom wasn't even sure his friend was listening until Peter muttered, "Who knows? Maybe the end is near."

"You've got to snap out of it, Peter. You're really getting to be a downer these days."

Peter turned up the radio as the two drove past the Gateway Arch in St. Louis.

That evening, Sarah sat in her bedroom, thinking about all the changes her friends had experienced over the past four years. She realized that she hadn't talked to Kathy Cohen in a while, so she reached for the phone to give her a call.

"What's up, Kathy? Have you got a minute to talk?"

"Sure. How are you? It's been a while. What's up?"

"Nothing. I just thought I'd give you a call. Have you heard from Jerry recently? He's certainly getting a lot of press from his heroics in Evansville. I've been meaning to give him a call."

"Yeah, I tried to call him the other night. His phone was busy all night. He must be a pretty popular guy these days."

Sarah chuckled. "And to think we knew him way back when....before he was famous!" After a brief pause she continued: "So...how was your date the other week? Are you guys becoming an item?"

"I don't know. Jerry's a hard guy to read. He keeps things to himself. It drives me crazy! I think he's worried about some people still not accepting a black guy going out with a white girl. He's got a lot of pride."

"Kathy, pride screws up some of the best intentions. It's usually just a way of masking our insecurities. You've got to remember, Jerry's been through a lot with his dad in jail and his brother's death. You've just got to give him some time. What about your mom? Does she have any concerns about you going out with someone who's not Jewish?"

"I don't know. She hasn't said anything. Then again, I don't think she even has a clue we're seeing each other. Heck!

I don't even know if we *are* seeing each other. I think it's still more of a friendship than anything else. This was the first time we ever went out alone."

"Soo…did he kiss you?"

There was silence on the other side of the phone line.

"Kathy! Did he kiss you?!"

"Yeah…it was nice. It wasn't like one of those awkward kisses when friends kiss just to see if it feels right. There was actually some good chemistry going on between us." Kathy laughed. The two girls continued talking for an hour, discussing race, religion, and their deepest feelings. The conversation reaffirmed their belief that their friendship had no boundaries.

✧ ✧ ✧

Within a few hours, Peter and Tom were just outside Cape Girardeau. Tom was scanning the directions he had used to guide him on his first trip.

"Look for Nash Road, Peter; we should be close to the Rivermass lab. If I remember right, it's near a local airport around here."

"Just point me in the right direction. However, I've got to tell you, Tom, this area doesn't seem like a hub of activity."

The two friends drove down a dusty road, past the regional airport. Tom was sure that he recognized the old industrial complex. Nonetheless, Peter was right. There was no sign of life in the immediate area. It was as if the earth had swallowed the area and passed it out through its digestive tract. It looked like a wasteland. Tom was beginning to worry that his hope to find Dr. Cregar was in vain. Still, there was one last place to look.

"See that small house over there, Peter? It looks familiar. I'm pretty sure that's where I stayed the last time I was down here."

Tom looked with dismay as the car slowly approached the house. The once modest, although well-kept home, looked in complete disarray. Two of the outside windows were broken and trash bags lay outside the home, strewing food for scavengers. The place looked completely abandoned.

Peter stopped the car, allowing the boys to walk cautiously toward the house. Grabbing the doorknob, Tom heard a ghastly screech from the other side of the house. A stray cat jumped out, its back hunched like an archway, and sprinted toward the car. Peter hurried over to see what had frightened the cat. A large stray dog was picking over the scraps of trash that had been left outside. He had obviously not taken kindly to the cat trespassing on his bounty.

"This looks like one mean dog," Peter called back to Tom. "Hurry and see if anyone's in the house."

With a half-turn of the doorknob, Tom and Peter entered the house. Newspapers, magazines, grocery bags, and writing papers lay strewn across the floor. Some piles were three-feet high, making their footing precarious. Tom and Peter carefully made their way to the kitchen, only to discover empty cans, dirty dishes, and discarded food containers lying carelessly about the kitchen table, counters, and floor. Two stray cats prowled the floor, looking for additional food.

Peter finally broke the silence. "Geez, Tom, did you forget to clean the place after you left here last time?"

"This isn't funny, Peter. I mean...Dr. Cregar might be a little eccentric, but I don't think he would ever live like this. I think something must have happened to him."

"What the hell are you kids doing in my house!"

Peter and Tom turned around quickly to see Dr. Cregar brandishing a two-foot long club in his right hand.

Slamming the club on the kitchen table, Cregar swept away a glass, one-quarter filled with spoiled milk, onto the floor. His appearance lacked any resemblance to the image Tom last remembered. His muscular frame now bore stained and shabby clothing. His eyes had a distant look, half-hidden by his long, bedraggled hair and scraggly beard.

"Doctor Cregar! It's me—Tom Nelson! Are you okay? We were worried about you."

"Worried about me? Like hell you were! No one gives a damn about me."

"That's not true. The people at Care4 don't know what happened to you. Are you okay?"

Cregar seemed to recognize Tom, and lowered his voice to a more sane tone.

"The people at Care4 are worried about me, eh? And just which people are you speaking of, Tom? Come here and let me show you how much the people at Care4 are worried."

Tom and Peter followed Doctor Cregar through a littered pathway that led to a room stacked with boxes. In one corner of the room were a chair and desk, piled high with papers and discarded mail. In another corner of the room, a single bed was set against the wall. The bedding smelled as if it had not been washed in months.

Cregar sifted through the piles of letters and envelopes scattered over the desk and the floor below. He grew more agitated as he continued his search.

"Aha! Here it is! Here—let me show you how much the people at Care4 miss me."

Doctor Cregar waved a letter in Tom's direction, encouraging him to take it from his hand. Tom reached out to grab the letter from Cregar's visibly shaking hand.

"Go on—read it, Tom. See how much they care."

Tom unfolded the letter and began to read.

Re: Termination for Just Cause

Dear Doctor Cregar:

As a result of your decision to disregard our invitation for a meeting on Friday, August 19th, I regretfully confirm that your employment with Care4 Pharmaceuticals is terminated with immediate effect.

As stated, in an original letter dated August 12th, the reasons for terminating your employment with us are as follows:

- *Excessive unexcused absences over the past three months;*
- *Your continued work on activities outside the Company's domain, specifically the work you are currently marketing under the label of "Rivermass";*
- *Specific belligerent emails and dishonest assertions you have made against Senior Management at Care4 Pharmaceuticals.*

On three separate occasions we have sent warnings and asked you to immediately cease all work on Rivermass. You have decided to disregard our request...

Tom quietly read the remainder of the letter to himself.

"Doctor Cregar, this letter says you have the right to appeal this decision. They must know the stress you've been under since the loss of your family. Why don't you meet with them and discuss this? I can try to get my dad to help you."

"What makes you believe your dad would want to help me, Tom? What makes you think *anyone* would want to help me? Do you think that's the only letter I received? There's another letter here from the American Medical Association. The AMA voted this past week to seek stricter FDA oversight and regulation for Rivermass. They think Rivermass presents undue risks. Don't you get it, Tom? You can't beat the system. But it doesn't matter. We're not going to let it stop us. Doctor Lake and I are going full steam ahead with our plan."

Tom was feeling nervous regarding Cregar's irrational ramblings. He knew he had to ask the next question.

"What exactly *is* your plan?"

"To get rich, of course! To help people achieve the same results I've achieved. I've got to find Doctor Lake. He gave me this coin. He told me to trust in this coin. That's all we have to do, Tommy! It will get people to buy anything from me."

Like a wild man, Doctor Cregar reached deep into the pocket of his pants, withdrew a gold coin, and threw it across the room. Suddenly, Cregar's attention was diverted to a stack of boxes on the other side of the room.

"Look, Tom! Here's the fruit of my labor."

Cregar ripped open some of the boxes. Each box contained dozens of packaged bottles of Rivermass. Shaking the bottles, Cregar continued on his tirade.

"You don't think this stuff works?! Look at me! I'm five times stronger than I was a few months ago. I have the strength to rip the hearts out of the people who are writing me these letters. Do I look like I'm suffering from any ill-effects?"

"Okay, Doctor Cregar. I'm on your side! I believe you." Tom didn't want to further agitate his one-time mentor. "We'll prove the safety of Rivermass. We'll prove everyone wrong. I already gave some of the pills to my dad. He knows people at Care4 who can check it out."

"What! You stupid fool! Don't you get it? The people at Care4 don't want something outside their company to be successful. Didn't you read that letter? They don't want any part of me. Hell, you're probably the reason they came after me."

Suddenly Doctor Cregar lunged at Tom with the eyes of a madman. Peter immediately jumped on top of Doctor Cregar, and all three bodies wrestled to the ground.

"Get off of him! It's not his fault," Peter yelled, grabbing at Cregar's hands to restrain him. Cregar did not struggle any further. He lay passively for a few seconds and then slowly rose to his feet. His intense anger gave way to feelings of despair. He turned his back on the two intruders and went over to the chair by his desk to sit down. Propping his elbows on his desk, he placed his hands on each side of his head and pulled at his shoulder-length hair as if trying to exorcise the demons in his head.

"Not his fault? Whose fault is it? Whose fault is it that my family is lost? Whose fault is it that I no longer have a job? I've lost the respect of my peers..."

Tom stared at Doctor Cregar in silence, as Peter walked around the room. Peter reached down and grabbed something and then walked back to Tom's side.

"I think we ought to get out of here, Tom."

Tom looked at Peter and then called to Doctor Cregar.

"I'm sorry if I made things worse. I only wanted to help."

PETER JANGLE AND THE NEW MADRID DISCOVERY

"I'm sure you did. Just listen to your friend and please leave me. If you want to help me, please leave me now, okay?"

Tom and Peter walked in silence back to the car. They were two miles down the road before Peter finally spoke.

"We need to find Doctor Lake. We need to stop him."

"What are you talking about, Peter?"

"I think he's dangerous."

"Dangerous?! Perhaps he's a bit mysterious, and maybe a little unethical. But why do you think he's dangerous?"

Peter slowly opened his hand, revealing the object he had picked up from Doctor Cregar's bedroom floor. Resting in Peter's palm was a gold, hexagon-shaped coin. On one side of the coin was a pyramid, with an eye in the middle. On the other side were the words, "In This I Trust." Peter recognized it as the calling card of the Sandman.

"Trust me on this one, Tom. We've got to find Doctor Lake."

CHAPTER TWENTY NINE

It was the last week in August. Peter tossed in his bed, dressed in nothing but his underwear. The sweat from his body had soaked the bed sheets. Looking at his alarm clock, he saw it would soon be time to get up and prepare for another week of work. Peter felt limp as he rolled out of bed and walked over to the bathroom to relieve himself. After finishing his business he walked toward Tom's room and called out, "Tom, did you turn off the air conditioning? It feels like a furnace in here!"

"Yeah...good morning to you, too. I didn't touch the air. It's just hot."

Peter turned on the news and the weather report confirmed Tom's comments.

A short, stubby fellow, dressed in a tropical shirt and sunglasses, was doing his best to entertain the television audience.

"It's going to be a hot one this week, folks! Heat advisories are in effect for the entire Midwest. If you're planning on spending any time outdoors this week, remember to drink plenty of fluids."

Peter remembered the last time the weather had been so unseasonably hot. The Sandman seemed to thrive in the heat. Michigan City lost ten of its fellow citizens that year. One of them was Peter's friend. He then thought about all those who had lost their lives in the New Madrid earthquake. He knew he had to find Dr. Lake. He was sure that Dr. Lake would lead him to the Sandman.

Peter's obsessive thoughts about the Sandman haunted him all day at work. He felt alone, as Fran Solli, David Koslow, Terri Tanaka, and Tony Salami worked on finalizing their presentation for the World Hunger Foundation. The morning seemed to fly by, and there were only three hours remaining in the workday. He welcomed the distraction when Terri Tanaka walked into his cubicle to chat.

"What are you working on, Peter?"

"I'm just doing some work for Dave Koslow. He wanted me to do some research on a couple of companies. Why? Do you have something for me to do?"

"No. That's fine."

Peter eyed Terri as she lingered in his office. She was a beautiful and intelligent woman. A Harvard undergrad, she had subsequently received her MBA from the University of Chicago. He guessed she was probably 35 years old. He wondered why she had never married. *Probably too devoted to her work*, he thought. It seemed that something was troubling her. "Are you all right?" he asked.

"Sure."

"Are you guys all ready for your presentation tomorrow?"

"We're ready, but I don't think I'll be going with them. It'll just be Fran, David, and Tony."

"Why aren't you going?"

"Apparently Tony thinks we'll overwhelm them if we take too many people."

"Didn't you want to go?"

Terri had never really considered the thought. She hesitated before answering affirmatively.

"Sure I did. I think I could explain our process as well as any of them."

Peter looked into Terri's eyes. He could tell she was upset, but he didn't know how to react. He felt an urge to hug her, but he was worried reaching out to her would be considered inappropriate. After an awkward minute of silence, Terri finally asked, "Didn't you say that you knew someone at Hoosier Insurance in Indianapolis?"

Peter was surprised by the question. "Yeah, one of my good friends is working there this summer."

Terri hesitated, and then looked around and said in a hushed tone, "I got a call from a headhunter today. She said Hoosier Insurance was searching for a new CIO. Do you know anything about the job?"

"Yeah, my friend mentioned it, and I gave him your name. I hope you don't mind."

"No. I appreciate it. I just don't know if I want to leave Chicago."

"Indianapolis is a nice city. Have you ever been there?"

"I've driven through. I've never spent much time there. I guess I've always considered myself more of a big city girl."

Peter smiled. Growing up in Michigan City, he had always thought it necessary to leave Indiana to establish a successful career. He thought about the large manufacturing plants in Indiana that had shut down in favor of cheap labor overseas. If his home state was going to lose its manufacturing workforce, he hoped it could replace them with intellectual resources. He figured that Terri was the type of individual Indianapolis needed. "Give Indianapolis a chance," he urged. "I'm sure you'll like it."

Terri smiled and placed her hand on Peter's arm. "Thanks, Peter. I'll think about it."

After Terri left, Peter picked up the phone to call Sarah. "Hello."

Peter looked around and whispered into the phone. "Hi, Sarah. It's Peter. Listen, when you give your presentation to the World Hunger Foundation tomorrow, be sure to take an analyst with you."

"Why?"

"Because the people here aren't going to take our analyst. I think it might work to your advantage if you can show the depth of your team."

"I think you guys have a deeper team than us." she replied.

"It's all about marketing, Sarah."

"I'll have to talk to Doug about it."

"Just think about it. I have to go. I love you."

Peter hung up the phone, reflecting on whether it was ethical to pass on his inside information to Sarah. Peter thought about his father, a man of unquestionable integrity. He idolized his father, and did not want to let him down. He recalled one of the many quotes his father had always told him.

"If you lose your wealth, you have lost nothing, But if you lose your character, you have lost everything."

Peter lived in constant fear that the Sandman was affecting his actions. His father had told him that life would be filled with difficult choices. He prayed he could live up to the same moral standards as his father. Deep in thought, he almost jumped out of his seat when the phone rang. It was Tom Nelson, speaking in a hushed and hurried tone.

"Hey, Peter. I just got off the phone with Doctor Cregar. He seems to have settled down a bit. He said he could take us to meet Doctor Lake this weekend."

CHAPTER THIRTY

Peter woke up early Tuesday to take a quick run. The morning heat weighed on him like an anchor. Each gasp of breath was a struggle, as he crossed Michigan Avenue toward the lakefront. Reaching the beach, he took off his shoes and let his feet sink in the sand. Closing his eyes, he thought back on his high school days in Michigan City. He remembered his football training routine of sprinting up and down Mount Baldy. Life was simpler back then—he could recognize his enemies.

Now I'm beginning a different type of training. I'm training for my spiritual life. My enemy isn't as easy to recognize. As he resumed his run, the sand seemed to swallow each of his steps. He pushed himself to run consecutive sprints, resting a minute between each dash. *I'm not battling to win a game, I'm battling for my soul.*

Looking up, Peter admired the Chicago skyline. The large structures before him resonated with power. He understood why Terri felt safe here. The city accepted all, and gave each race, religion, and gender equal opportunity. Peter prayed he wouldn't be swayed by the lure of power. He yearned for something more. Falling to his knees, he bowed his head and quietly recited, *"Lord, lead me not into temptation, but deliver me from evil."* Taking a deep breath, he grabbed his shoes and pulled them on to his feet. After tying his laces, he rose to his feet and plodded home, his body drenched with sweat.

✡ ✡ ✡

It was past 3 p.m. when Fran, Tony, and David returned from their meeting with the World Hunger Foundation. They exchanged few words. Peter could sense something was wrong, but he didn't want to say anything that would set Tony off. After ten minutes, Peter noticed David and Terri in a private conversation by the copy machine. Peter grabbed some work he had promised David and walked over toward them. He could overhear the conversation.

"We could have used you at the presentation."

"I'm sure you could have. But if I remember right, you and Tony thought that too many people would overwhelm them," Terri replied sarcastically.

"Don't blame that on me. That was Tony's decision. You know that."

"So how did it go?"

"It was going fine until they asked about our analyst team. They wondered why we didn't bring any analysts. We explained our process, and we thought we covered ourselves pretty well. Then they looked straight at Tony and told him that our competition brought along their analysts."

David smiled. "You should have heard Tony on the car ride back. He was livid."

"Should I go rub it in his face?"

"I wouldn't go near him right now."

Peter glanced over at the trading desk. Tony was castigating a broker over the phone line. Peter smiled and handed David his completed work.

"I finished the research you wanted on these companies."

"Thanks, Peter. Hey, when do you go back to school?"

"My last day of work will be next Thursday. We don't have to go back to school until the Wednesday after that, September 10th."

"We'll have to have a party next week before you go. I think you've done a really good job here this summer. So what are you going to do when you graduate? Do you want to come back to Chicago?"

"I don't know," Peter answered. "I guess I'll just go wherever God leads me."

Peter smiled, and then turned and walked back to his cubicle. He was proud of his answer.

That evening Peter called Sarah to ask about her presentation to the World Hunger Foundation.

"It went well," Sarah replied.

"Did you follow my tip to bring an analyst along?"

"Of course I did. Doug spent the whole day instructing her on what companies to highlight. She did a great job. Doug said it was the first time he ever took an analyst to a presentation. It was a great learning experience for her, and I think that she was one of the primary reasons we might get the business." Sarah paused briefly—but could no longer contain herself. "Oh...by the way...did I mention that 'the analyst' that Doug took on the trip was *me?*"

Peter smiled in admiration of Sarah.

Sarah suddenly realized that she had forgotten to ask Peter about his trip to Cape Girardeau.

"So how did your trip with Tom go last weekend?"

Peter hesitated, not knowing how much information he should divulge. "I'm not sure. His friend Doctor Cregar was acting pretty wild. He actually attacked Tom at one point."

"What do you mean, he attacked him?"

"I mean that he was really irrational. He was angry because he lost his job, and I think he's having problems with his business partner in this Rivermass deal. I don't know...he was just really depressed."

"Speaking of depressed people, have you talked with Jerry lately?"

"No. Is he still down in Indianapolis?"

"No. He finished work last week and went back to IU to start football practice. Kathy told me she's been talking with him periodically. She says he's been acting a bit weird lately."

"Believe me, Sarah, the first few weeks of football practice are intense. That might be what's affecting his behavior. I'm sure the coaches are pushing him. There's a lot of pressure to keep your job. In addition, I'm sure the incident in Evansville had an effect on him. One moment he's a hero, and the next moment his coaches are probably riding his ass. He'll be all right. I'll give him a call later to check on him."

Despite his reassurance, Sarah sensed that Peter was withholding something.

"Are you sure you're okay?"

Again, Peter hesitated. "Something happened this weekend that convinces me the Sandman is back. Do you remember the coin he gave me three years ago, when all of those bad things happened?"

"I'm not sure, Peter. I've tried my hardest to forget. What coin are you talking about?"

"Three years ago, the genie gave me a gold coin. On one side of the coin was a pyramid, with an eye in the middle. On the other side were the words, "In This I Trust." The genie told me to trust in the coin when I needed anything. I used that coin to get a bank loan for my father when he was out of work, and I used the coin to influence the Federal Reserve Board to lower interest rates. That's when all the trouble started three years ago. People started drowning in the lake and panicking because the inflation rate was skyrocketing out of control. That's when I almost lost you, Sarah. All of that was my fault. And it was all because of the genie and that damn coin."

Sarah gulped. Unlike others, she had seen the Sandman. She felt sure that Peter wasn't crazy. She knew he would always be tormented by that experience.

"I guess I've tried to forget all that," Sarah repeated. "But you threw that coin back into the lake, didn't you? And I thought the genie told you that the coin wasn't magical. Didn't he say that it just opened people up to suggestions? People have the power to resist."

"Yes, that's what the genie said. But why should I trust him? Anyway...you're right, I threw the coin in the lake. But when we went to visit Doctor Cregar this weekend, he had the same coin. The only way he could have gotten that coin is from the Sandman."

"So what are you going to do?"

"Tom told me that Doctor Cregar is going to take us to meet Doctor Lake this weekend." Peter hesitated and then said in a hushed voice, "I'm starting to think that Doctor Lake is the Sandman."

"I want to go with you, Peter."

"I don't know, Sarah. Who knows what this guy wants? It could be dangerous."

"Have you told Tom about your suspicions?"

"No. I haven't told anyone about the Sandman except you and my dad. You saw him. You know he exists. And I had to tell my dad. Funny thing is…my dad said that maybe the Sandman tried to influence him, but he won't tell me how. And the Sandman once mentioned that my father's love defeated him. They obviously have some connection they won't tell me about. The key is…somehow we need to show evidence of love to defeat the Sandman's evil."

"Listen, Peter, if love is one of the weaknesses of the Sandman, you and I are much stronger together. Maybe, if he sees our love for one another, it will be enough to defeat him."

Peter could not argue against Sarah's logic. As much as he wanted to protect Sarah, he felt comfort in knowing that she would be at his side. He continued to think of ways to defeat the genie.

"I also think he's vulnerable to water. I remember that he almost drowned the last time when I filled his bottle with water. If I could only find his bottle…maybe Doctor Lake has it."

"Then I guess we need to visit Doctor Lake," Sarah replied.

CHAPTER THIRTY ONE

Jerry Parker returned to his Bloomington apartment after a particularly brutal Wednesday afternoon football practice. His face was flush, and his body tired. Although he was doing well at practice, he found that he was getting increasingly agitated with his teammates and the coaches. After sitting down to relax, he was interrupted by the sound of the phone. He didn't want to answer, but the ringing would not stop. He answered on the seventh ring.

"Hello."

"Hi, Jerry. It's Kathy. It seems like I can never get in touch with you these days. What's up? You're not ignoring my phone messages, are you?"

"I'm sorry, Kathy. I just haven't had time."

"How's practice going?"

"The coaches are pretty impressed. They've said that I might be the starting tailback this fall."

"That's great! Congratulations! I mean…granted, we're talking about IU football, not Purdue. Still, you've got to feel pretty good about that."

"I don't know what I feel good about anymore."

Kathy could sense the sullenness in Jerry's voice. "What does that mean?"

"It means that nothing is that much fun anymore. I'm doing well…but I feel worthless."

"That's crazy, Jerry. You're a hero. Everyone's saying great things about you."

"Come on, Kathy! I'm so tired of hearing about what happened in Evansville. I'm not a hero! I did what anyone else would have done."

"But the fact is that no one else did anything, Jerry, until you led the way. You should be proud of what you did."

"Yeah, I know. And I should be proud that I got the starting tailback job. Everyone tells me all the things I should be proud about. So why do I feel like crap?"

"I don't know. Stress maybe? What do you say I come down to visit you this weekend and we just relax a bit?"

"Not this weekend, Kathy. I'm just not up for it. Maybe sometime later."

Kathy was starting to get the impression that Jerry didn't want to see her. She wondered if she had done anything to hurt him. Perhaps he was having second thoughts about dating a white Jewish girl. She was determined to confront him.

"Jerry, this isn't about us, is it? I mean, have I done anything to get you upset with me?"

"It's got nothing to do with you, Kathy. I've just got to figure it out on my own, okay?"

"All right. I just want you to know that I care for you. I'm here to help if you need me."

"I appreciate it. Thanks, Kathy. I'll talk to you later."

Jerry hung up the phone and walked over to the sink in the corner of his dorm room. He stared at his face in the mirror for a minute, and then he washed his hands vigorously with soap and water for the third time since he had returned to his room.

Kathy sat motionless, her hand still clinging to the phone. She wondered if she should change her behavior. *Did other people view her as too abrasive?* A knot was developing in her stomach. She remembered how her mother suggested she deal with hurt feelings. She went straight to the kitchen for a bowl of ice cream.

While Jerry and Kathy were attempting to alleviate their anxiety, Peter was in his Chicago apartment, watching the Cubs battle the New York Mets. Suddenly, he heard Tom call from the next room, "Peter, come here!" Knowing that a Cubs victory would be meaningless this late in the season, he got up and walked over to Tom's room.

"What's up?"

"I just got off the phone with my dad. Do you remember me telling you I was going to try to convince my dad to get doctors to recommend Rivermass?"

"Yeah, I remember you saying something about it. I didn't know that you actually had the conversation with him."

"Well, I did. And I just found out that my dad took the capsules to some of the chemists at Care4 for testing. Well, my dad just called me with the results of the tests they ran.

He warned me that there might be some potentially danger-ous side effects associated with the pills."

"What do you mean, dangerous?"

"According to my dad, the protein found in this capsule might cause severe depression in people. He was trying to explain to me something about a neurotransmitter in our bodies called serotonin. Supposedly, serotonin controls all kinds of functions in our body, including appetite, learning ability, muscle contractions, and our moods—scientists think serotonin is linked to severe mood swings and depression."

"You're losing me."

"I don't exactly understand it either. But supposedly most anti-depressant drugs, like Prozac, work by making more serotonin available to the brain cells. But in order for the serotonin to work, it needs to bind to some kind of receptors on the cell surface. My dad said that his chemists believe that Rivermass might inhibit this binding process. And if the chemists are right, long-time use of this product might cause some serious problems."

Peter stood in silence, trying to fathom what Tom was telling him.

"We've got to talk to Doctor Lake this weekend," Tom said. "We've got to warn him to stop selling this stuff before it hurts someone."

Peter was trying to figure out if this was all part of the Sandman's plan. His mind was a whirlwind; he wasn't sure what to do. The phone rang, interrupting his thoughts. Tom rushed to pick it up, thinking it was his dad with more information. It was Jerry Parker.

"Hey, Tom, I need some more of those Rivermass pills you gave me."

Tom had a sinking feeling in the pit of his stomach.

"Jerry, how many of those pills have you taken? You've got to stop taking them."

"What do you mean I've got to stop taking them? They work! I'm bench-pressing 310 pounds now, and I've cut my time in the 40-yard dash by five-tenths of a second. Dude, I'm going to be the starting tailback this year. This could be my ticket! I'm not going to stop taking the pills. Heck, I'm going to get the other guys on the team to start taking them. They're great!"

"They aren't great, Jerry. They're dangerous. My dad just told me they can really mess up your emotions."

"What are you talking about? I thought you said they were safe."

"I thought they were. But I might be wrong."

"What do you mean, 'might' be wrong? Are they safe or not?"

"I don't know. But I don't think you should take them any more until we can prove whether or not they are safe."

"Listen. I've seen the ads on television. They're not going to be selling something if it's dangerous."

"Jerry, these are non-prescription pills. That means they aren't regulated in the same way as prescription pills. These pills haven't been tested for safety. Since they aren't regulated, they don't have the same legal disclosure requirements that regulated drugs have. So you don't know exactly what you're taking, or what side effects to expect."

"Well, it doesn't sound to me like you know either. So... are you going to get me more or not?"

"Jerry, as a friend, I'm not going to give you any more pills until I find out more information."

"Fine. To hell with our friendship." Jerry slammed the receiver down and went to the sink to wash his hands.

CHAPTER THIRTY TWO

Peter kicked his legs out from underneath his bed sheets. He rolled over onto to his stomach and punched at his pillow in frustration—it was damp from perspiration. He couldn't sleep. He glanced at the alarm clock to see that it had just turned 3 a.m. Realizing that sleep was a battle he wouldn't win this evening, he rolled out of bed and headed for the kitchen.

Pouring himself a cup of coffee, Peter knew that sleep was not the only battle he faced. Doctor Cregar told Tom that Doctor Lake was renting a small cabin in Michiana Shores, a small town adjacent to Michigan City. Now it all made sense to Peter. *The Sandman has come back to battle me in my hometown.*

Peter had already called Sarah to tell her he was coming home tonight. They were planning on surprising Doctor Lake at his cabin on Saturday morning. Peter again looked at the clock. It was 3:15 a.m. He didn't need to be at work for hours and he knew that going back to sleep was futile. He wondered how he should approach Doctor Lake. *How will I be sure that Doctor Lake is the Sandman?* Peter felt in need of spiritual guidance. He knew of a Catholic church two blocks away. *A church is as good a spot as any for divine inspiration.*

The humid Chicago air seemed to weigh Peter down as he approached the church. The inscription "Saint Peter and Paul Catholic Church" was engraved on a large gold plate, embedded in the colossal mahogany doors that stood before him. Peter tugged on the iron handle, but the door would not budge. Looking for another possible entrance, Peter walked over toward the side of the church. He walked cautiously through the dark alley. The city was still sleeping. A faint light illuminated three steps that led to a more modest side door. A small plaque on the door read, "Adoration Chapel." The familiarity of the Adoration Chapel brought a smile to Peter's face as he opened the door and walked inside.

The chapel was a small, modest room, with a connecting door leading to the main church. Peter blessed himself by dipping his hand in the holy water, located just inside the door, and making the Sign of the Cross with his wet finger-tips. The room was much like the chapel in his hometown church. There were five rows of votive candles set against one of the walls. Most of the candles were lit, their flames flickering in the night air, as if dancing to a familiar beat. Peter knew that the lit candles represented special intentions or prayers of parishioners in need.

Immediately in front of Peter was a small altar covered by white linen. A large, ornate, gold-plated box, called a tabernacle, rested on the altar. In front of the tabernacle stood the monstrance. The monstrance looked like a gold trophy, standing on three raised legs. The stem of the monstrance led to a round glass container, made to look like a sun, with golden rays emanating from the center. Peter knew that the consecrated Eucharistic host was contained in the circular glass. Peter was in the presence of Christ.

An older man, probably in his sixties, was kneeling in the front pew with a rosary in his hands. Peter did not want to disturb the man's prayers. Without saying a word, Peter walked by the stranger and knelt down two pews behind him. Peter looked up at the crucifix hanging on the wall behind the altar. Strengthened in his faith, he prayed for all those who died in the earthquake, and he prayed for help in his battle with the Sandman.

After a few moments of silent prayer, another man entered the chapel. Once again, no words were exchanged. The man merely nodded his head toward Peter and the other man. He then dropped to his knees in prayer. After a few minutes, the older man got up and walked out the door. Peter figured it must have been the start of a new hour. The intent of the Adoration chapel was to worship Christ twenty-four hours a day. At the top of each hour, a new individual would enter the chapel to relieve the worshipper before him. Watching the old man quietly exit, Peter wondered what intention the man had prayed for. Peter thought of those who had died in Lake Michigan three years ago, and wondered if people were still praying for them. Peter got up and walked over to the five rows of flickering candles. One by one, he lit a candle for each of the victims who had drowned in Lake Michigan. He then returned to his kneeling position and prayed.

"Oh God, if this is my cross to bear, please give me the strength to make things right. Please protect my dad. Protect him from any influence of the Sandman. If it's your will for me to give up my life,

I do it willingly. But please protect my family and my friends. I also ask that you protect Sarah. If love can, indeed, defeat the Sandman, please fill Sarah's heart with as great a love for me, as I have for her. I ask all of this in Jesus' name. Amen."

After another ten minutes, Peter rose from his knees and walked out the door.

✵ ✵ ✵

Peter grew wearier as the day dragged on. Terri Tanaka was not at work that day, and the financial markets were relatively quiet. The markets had been volatile over the past couple of months, trying to determine what impact the New Madrid earthquake would have on the overall economy. Consumer spending over the past month had slowed considerably, as Midwest consumers were more occupied with surviving, rather than buying. Nonetheless, most investors knew that property disasters had historically been a source of strength for the financial markets. Companies would eventually profit from the demand for new homes, roads, and bridges. The new construction would lead to new jobs, which would lead to more consumer purchases.

However, the only moment of excitement on this quiet day was when Tony Salami brought some goldfish in from his lunch break and promptly fed them to the piranhas.

It was around three o'clock in the afternoon when Peter decided to call Tom.

"Hi, Tom. Did you hear anything new today from Doctor Cregar?"

"Yeah. He told me that he's going to go to Doctor Lake's cabin tonight. He said he'll make sure that Doctor Lake will be there when we come by tomorrow. He gave me the address of the cabin."

"What do you think they're going to discuss tonight?"

"I don't know."

"Do you trust Cregar?"

"I don't know. I guess we'll find out tomorrow."

"Yeah, okay. So, what time do you want to catch the train tonight?"

"Do you think you can get ready in time to catch the 5:15?"

"Yeah. It's quiet here. I should be able to leave early. I'll see you later."

Friday evening, before Peter went to bed, he went to talk with his father. Peter was noticeably apprehensive over what would happen the next day. He wanted to ask his dad whether or not he should take Sarah. In some way he was hoping his father would discourage any of them from going.

"So, Peter...do you believe that this Doctor Lake is the genie?"

"I don't know, Dad. That's what I need to find out."

"I think I should go with you."

"Dad, I don't want you to go. I have my cell phone, and I promise to call you if there's any trouble. Tom knows Doctor Cregar. I don't think they're going to try to hurt us."

"So why do you think it might be dangerous for Sarah to go?"

"I don't know. It probably won't be dangerous. I think he's still trying to teach me a lesson. Maybe he's trying to tempt me or test my faith. He seems to get a kick out of taunting me. I still remember what he said three years ago, when Sarah was drowning in the lake. I think that I could have killed him that day. But I didn't. I thought that if

I destroyed him, I would lose Sarah. I think he realizes that I saved his life. Maybe he feels like he owes me something. Maybe he'll never kill me and I'll never kill him. We'll just coexist. He'll continue trying to influence people to make bad choices. And he's going to defy me to stop him. That's what he's all about. He's not a killer. He's worse. He's someone who promises false dreams and ultimately causes people to lose all hope. He represents despair. I guess my job is to promote hope."

David Jangle smiled. "Unfortunately, Peter, the world is full of people who are similar to the genie you just described." Struggling to come up with good advice to give his son, David asked, "Do you remember that story I told you years ago, about the difference between moths and butterflies?"

Peter smiled and laughed. "You said that butterflies have vision. Moths, on the other hand, come out at night and get fried by the bug zappers."

David sheepishly bit his lip, hoping his story had left a more lasting impression than bug zappers.

"The point is that everyone needs a vision...some kind of purpose in life. I'm extremely proud of you, Peter. You've learned a lesson that too many people never learn. You've learned that sometimes you must sacrifice your own wants and needs for the greater good of mankind. That's your mission. It's not going to be easy. We all have demons we need to conquer along the way. But God has a plan for you. So go ahead and set out on your journey, but don't jump to conclusions. Doctor Lake might just be a misguided man. Don't be disappointed if nothing gets resolved tomorrow. Don't let the bug zapper get you."

Peter smiled.

After a pause, David asked, "You do love Sarah, don't you?"

"I think so, Dad. I keep messing up our relationship. But I do love her."

"As I told you before, Peter. I think that love will ultimately defeat this genie. That's why you should take Sarah. And that's also why I'd be happy to go with you. Our love is stronger than any influence this genie could have. The important thing is that you don't try to battle him alone."

Peter looked at his father in admiration and hastened to give him a hug. Peter thought back to the remarkable peace he had felt in the Adoration Chapel earlier that morning. He now felt the same peace with his earthly father.

CHAPTER THIRTY THREE

Peter heard his mother call from the bottom of the stairs. "Peter, the phone is for you." He struggled to reorient himself to his surroundings. A quick glance at his alarm clock showed it was almost 11 a.m. He did not usually sleep in so late. Reacting as if he had overslept for a final exam, Peter sprang from his bed to get dressed. Again, his mother called, "Peter, are you awake?"

"Yeah, Mom. Just a minute." Peter slipped on a pair of pants and bounded down the stairs to get the phone. It was Tom Nelson.

"Peter, I just tried to get in touch with Doctor Cregar and no one answered the phone. What time were you thinking about going over there?"

Tom's words struck Peter like a body blow. He had just awakened from such a peaceful sleep. It was as if Cregar, Lake, and the Sandman were all just a bad dream. *Why do*

I have to deal with this today? Pausing, and realizing something had to be done, Peter answered Tom.

"I'm sorry. I just woke up. I told Sarah that we'd call her before going over there. Let me take a shower and then I'll give Sarah a call and come by your house around one o'clock. How's that sound?"

"That's fine with me. But what if Doctor Cregar still doesn't answer? What if no one's there?"

"I don't care. We have to find out what they're doing in Michigan City. I'll see you at one."

Peter hung up the phone, and then heard a thunderous boom that shook the house. He raced to the window and looked outside to see a dark, ominous sky. Lightning pierced the darkness, followed by the rolling sound of thunder. *I guess Sandman is expecting us,* Peter thought to himself as he went upstairs to take his shower.

By the time Peter left his house, a torrential downpour of horizontal rain, pushed by forceful wind gusts, seemed destined to impede the boys' mission. Peter kept hoping that the water would work to his advantage in his battle with the Sandman. Peter picked up Sarah and then proceeded to Tom's house. Peter leaned on the car horn to get Tom's attention. He didn't want to have to go in and discuss the day's agenda with Tom's parents. Tom ran out, shielding himself from the rain, and was surprised to see Sarah in the car. He knew Peter was planning on calling Sarah, but didn't know he was planning on inviting her to come along. After the last confrontation with Cregar, he thought this mission would be best handled by the men.

Peter tried to think up a good explanation for Sarah's presence. "Sarah told me that she has some family commitments tomorrow, and this was the only chance that I would get to see her. Chances are that Cregar and Lake won't even be there. I told Sarah you wouldn't mind if she came along." Peter winced at his own lame attempt to keep Tom from asking additional questions.

Tom stared at Peter. He suspected Peter was hiding something. Nonetheless, he didn't think it was worth pursuing.

"Hi, Tom." Sarah smiled nervously. She didn't know how much information Peter had shared with Tom. She thought it best that she feigned ignorance regarding their destination. She tried to change the subject.

"I was talking with Kathy this morning. She's pretty worried about Jerry."

This was not a good conversation for Sarah to initiate. Tom was becoming increasingly paranoid over his role with the Rivermass pills.

"Did Peter tell you about the Rivermass pills?"

The response caught Sarah completely off guard.

"What pills are you talking about?" Sarah cast a sharp look of suspicion in Peter's direction.

Tom was eager to share his knowledge with Sarah. "This guy that we're going to visit is a chemist. He manufactured some pills that are supposed to help you lose weight and increase your strength. The problem is that we think they might have some dangerous side effects. Didn't Peter tell you anything about this?"

Peter cringed, bracing for Sarah's verbal onslaught.

"Peter, you didn't tell me about any pills."

"I'm sorry. I was going to. I've had a lot on my mind. The point of Tom's story is that Jerry's been taking some of the pills, and he called Tom the other night, asking for more. We're worried that they might be affecting his behavior."

"When are you going to learn to tell me this stuff?" Sarah insisted. "We need to share this with Kathy right away. She told me she was driving down to Bloomington today to surprise Jerry."

"Don't worry," Peter replied. "We'll call her after we talk to Doctor Lake. He should be able to tell us more about these pills."

The three companions fell silent as they contemplated their upcoming confrontation. Driving north on Lakeshore Drive, Peter looked out to his left, still haunted by the sight of the storm surge pounding the beachfront. Steam was rising from the road as the cold rain pelted the heated pavement. Peter's thoughts turned to the inflation monster that had tormented swimmers in Lake Michigan three years ago. He was still consumed with guilt and anger.

A red warning sign marked stop 41 on Lakeshore Drive. The road ended a short mile ahead. Peter turned right, away from the lake, and continued to the entrance of Michiana Shores. Like other towns that lined Lakeshore Drive, the area was comprised largely of summer homes and rental cabins. It was purely residential, with no commercial establishments. Nestled within a forest of large oak trees, it was the perfect hiding spot. Tom used the directions provided by Doctor Cregar to guide Peter to the appropriate house.

Peter slowly turned down Totem Lane. Each of the passengers in the car began to search for the address—636 Totem Lane. They soon came upon a small log cabin, hidden among mature pine trees, with the numbers "636" dangling loosely from a mailbox that looked like it had been a frequent target of vandals. Peter parked the car and all three of the passengers stared at the house in silence. The full-grown trees swayed under the onslaught of the wind. A crash of thunder shook the car.

"Are you sure this is the house?" Peter asked.

"It's the address he gave me."

Peter looked directly at Tom and Sarah. He could see they were both apprehensive. He recognized this was a situation where he would have to lead. "Are you guys ready?" Without waiting for a reply, he commanded, "Let's roll."

The three of them ran to the front door of the cabin, trying to stay as dry as possible. Tom pounded on the wooden door, with no response. The thunder increased in intensity. Peter knocked five times hard on the door. Still no answer.

"I don't think anyone's here," Tom yelled over the wind.

Peering through the window, Sarah saw a figure dart out the back door. "I think someone just ran out the back door."

Peter grabbed Sarah by the hand and urged, "Come on!"

Sarah and Tom followed Peter's lead around the side of the cabin. The back door of the cabin opened out to a dirt path that led to a dense forest.

Peter tried to yell over the howling wind. "Is anyone there?"

The rain increased in intensity, causing the three uninvited guests to stop short of entering the woods. Peter was the first to call out, "Doctor Cregar, is that you?"

There was no answer. Tom took a few steps into the woods and looked around. The dark sky and falling rain made it difficult to see. A bolt of lightning suddenly lit up the sullen sky. For a brief moment, Tom spied the muscular image of Doctor Cregar trying to hide behind a mature pine.

"Doctor Cregar, it's me! Tom Nelson! You told us to meet you here. Why are you hiding from us?"

Like a fleeing deer, Doctor Cregar started running deeper into the woods. One of Tom Nelson's greatest physical attributes was his speed. He was determined not to let the older man outrun him. Peter and Sarah brought up the rear. Doctor Cregar stopped and turned to face Tom; his desperate eyes were those of a mother bear protecting her cubs. Tom stopped, bracing for Cregar's charge. Suddenly Cregar dashed between two large pines, just beyond Tom's grasp. Tom started after Cregar when, with a sharp thud, a branch from one of the pines snapped back and hit Tom square in the chest. The impact knocked Tom off balance, causing him to slip in the rain-drenched mud. He tried to catch himself with his right hand, but the mud offered no traction. His head came down hard on a large rock protruding from the ground. Tom's world went dark.

Peter and Sarah ran to their friend to help.

Peter bent down over Tom's still body. "Is he okay?" Sarah yelled.

"I don't know. He's unconscious." Helpless, Peter stood up and yelled into the woods. "Doctor Cregar...Tom's hurt! He's not moving. We need to get him out of the rain and bring him into the house."

There was no response. Peter looked toward Sarah and said, "Go see if the door's open. I'll drag Tom over to the house."

Sarah ran to the back door and swung it open. She then helped Peter drag Tom's body over to the carpeted floor. A thunderous boom shook the house and a bright flash of lightning illuminated the cabin from the open back door. Peter and Sarah both looked up to see the hulking image of Doctor Cregar blocking the doorway.

"What are you kids doing here?"

Peter stood up, preparing himself for a fight. Sarah then stood, positioning herself between Peter and Doctor Cregar. Sarah held out her hands as she began to speak. "Doctor Cregar, my name is Sarah Banks. I'm a friend of Tom and Peter. We don't mean you any harm. Tom is hurt. Please let us help him."

"Why did you kids come out here after me?"

Peter interjected. "Tom told us that you invited him out here. He wanted to warn you and Doctor Lake about some of the dangerous side effects of the Rivermass pills. Don't you remember any of this?"

Cregar looked genuinely confused. He began fidgeting with his fingers and looked down at his hands. He had the look of a small adolescent being scolded by his parents.

Sarah continued. "Doctor Cregar, Tom told us about the loss of your family. I am sorry. I offer my sincere condolences. Still, we have to make sure that no one else gets harmed by these pills."

The mere mention of Cregar's family seemed to strike a nerve. He snapped back in anger, "Don't pretend that you care about my family. Nobody cares about my family. Didn't Tom tell you that my company—where I've been a loyal employee—fired me? There is no such thing as loyalty. Rivermass is all I have. I've taken it. It works! I'm twice as strong as my former self. Look at me!" Doctor Cregar stretched his arms toward the sky, as if issuing a command for all to hear.

"Doctor Cregar, please, just consider the possibility that Rivermass could harm others. You're a scientist. You should understand that the pills might need further testing. One of my friends has been taking these pills, and I'm worried that they're changing him. It's changed his whole personality. What if the pills are changing you, too?"

In an agitated state, Cregar began pacing the floor, considering the possibility.

"Bravo, Peter. Bravo." Peter recognized the sinister voice emanating from the back bedroom. The Sandman emerged from the dark shadows, clapping and smiling, applauding the drama unfolding before him. The Sandman looked toward Cregar and spoke in a chiding manner.

"Are you going to listen to these kids, Cregar? You've been listening and obeying all of your life, haven't you? You dutifully obeyed when your employer told you to abandon one research project after another. *It wasn't profitable*, they told you, didn't they? What has listening to others accomplished for you? You've lost your family, and the employer that you were so loyal to has abandoned you in your time of need. They dumped you the same way that they discarded your family, and all of the other lifeless bodies hit by the earthquake. It seems to me that I'm the only one who wants you to succeed. You and I have discovered something that can finally make you rich. Are you going to let your dreams slip away again?"

"Doctor Cregar, don't listen to him. He's evil. You'll regret it!" Peter looked down at the floor and spoke softly. "I know. He tried to satisfy all of my dreams, too. He gave me all the power I ever wanted." Looking up at Cregar, Peter asked, "Has he allowed you to assume the roles of other people? He let me assume the role of President of the United States. He could probably allow you to assume the role of CEO of Care4. Then you could get your job back. Wouldn't he do that if he really wanted to help you?"

Cregar looked to Doctor Lake for an answer.

"Don't listen to him, Cregar! He's talking nonsense. He's just a stupid kid who's trying to keep you from the fame and recognition that you deserve."

"No. That's not true. Don't you see, Doctor Cregar? He promised me fame also. It was only later that I found that the price for fame was too great. Innocent people were hurt because of what I did. Similarly, innocent people might get hurt from these Rivermass pills. Don't let it happen to you. Believe me, you'll regret it."

The Sandman sneered and resumed his clapping. He was thoroughly amused by the theater that he had orchestrated.

"That's right, Petey. Share with us what an enlightened soul you've become. We're all so touched by your sentiment."

Lake then cast his eyes on Sarah, acknowledging her for the first time.

"How thoughtful of you to bring your girlfriend here. She is still your girlfriend, isn't she? Or did that sinister Doug Keyster lure her away from you?" The Sandman laughed deviously at his words. "Do you really think she's going to protect you?" The Sandman took obvious pleasure in watching Peter boil with anger.

"I should have drowned you when I had the chance," Peter snarled. "Doctor Cregar, I picked up the gold coin that you threw at us in Cape Girardeau." Peter reached into his pocket and pulled out two identical coins. Unbeknownst to Sarah, he had kept one of the coins from three years ago. He had vowed never to use it again. Holding one coin in each hand for Cregar to see, he said, "Look, I have a coin just like it. I know that it seems this coin has power over others, but we don't need to use it. This coin is seductive and dangerous. The Sandman can't make us do things against our will."

While Cregar stood motionless, unresponsive, Peter frantically began looking around the house. He searched through the cabinets and even pulled the sofa cushions off the couch, continuing to speak while looking for the genie's bottle.

"Did Doctor Lake show you his bottle? He's not human, Doctor Cregar. Did you know that? The first time I met him, he washed up on Lake Michigan in a bottle. If we can find that bottle, we can defeat him."

Peter found a vase in one of the kitchen cabinets, and acting on a hunch, he began filling it up with water. Grabbing the full vase and running toward the Sandman, he splashed the water in the Sandman's face and yelled, "Look! He hates water!"

The Sandman began clutching at his throat as if his very breath was being taken away. His face began turning a reddish, purple color, and his body fell to the floor in convulsions.

Reaching out to Doctor Cregar, the Sandman yelled. "Augh, help me, Jonah, I'm melting!"

Cregar instinctively moved in to help. But slowly the Sandman's screams morphed into hysterical laughter. He seemed thoroughly amused by his reference to *The Wizard of Oz*. His laughter gave way to a hideous grin, as he turned to face Peter Jangle.

"Petey, my boy, do you really think that if you sprinkle me with water, I'm just going to fade away? It's been years since that trick worked. I've been promoted. I've been set free of the old chains of my bottle." The genie raised his arms and looked up to the sky to proclaim. "The genie's been let out of the bottle, Petey! You can no longer put a cork in it! I'm much more engrained in your society today. You're losing the battle."

Looking toward Jonah Cregar, the Sandman ordered, "Get rid of these kids, Jonah. They stand between us and our dreams."

CHAPTER THIRTY FOUR

After a four-hour drive, Kathy arrived at Jerry Parker's apartment in Bloomington. At the same time her friends were battling the Sandman, she was preparing to confront Jerry. She was not sure how he would react to her unannounced visit. Closing the car door behind her, she approached Jerry's apartment with an uneasy feeling in her gut. She was tempted to turn around and retreat. She didn't want to appear too aggressive. Standing outside Jerry's apartment door, she realized there was no turning back. Jerry was too important to her. She needed to discuss their relationship. Mustering up her courage, she knocked firmly on the door. There was no answer. She knocked again. Finally, as she was about to turn back to her car, the door opened barely enough so she could hear a faint whisper from inside.

"Kathy, what are you doing here?"

"I'm sorry, Jerry. I know I should have called you. But I was worried about you. Can I come in?"

After a moment's hesitation, Jerry opened the door, inviting her in. Looking around the apartment, Kathy noticed dirty clothes lying neglected on the floor. Unwashed dishes were stacked in the kitchen sink.

"It's a good thing I came," Kathy laughed nervously. "You're in obvious need of a maid."

"Yeah. I guess I haven't gotten around to cleaning up," Jerry replied sullenly. "I've been pretty busy with football and all." His voice trailed off.

"Jerry. Are you sure you're all right? You seem kind of lethargic."

"I'm sorry. I told you not to come down here. I don't know. I haven't been getting much sleep lately."

"Maybe you ought to take it easy for a bit."

"I can't!" Jerry snapped back. "I've got football practice... I've got people calling me all the time to tell me what a hero I am...I just want to be left alone!"

Regaining his composure, Jerry said, "I'm sorry, Kathy. I don't want to bother you with my problems."

Kathy stared at the once-confident figure before her. Despite his strong build, he had the look of a broken man. She instinctively opened her arms and walked toward Jerry to comfort him. Jerry half-heartedly returned her embrace.

"Jerry, you aren't bothering me with your problems. I care about you. I want you to share things with me." She tightened her grip around Jerry.

Jerry self-consciously broke away. "Listen, Kathy. I don't think this will work. I'm not like you. I'm black. You're Jewish. We come from different backgrounds. You can do better than me."

"What are you talking about?"

"Listen. You're smart, you're going to make an impact in the world with your knowledge. That's not who I am. I'm just a physical body. I play football. I rescued some people because I was physically capable of rescuing them. Once my body breaks down, I'm nothing. We would eventually drift apart. Why put off the inevitable?"

Kathy's compassion turned to anger at the sound of Jerry's self-pity. "Don't you give me that shit, Jerry! I am so tired of hearing about how you're so different. When you first came to Michigan City, you tried to set yourself apart as 'the kid from Gary.' But then you became part of the team. You were no longer a detractor; instead, you made us better. You inspired the team and you inspired me. So quit talking like a loser."

Jerry gave Kathy a shallow hug and replied, "Kathy, I appreciate your words, but really, you'd be better off without me. I'd just be trouble for you. I know I've got issues I need to work through. Just let me deal with it."

"Damn you, Jerry! You're acting just as ignorant as any other racist! I know you've had to struggle. Do you really think you're the only one who's had to struggle? My mom had to struggle to raise a child by herself. My people have had to struggle. Yeah, I know you've been discriminated against, but what about us? Half of the world doesn't even recognize that a Jewish state exists. Half of the world wants us wiped off of the planet, Jerry. And you know what we do? We persevere. We fight—with our head, and our body, and our spirit. And guess what, Jerry? You've got a good head and you've got a great spirit. And yet, you're choosing to throw away your greatest attributes."

Kathy turned around and headed toward the door.

"Kathy! Wait! I'm sorry. I'm so lost. I'm barely here. Thank you for believing in me...I do love you. I just don't want to hurt you."

Kathy smiled, wiping a tear from her eyes. She ran into Jerry's open arms. They embraced tightly, gaining strength from each other.

"Don't you get it, Jerry? I'm here to help relieve your pain. You and I share a bond. We both lost our fathers. Maybe we need to admit that we need each other."

Jerry forced a smile. "Are you sure you can do that?" he asked.

Kathy stared deep into Jerry's eyes and replied, "I can if you can."

Tears welled up in Jerry's eyes as he tightened his grip around Kathy. A flood of emotions raced through his head. He felt himself feeding off of Kathy's strength.

After a long embrace, Kathy opened her eyes and looked out the balcony window. The sun was breaking through the clouds. Taking Jerry by the hand, she led him toward the balcony. "Look, it's clearing up. It's going to be a beautiful day. What do you say we enjoy it together?"

Jerry opened the sliding glass door and led Kathy outside. He put his arm around her as they looked out over the horizon. Pointing to the distance, he said, "Look over there." The couple observed a faint rainbow where the rain met the sky. Jerry was currently experiencing one of the highs he had become familiar with since taking the Rivermass pills. Unfortunately, he knew they were often followed by deeper lows.

CHAPTER THIRTY FIVE

A loud crash of thunder shook the small cabin in Michiana. Jonah Cregar rushed past Peter and grabbed Sarah around the waist.

"Let her go!" Peter yelled.

Cregar tightened his grip. "If you want to save your girlfriend, get the hell out of here and leave us alone."

"You can't let them go," the Sandman commanded. "They'll stop us. We need to finish this now."

Peter rushed toward Cregar, trying to pry Sarah from his grip, but Cregar was too strong. Throwing Sarah to the floor, Cregar took Peter by the shoulders and slammed him against the wall.

Despite all his efforts, Peter was no match for Cregar. Cregar gave Peter a quick punch to the stomach, knocking the wind out of him, and then shoved him to the floor. Sarah ran to Peter's aid, shielding him from further attack.

Looking up at Cregar, she implored, "Why are you doing this? We don't want to harm you. We aren't your enemy. He's the enemy!" she yelled, pointing toward the Sandman.

The Sandman was noticeably amused, and seemed to gain strength from the battle taking place before him. He emerged from the shadows of the room, his eyes gleaming a bright yellow tint. Flashing a sinister smile, he goaded Cregar to finish the job. "Get rid of them," he instructed coldly.

Cregar recognized the hatred in the Sandman's voice. He covered his ears and winced, as if trying to force the evil thoughts from his head. Cregar desperately wanted to overcome the temptation to do harm. Nonetheless, he was driven by a promise Doctor Lake had made to him—and he wanted to be sure Doctor Lake could deliver on that promise. He asked one final question of his partner.

"Just who are you, Doctor Lake? Where did you come from?"

"What does it matter, Cregar? I'm a time traveler. I came from the beginning of humanity. I offer a last hope for those of you abandoned by your God. You, who have no hope left."

Catching his breath, Peter cried out, "Don't you get it? He doesn't offer hope. He sucks hope out of you. He's the source behind the earthquake. He's the one responsible for the loss of your family."

The words resonated with Cregar. He had been so filled with ambition to bring Rivermass to market that he had completely blocked his family from his mind. His thoughts turned to his loving wife and his beautiful daughters. He recalled with pride the lack of fear he felt when he rescued his daughter from drowning—and he longed for the love and faith he had seen in his little girl's eyes, as she clung desperately to his neck for safety. Looking down, Cregar was ashamed of what he had become. He studied his large frame and muscles, and realized it had come at a price. His new muscle mass had intruded upon his heart. He felt his heart was empty. The love that had once resonated within him had been replaced with feelings of paranoia, greed, distrust, and despair.

Cregar looked down at Sarah's cowering figure as she attempted to shield Peter from further harm. He remembered that he would lovingly make any sacrifice to shield his own family from harm. His thoughts were suddenly interrupted by the caustic barbs from the Sandman.

"Why are you just standing there, Cregar? Don't you get it? If you let them escape, everything we've worked for will be lost. They'll have won. You'll be alone, unemployed and miserable. And you'll never see your family again."

He promised me I'd get my family back, Cregar recalled.

Peter slowly rose to his feet. He bent over, clutching his side with his left hand. He felt as if one of his ribs had been broken. Reaching into his right pocket, he pulled out one of the six-sided gold coins. Extending the coin toward Cregar, he said, "I know the power of this coin. I also know the man you refer to as Doctor Lake. He came to me three years ago when I was a senior in high school, and my dad was unemployed. I felt the same anger that you're feeling now. I thought he was the answer to my prayers. He gave me great power, and he filled my head with the promise of fortune and fame." He paused. "But he's a liar—full of deceit...and all he'll leave you with is regret."

Peter tried to stand tall, and then grimaced as a sharp pain stabbed his side. "I still get tempted by the pursuit of fortune. But I know that the people I love will keep me grounded. I've already hurt people...you don't have to.

Believe me, no personal gain is worth the cost of the hurt I've caused others. I know you're physically stronger than me, and I know you can take his advice and destroy me, if you like. I can only warn you about the path you're traveling down. Believe me, with my last breath, I'll pray that God has mercy on me for the harm I've already caused. In the end, I truly believe we won't be seeking fame and fortune…we'll be seeking mercy."

The Sandman walked to Cregar's side. In a low, malevolent voice, he whispered into Cregar's ear, "Look at him. He's weak. He's a fool. Finish him."

Slowly Cregar reached into his pocket and pulled out a gold coin similar to the one Peter held in his hand.

"Did you think that was my only coin?" the Sandman asked. "This has always been about getting you here, Petey. You followed our plan perfectly. Get rid of him, Cregar, and I'll give you the opportunity to see your family again," he stated coldly.

Doctor Cregar looked at Sarah and stated, "I have no use for you, girl. This is between Peter and me. You said you're looking for mercy, Peter? As my last gesture of mercy, I'll let your girlfriend stay here and take care of Tom Nelson."

"No, I'm not leaving Peter!" Sarah cried.

Resigned that it was his battle alone, Peter held up his coin toward Sarah and said, "You stay here with Tom. Let me go."

Sarah was powerless to resist Peter's wishes. She reluctantly turned her back and walked to the couch where Tom Nelson lay unconscious.

Cregar extended his right hand to grab Peter by the scruff of his neck. With his left hand, Cregar cupped Peter's chin and twisted his head so that Cregar could look directly into Peter's eyes. "Was that enough mercy for you, Peter?"

Peter realized he lacked the strength to fight Cregar.

"Come with us, Doctor Lake," Cregar invited, "I think you'll find that I've come up with a fitting solution to our problem. We're going to take Mr. Jangle to Lake Michigan. I believe you told me that was where you two first met, right?"

The Sandman leered in acknowledgement. Cregar led Peter to the kitchen and opened a drawer that contained some scissors and duct tape. Seeing that Cregar meant to restrain him, Peter struggled to fight free. He swung a fist with all his might toward Cregar's head. Cregar blocked the blow and delivered a sharp left punch to Peter's stomach, followed by a hard right across Peter's head. Peter slumped to the floor. There was no fight left in him. He looked at Sarah on the couch, before lapsing into a state of unconsciousness. Grabbing Peter by the collar, Cregar dragged him across the floor.

"Come on, Doctor Lake. You don't want to miss this!" he yelled as he swung open the door to the cabin and hauled Peter outside. Lightning punctuated the dark sky, as the rain continued to fall. When the cabin door slammed shut, Sarah raced to the window to see where they were going. She saw Cregar and Lake push Peter into the front passenger side of their car. Cregar then jumped into the driver's seat and started the car. The Sandman looked back at Sarah, staring through the cabin window, and leered as he got into the back seat of the car.

CHAPTER THIRTY SIX

Peter slowly regained consciousness, only to discover his hands and ankles were bound tight with the duct tape that Cregar had retrieved from the kitchen drawer.

"Ah...Peter, you're back with us, I see." Peter didn't need to open his swollen eye to recognize the voice of his nemesis.

"Please, get up, Peter." From the back seat of the car, the Sandman pulled Peter up by the shoulders.

Still aching from the blows that Cregar had delivered, Peter squinted to look out the windshield of the car. He discerned the beach was ahead of him by the sound of the pounding surf.

"Remember the inflation monster, Petey?" The Sandman asked. "It looks like he's back, doesn't it? And it looks like he's come for you."

Peter could hardly believe what was happening. *Was he really going to meet his fate in Lake Michigan?* The memory of swimming in the lake, trying to save Steve Shindler, and later Sarah, was vivid in his head. *Could it be true that the inflation monster, his creation, had returned?* The pain of that summer haunted Peter much more than the physical pain he now endured.

Peter turned his head toward the back of the car to look at the Sandman. "I don't get it. If you wanted to kill me, why didn't you kill me three years ago? You certainly had the chance."

"You're right, Peter. You don't get it. I'm not the same person you battled three years ago. The gates of hell have numerous foot soldiers. The last sandman you faced was much too weak. He also broke the rules. Believe it or not, we do have to adhere to certain rules. We're not allowed to create monsters. We're only allowed to tempt humans. We can't physically harm anyone. We let you humans do our dirty work. Here's a newsflash: I didn't cause the earthquake, I merely took advantage of the opportunity. I'm here as nothing more than a spectator. Observing mankind is like watching a continuous tragedy, and the ending is always the same. You people never disappoint. You always pursue your own interests, regardless of the harm you might cause others.

"Isn't that right, Cregar? This kid is nothing more than a bit player... an obstacle to our goal... a pawn in our game. His life means nothing."

"Is that how you feel, Doctor Cregar?" Peter asked. "He fed on my greed once. But I guess I was luckier than you. He didn't kill everyone that I loved. I know he said he didn't cause the earthquake, but do you really believe him? Do you remember how your family used to support you? My dad always tells me that it's not important what you get in life, but rather what you give. And that we'll ultimately be remembered by what comes *from* us, not what comes *to* us."

Cregar's ashen face suddenly grew red with searing shame. He looked agitated as he rubbed his forehead between his thumb and index finger. "Do you ever stop preaching?" He slammed his fist against the car dashboard and yelled, "I can't stand it any longer! Who the hell do you think you are, Jangle? You annoy people. Do you really think you're any better than us? I lost my family...I lost everything!"

"Yeah, thanks to the creature in the back seat...and now you're helping him."

Cregar began mumbling inaudibly as he stomped on the gas pedal and tightened his grip on the steering wheel. Peter could see that the car was gaining speed through the sand as it approached the water's edge. Peter heard the hideous laugh of the Sandman coming from the back seat. He knew they were going into the lake. He was struggling to free the binding from his legs and arms when Cregar suddenly reached across his body and grabbed at the passenger side door handle. Cregar stared at Peter, his eyes full of remorse, and said, "Tell your friend Tom that the water made me a hero once again. Remember me in your prayers."

In the next instant, Cregar flung open the passenger side door and shoved Peter clear of the car. As Peter rolled over the wet sand, he saw the passenger door slam closed, just before the car was engulfed by the breaking waves. Within ten seconds, the car had disappeared.

Beneath the water's surface, the battle continued. Cregar reached back to grab hold of Doctor Lake, ensuring that he didn't escape. Suddenly, the genie's appearance morphed into an image of Cregar's daughter. *Don't deceive me!* Cregar willed as he continued to hold firm. As his lungs started filling with water, he closed his eyes and again saw the image of his daughter, Emily. She was smiling. Just before he blacked out, he took comfort in the thought that he would be reunited with his family.

Peter stared in disbelief, trying to comprehend what had just happened. He continued to focus on the pounding surf, waiting to see if anyone would emerge. After five minutes of waiting, he was convinced that he had seen the last of Doctor Cregar and the Sandman. Cregar had given his life to save Peter. Cregar had been redeemed. Looking up to the sky, Peter noticed that the rain had stopped and the clouds were breaking. Using his teeth, he ripped at the tape around his wrists, finally managing to free his arms. He quickly tore the tape from his legs and looked around to determine his location. He realized that he was less than two miles from where he had left Sarah and Tom. Gathering his strength, he started sprinting from the beach toward the cabin.

CHAPTER THIRTY SEVEN

"Tom, get up, we've got to help Peter," Sarah implored as she urgently shook Tom's limp body. Slowly Tom began to regain consciousness.

"What? What happened? Where's Cregar?"

"Cregar took Peter. I think the Rivermass pills were affecting him. He showed all the signs of a manic depressive. He was acting like a crazy man."

"Where did they go?"

"I don't know. We've got to find them. We've got to call for help."

Sarah pulled out her cell phone, searching her thoughts for someone to call. Suddenly a thought occurred to her. "Oh my gosh! Kathy! We've got to warn Kathy! What if the Rivermass pills have the same effect on Jerry as they had on Doctor Cregar? Kathy could be in trouble."

Sarah frantically punched in Kathy's cell phone number. Kathy answered on the third ring.

"Kathy, where are you?!"

"Hi, Sarah. What's up?"

"Are you with Jerry?"

Kathy could detect the worry in Sarah's panicked voice.

"Yes. I'm at Jerry's apartment. Why? What's the matter?"

"How is he? Is he okay?"

Kathy looked at Jerry, who was still leaning on the balcony, staring blankly at the horizon. She walked inside the apartment to continue the conversation in private.

"I guess he's okay...a little bit stressed maybe. Why? What's wrong?"

"He's been taking some kind of pills that Tom gave him. They're supposed to help him build muscle, but they have bad side effects. They cause severe depression. Are you free to talk now?"

"Yeah. He can't hear me. He's outside."

"Look at him, Kathy. Does he look stable? Do you think you can have a coherent conversation with him?

"Sarah, you're freaking me out. What do you think is wrong?"

"I've seen what these pills can do to a person. They not only affect the body, they affect the mind. Look around the apartment, and see if you can find any pills—they're dangerous. The people who created the pills are dangerous. I met them, and they took Peter. These people are evil, and they want people to suffer."

"Sarah! Chill out! You're not making any sense. Who's evil? What do you mean, they took Peter?...... Oh, noo! I've got to go!"

"Wait! Kathy! Don't hang up!"

It was too late. The phone went dead.

Sarah was about to redial when Tom grabbed her hand that held the phone.

"Sarah, you've got to tell me what happened. Where are Peter and Cregar? Was Doctor Lake here? What happened? I don't remember anything."

Sarah didn't know what to tell Tom. *Should she tell him about Doctor Lake? Should she tell him that she believed Lake was the genie who had befriended Peter years ago and caused so much havoc? No. She had promised Peter she would tell no one.* She stammered to answer Tom's questions.

Suddenly the cabin door swung open. Peter stood exhausted in the doorway. One hand clung to the doorknob, barely supporting his slumped body. He had sprinted back from the beach as fast as he could, and now struggled to speak between gasps for air.

"Peter! What happened?!" Sarah cried out as she helped him over to the couch. Tom and Sarah positioned Peter between them on the couch.

"Where's Doctor Cregar?" Tom asked. "What did he want with you?"

Peter raised his arm as a gesture to stop the barrage of questions. After a couple more deep breaths, Peter told them, "Doctor Cregar and Lake are gone. I think they're both dead."

Sarah stopped asking questions. She knew that Peter would try to craft some type of believable story. She wanted to see if Peter would mention the genie in Tom's presence. He didn't. Tom continued with his questions.

"What are you talking about? How did they die?"

"The pills." Peter replied. "The Rivermass pills had a terrible effect on Doctor Cregar. Doctor Lake knew the pills caused severe depression, yet he continued to encourage Cregar to take them. He was using Cregar as a lab experiment. He thought maybe the effects would wear off, but they only got worse. Doctor Cregar wasn't a bad guy. Doctor Lake took advantage of him."

"So what happened? How did they die?" Tom interrupted.

"Doctor Lake kept telling Cregar that I would expose the negative side effects of the pills. He was trying to convince Cregar that I was an obstacle that needed to be eliminated. I think Lake wanted me dead."

Peter glanced briefly at Sarah, seeking reassurance regarding the credibility of his story. He wanted to rehearse his story on Tom, figuring that if Tom accepted it, he would never have to mention the genie again.

"This is crazy!" Tom replied. "Why would Lake want to kill only you, and not Sarah and me?"

For the first time, Peter looked Tom directly in the eyes to answer. "Cregar didn't want you hurt. He liked you. And he certainly didn't want to harm Sarah. In fact, Cregar didn't want to hurt anyone. He saved my life. He pushed me out of the car right before he drove the Sandman, uh….I mean Doctor Lake…into Lake Michigan. I watched as their car sank under the water. I waited to see if anyone would swim out. No one did. I'm pretty sure they both drowned."

All three sat in silence, reflecting on Peter's words. After thirty seconds, Peter resumed. "Doctor Cregar was a good man. I could see it in his eyes. Lake tried hard to tempt him. He tried to make him vengeful for the loss of his family and the loss of his job. Cregar was a perfect candidate for the Rivermass pills. The pills made him more self-consumed…. and more depressed."

"The pills!" Sarah blurted out. "I forgot about Kathy. She hung up on me. What if the pills affected Jerry in the same way? What if he's attacking her for talking with me?"

Sarah began punching Kathy's cell number into her phone.

"Hello."

"Kathy! Is everything okay? Why did you hang up on me?"

"Don't worry, Sarah. Everything's okay. I told Jerry what you said about the pills he was taking. We flushed them down the toilet. He's not going to take any more. Everything's going to be okay."

Sarah was overcome with emotion, as tears of relief rolled down her cheeks. Kathy smiled, and soon her eyes welled up, too. Tears seemed to be the best outlet of their anxiety from the past couple of days.

"Why did you hang up on me?"

Kathy sniffled and then replied. "When I looked out on the balcony, Jerry had collapsed. He was so sad. He was hunched over in the corner crying. He didn't know what was wrong with him. I told him what you said about the pills, and that they cause depression. That's when he and I both agreed to grab them and flush them down the toilet. He's smiling at me right now…but I don't think he's happy I told you he was crying." Kathy laughed.

"Why don't you guys drive up here tonight? It looks like the weather's clearing. We can all go out and grab a pizza and go to a movie. It'll be a good way to celebrate before Tom and Peter go back to Chicago for their last week of work."

"No. I think we're just going to stay here tonight. I told Jerry I would help him clean up his apartment. Believe me, it needs it."

Sarah smiled. "Okay. Love you."

"Love you too," Kathy replied. "Bye."

✵ ✵ ✵

Later that evening, Peter's dad came to visit him as he was preparing for bed. Peter had managed to slip in the house unnoticed, while his parents were watching the evening news. A large bruise was now forming under Peter's eye.

"Oh geez, Peter, are you okay? I've been worried about you all day. Tell me what happened."

"I don't know, Dad. I thought it was him. I thought the Sandman came back. But he talked as if he was someone different. I don't know how many exist. But I do think that this guy actually wanted to kill me."

For the next thirty minutes, Peter related the day's events to his father. David Jangle listened patiently and only gave advice when asked. When Peter was done, David put his arm around his son and asked, "Do you think he's gone for good?"

"I don't know," Peter replied. "Probably not. Even if this one is gone, he's likely to be followed by another. It's scary. I feel like no one around me is safe."

"Peter, don't worry about us—just know that we'll always be here for you. You're not the only one who has to deal with demons—we all do. Unfortunately, your demons just seem to be more obvious about revealing themselves. You should be proud that you defeated them once again."

"I don't think I defeated him this time. I think it was Cregar who defeated him. Of course, I think this sandman was after Cregar more than he was after me. I was just a pawn—an expendable one. He wanted Cregar to kill me so that he could strengthen his hold over Cregar. I still don't understand. Maybe the other sandman was his brother, and he wanted to get revenge. Maybe it was the same guy and he was just lying to me. I don't know."

"Well, you can't worry about it, Peter. You just need to learn from the experience. So how do you think Cregar resisted him?"

"I actually think he did it the same way I did. I think it was his love for his family that saved him. I could see it in his eyes. He may have been looking at me, but it was like he was looking at his wife and daughter. I could feel the connection."

David Jangle smiled and hugged his son. "Good night, my man. Remember to say your prayers. We've both got lots to be thankful for."

As David Jangle was leaving his son's room, he looked back and asked, "So, how are you going to explain that shiner to your mother?"

Peter smiled and replied sheepishly, "Do you think she'd buy it if I told her I was mugged?"

"I think that would unleash a barrage of never-ending questions. How about we just attribute it to clumsiness? That's a story she's more likely to believe."

Peter lay in his bed with a peaceful smile on his face. He felt filled with joy. He knew the power of love. Then his thoughts turned to what he should try to accomplish in his last week at work. He started thinking about Tony Salami. His brief experience of heaven was over.

CHAPTER THIRTY EIGHT

Monday, September fourth.
Peter's alarm clock went off at five in the morning. Peter had mixed feelings about his last week at work. It had been a difficult summer internship. He had gone into the summer believing that he would prove himself extremely successful in the money management business. His goal had been to remain focused. His encounter with the Sandman distracted him from his original goal. He was now more uncertain than ever about his eventual career path.

Terri Tanaka greeted Peter as soon as he walked through the door at American Dinero.

"Peter! I've been waiting for you. Listen—I need to talk to you."

"And a good morning to you, too," Peter said with a smile.

Terri led Peter to one of the conference rooms where she could close the door to ensure privacy.

Terri began in a hushed, but hurried voice.

"Peter, I swear to God…I almost completely lost it with Tony this morning. I can't take his crap any more."

"Why? What happened?"

"I was told late Friday afternoon that Tony bought a large position in this small stock that we have never followed. So he comes to me, first thing this morning, and tells me to write a bullish report on the stock. It's like…he wants me to promote this company that I know nothing about. Even if I do end up liking the company, the whole thing stinks. He never should have purchased this stock without giving us the opportunity to research the company."

"I agree with you, Terri. But what do you want me to do?"

"I don't know. You seem so religious. Calm me down. Tell me I should forgive him."

Terri's words struck Peter. No one had ever called him religious before. *Was he more religious than other folks?* He smiled. *Maybe his greatest contribution to society could be his moral beliefs rather than his financial expertise.*

"Listen, Terri, I don't know what you want me to say. You know that the world's full of people who get tempted by greed. There have been scandals in the mutual fund industry, there have been accounting scandals at large companies, and for all we know, Tony might be engaging in insider trading. In fact, one of my friends was interning at a law firm this year and got fired because she told her boss she thought some lawyers were over-billing their clients. It sucks. The fact is that there are dishonest people. I guess the best advice I can give you is to not be one of them."

"So are you saying that I should forgive Tony? Why does God even allow people to cheat others?"

Peter smiled. "Terri, I really don't have the answers. All I can tell you is what I believe. I believe that God's gift to us is the gift of free choice. We can choose to behave badly or choose to behave honestly. We can choose to forgive others or choose not to forgive others. All the other creatures God created act on instinct. They don't have a conscience or a soul. They act in the interest of survival. By contrast, God created us in his image. He gave us a soul. Without our conscience, we would act just like the other animals. We would cheat, steal, and maybe even kill if we thought that was necessary to survive. But our soul keeps us from always acting instinctively. Our soul is God's conscience within us. So each time we're at a crossroads, we have a choice to make. We can follow our instinct, or we can follow our soul. Hopefully, over our lifetime, we make more good choices than bad ones."

Terri hugged Peter. "Thanks, Peter. I'm really glad you came to work with us this summer."

Peter thought back on the words he had just spoken. *Maybe I should consider a career in ministry, or maybe counseling?* Peter followed Terri out of the conference room and headed toward the office of David Koslow. David was busy poring over various stock research reports. Noticing Peter approaching, David turned to greet him.

"Hey, short-timer. This is your last week, isn't it?"

"Yeah. My last day is Thursday. I just wanted to thank you for the stuff you've had me work on this summer. I was wondering if there's anything else I can do for you before I leave?"

"No. Why don't you just take it easy?"

Koslow was trying to be nice, but the look on Peter's face indicated that those were not the words Peter wanted to hear.

Sensing Peter's disappointment, David decided to assign him one last project.

"Wait. On second thought, I know what you can do for me. I'm trying to find some stocks for one of my investment portfolios that need income-producing stocks. My goal is to have good industry diversification. I still need one or two bank stocks to put in my portfolio. Here's a list of five stocks; why don't you give me the two stocks you'd recommend and tell me why you'd recommend them."

Right away Peter's face lit up with enthusiasm. He loved a challenge, and he appreciated the faith that David had placed in him.

Peter went back to his cubicle and began searching various websites for the latest information on the five banks under consideration. He welcomed a purely intellectual challenge without any moral implications and dove into the research, leaving his cubicle only once to go to the restroom.

Tom was already home when Peter got back to the apartment. He appeared anxious and eager to address Peter.

"Peter, are you sure we shouldn't tell anyone about what happened to Doctor Cregar and Doctor Lake? The thought's been bothering me all day at work."

"Why would you tell anyone at Care4? They fired him. They don't expect him to come in."

"I know. It just kind of haunts me. Don't you think we should at least have the police dredge the lake?"

"Tom. Listen to me. They'll ask us so many questions that it won't be worth it. Let's just give it time. Chances are someone will uncover the car soon. Neither one of them had family that we know of. Let's just wait a while and see what happens."

"Okay—if you say so." he said reluctantly. "But you've got to promise me that you're not holding any information from me."

"Tom, I promise. It happened just like I said."

"Fine. Tomorrow's my last day of work anyway. I won't worry about it. My plan for tomorrow is to line up some ladies who will be waiting for us when we make future road trips to Chicago."

Peter was glad to see that Tom was returning to his normal self.

Tuesday, September second.

Peter's alarm clock went off at five in the morning. He had worked hard the previous day, analyzing the list of banks that Dave Koslow had assigned him. He hoped to finish up the project that morning. Stretching his body as he rose from the bed, he decided to get in a quick workout before going into the office. By mid-morning the workday was beginning to drag. Suddenly, there was an uproar from the trading area. Peter had to go see what had set Tony off today.

"Are you shittin' me?!" Tony was yelling in the direction of Dave Koslow. "Koslow, are these people insane?"

"From what I heard, the Investment Committee was impressed with the presentation from that small bank in Michigan City. The consultant told me he tried to persuade the committee to give us some money, but they thought that your presentation was a bit too assuming."

"Too assuming?! Why? Because I told them that we were the best manager? Facts are facts. I'm not being assuming. I'm being honest."

The mention of Michigan City drew Peter closer to the discussion. Nonetheless, he did not want to get too close and risk Tony's wrath. It was too late. Tony spotted him.

"Guess what, Jangle? Your buddies down in Michigan City were awarded a part of the investment management mandate from the World Hunger Foundation—we got nothing. Zip. Zilch. Nada. Who got the fixed income money, Koslow?"

"The consultant said that all of the fixed income money went to PIMCO."

"Of course it did. The consultants always send the fixed income money to PIMCO. What's the purpose of even having a consultant?"

"So did the Michigan City bank get all of the equity money?"

"No. They gave half to Michigan City and half to some small investment boutique in Wisconsin."

"Oh, God. The cheese-heads."

Peter tried to slip out of the conversation unnoticed. But he was caught once again.

"Where are you going, Jangle? I want to hear your read on why you think your pals from Michigan City got the investment mandate over us."

"I really don't know, Tony."

"Oh, come on. Sure you do. You're a smart college kid. Who knows? Maybe you'll even work there and manage this money next year, huh?"

Terri Tanaka was quick to come to Peter's rescue.

"Peter, you don't have to listen to him. Tony, shut up. The only reason we lost the mandate was because of your arrogance. You have no one to blame but yourself. Come on, Peter. I have something to tell you."

"That's right, Peter, follow the little girl."

Tony placed his hands behind his head, and wiggled his hips like a cheerleader, as Peter and Terri walked away.

"Don't listen to him," Terri said.

"It's okay. Thanks for coming to my rescue."

"Well the fact is...I really do have something to tell you. In fact you'll be the first one I tell. I'm going to tell Fran Solli later this afternoon."

"What?"

"They offered me the CIO job at Hoosier Insurance. I think I'm going to take it."

"Congratulations, Terri. I think that's great. I'm really happy for you."

"In hindsight, it was a pretty easy decision. It's a great opportunity. And the fact is that I really can't stand Tony any longer. I'm going to tell Fran that's why I'm leaving."

"I'm really happy for you, Terri—you deserve it. Be sure to send me your new contact info once you get settled."

"Thanks for giving your friend my name." Terri leaned in to give Peter a kiss on the cheek.

Peter stood motionless, watching Terri in admiration, as she walked away. After a minute, his thoughts returned to Sarah. Peter went back to his cubicle to call her and inform her of the World Hunger win.

"I know!" Sarah exclaimed. "I just got off the phone with Doug Keyster. Peter, I know that we were both competing on this, but I am so psyched for my dad and the bank."

"You should be. It's a big win. Congratulate Doug for me."

"It's funny," Sarah replied. "For the first time, I actually heard Doug speak highly of the investment consultants."

"Yeah, it's funny how people tend to like the system when it benefits them."

"You know…he's really not a bad guy, Peter."

"I know he's not. I was just jealous. It's one of my many faults."

"Don't be such a martyr, Peter. We've all got faults. It's our ability to recognize our blemishes that keeps us grounded."

Peter smiled. He hadn't found a blemish in Sarah yet.

Later that afternoon Peter saw Terri walk into Fran Solli's office. Fran closed the door. Peter was surprised to see that Terri and Fran were still absorbed in their closed-door meeting, hours later, as he was preparing to leave the office for the day.

✵ ✵ ✵

Wednesday, September third.

Peter's alarm clock went off at five. Due to all the activity yesterday, Peter never had the opportunity to make his bank investment recommendation to David Koslow. He spent another three hours doing research overnight. He was confident that this was going to be the best report he had ever presented. He saw it as an opportunity to impress the money management community before returning to school. He rushed through his usual morning routine so he could catch Koslow before he got too busy. Arriving early at American Dinero, he realized he had forgotten to brush his teeth. "Can't make a good impression with morning breath," he muttered to himself. He rushed down to the building's main lobby to purchase a pack of breath mints. Within five minutes he was back at American Dinero, standing at the door of David Koslow's office.

"Hey, David, do you have time to go over these bank stocks?"

"Sure, Peter. What do you have for me?"

Peter handed Koslow his lengthy written research report. David briefly skimmed down the many numbers and ratios in the report. He then looked up and asked Peter to summarize his findings

"The two banks I like most are Peachtree Bank and Gold Coast Bank."

"Really? Why did you pick those two?"

"First off, Peachtree has the highest market share growth in Georgia, which is one of the fastest growing populations in the country. Likewise, Gold Coast Bank has the highest market share growth in Florida."

"How are you determining their market share growth?"

"By deposit growth. Not only are they both growing deposits, they're also low-cost demand deposits and checking deposits. In addition, their net interest margins are increasing. I read through the annual reports of these companies and it seems that they're both very successful in cross-selling other products to their customers. In other words, both of these banks have been successful in not only making loans to customers, but also opening checking accounts for those same customers and selling treasury management products to their corporate borrowers."

Koslow smiled at Peter. "I've got to admit, I'm pretty impressed. What about asset quality?"

"It looks pretty good. Their loan reserves represent 1.6 percent of total loans and the reserves cover non-performing assets by over three times."

"Are they pretty well diversified across loan types?"

"Yes, they are. And get this, assets under management in their trust department have increased at a rate of thirty percent annually over the past three years. Not only are they successful cross-selling on the bank side, but they've also achieved that same success on the wealth management side. And the best part is, as these two banks have grown, they've continued to add employees while controlling expenses. In other words, these banks aren't like others that just fire employees to control expenses. By contrast, these two are hiring some of the employees that their competitors are letting go. And those new employees are bringing new customers to the bank."

Koslow could see that Peter was getting excited. In fact, he was pleased with Peter—he had obviously done his homework. Nonetheless, he wanted to test Peter's knowledge of "value."

"I agree that these banks are pretty well run, but aren't they pretty expensive relative to other bank stocks?"

Peter was clearly prepared for that question. He pounced with his answer. "No. That's the best part." Waving his arms, he knocked over a cup of water sitting on Koslow's desk.

"Oh geez. I'm sorry." Peter lunged at the cup, trying to stop any more water from spilling. After setting the cup upright, Peter dashed to the restroom to grab some paper towels. He was back in thirty seconds, eagerly sopping up the water on Koslow's desk.

"Peter! Don't worry about it! My desk is fine. Now— what were you saying about the stock valuations?"

"Oh… yeah. That's the best part. Both of these stocks trade at approximately 1.3 times book value. The bank stock universe is currently trading at 1.1 times. So there's a small premium, but I really think these banks are in a better position for growth than the rest of the universe. I also think that their asset quality is better than that of their peers."

Finally, Peter stopped to catch his breath and prepare for Koslow's reaction to his report.

Koslow did not disappoint Peter. "I've got to admit, Peter—I think you did a great job. Your report is probably as good as any I've read from the most seasoned Wall Street analysts. I'll tell you what. This is your baby. Go over to the trading desk and tell the traders that I want them to get me a three percent position in each of these banks by the end of the week. They can work the trade however they think best."

"Thanks, David." Peter could hardly contain his excitement. "Oh, and I'm sorry about your desk."

"Don't worry about it. Go talk to the traders."

As Peter left Koslow's office, he felt a small knot develop in the core of his stomach. How was he going to convince Tony Salami that the traders should buy a large position in a stock based on his recommendation? He prepared himself for an argument. Thankfully, when he arrived at the trading desk, he found that Tony was nowhere in sight.

"Where's Tony?" he quietly asked Mike Bubnis, one of the junior traders. He and Mike had established a comfortable working relationship over the summer. Mike had confided to Peter that it was often pure hell working with Tony.

"He's been in Fran Solli's office for the past hour. Something must be up. Fran doesn't usually close his door for long conversations with Tony."

Relieved that Tony wasn't there to refute his trading idea, Peter told Mike that Koslow wanted to buy a three percent position in each of his two recommended banks. Mike acknowledged that he had already heard from Koslow and he promised to keep Peter informed on the trade progress. For the first time that summer, Peter left the trading area feeling confident about his job contribution. Best of all, it was work he had done on his own, with no help from the econometer and no help from the Sandman.

Terri Tanaka didn't come into the office until two in the afternoon. Peter couldn't decide what he wanted to discuss first—his successful trading ideas, or her conversation with Fran Solli.

"Terri! Where have you been all morning?"

"I was talking with the folks at Hoosier Insurance."

"So are you going to go there? How did your conversation with Fran go?"

"Fran and I had a good conversation, and I told him that I'm leaving." After a moment's hesitation, a smirk crossed Terri's face. "I told him a couple of other things also."

"Yeah...Go on...What else did you tell him?"

Terri looked around, surveying the trading floor.

"Where's Tony? Is he around?"

"No. He's been in with Fran all morning. I don't know what they discussed, but he was mad as hell when he came out. He didn't say a word to anyone. He just left."

"I have a feeling I know what they talked about."

Peter could see a certain glimmer in Terri's eyes.

"You do? What did they talk about?"

"I can't be sure. But during my conversation with Fran yesterday, a couple things came out about Tony."

Terri looked around and then whispered to Peter. "You've got to promise me that you won't say anything about this to anyone."

"Terri, I'm going to be gone tomorrow. I won't say anything."

"I mean you can't say it to *ANYONE*."

"I won't. I promise."

Terri leaned in closer to Peter. "It seems that we weren't the only people suspicious of where Tony gets his trading ideas. While I was talking with Fran yesterday, he started asking me a lot of questions about Tony. I guess the compliance folks have been monitoring some of Tony's personal trades, and I think they've even started recording some of his phone conversations. I think they're building an insider trading case against him. Fran even asked me if I would stay if Tony were to leave."

"Wow! That would explain his mood when he left today. He wasn't a happy camper."

"Well, let's just keep it quiet until I find out more. I told Fran I'd stop in and talk with him today. We need to wrap up a couple of things. There's a chance that tomorrow might be *my* last day as well as yours."

Peter could hardly get any work done when he went back to his cubicle. What a way to end his summer job! He couldn't wait to talk to Sarah when he got home.

That evening Peter propped his feet on the coffee table as he talked on the phone with Sarah. Tom had already returned to Michigan City. It was Peter's last night in his Chicago apartment.

"I've got to tell you, Sarah, I'm still curious about who was supplying Tony with his information. Do you think the Sandman could have been his source? Maybe the Sandman was the one who tipped Fran Solli off. That's the way he seems to work. He builds people up and then tears them down."

"Peter, don't be too quick to make judgments. Remember, you thought Doug Keyster was working with the Sandman, too. The fact is, there are many people who cave in to the temptations of greed and pride and power. There might be a little bit of sandman in all of us. It's what makes us human. Fortunately, our ability to resist these temptations is also what sets us apart as human. That's the human side we have to nurture."

"You sound like my father."

"I'll take that as a compliment. Now don't forget to say your prayers tonight."

Peter smiled. "Thanks, Dad. I love you." He joked.

"I love you too, Peter," Sarah said as she hung up the phone.

✡ ✡ ✡

Thursday, September fourth, the final day of Peter's summer internship.

Peter's alarm clock went off just after four in the morning. This was commencement day. He greeted it with mixed emotions. Peter planned to arrive at the office before anyone else. He wanted to leave a lasting impression. Nothing too dramatic, but something tangible, that people would remember.

First on his agenda was a brisk run down Lake Shore Drive. He wanted to admire the Chicago skyline one last time. The morning sun, rising over the lake, offered a beautiful greeting as he headed toward the beach. The lake was perfectly still.

Peter stopped running and stared out over the undisturbed water. *How long will it be before I see him again,* he wondered? Looking around to make sure no one could hear him, he softly called out to the water.

"I'll be ready for you next time. I'm not going to let you ruin people's lives. If you want to mess with someone, I dare you to try to mess with me."

Peter then turned his back to the water and ran to his apartment.

Peter arrived at the offices of American Dinero at six in the morning. Seeing no one was there, Peter searched to find where to turn on the lights. He surveyed the floor where he had spent his summer. Browsing through the portfolio managers' offices, and glancing at the work on their desks, he wondered what it would be like to be managing investment portfolios for clients. He soon approached Fran Solli's office. He admired the way Fran managed the office. He imagined that it would be a very difficult job managing the egos of the various traders, analysts, and portfolio managers. Nonetheless, not once during the summer did he hear anyone utter a disparaging remark about Mr. Solli. Peter appreciated Fran's effort to spend time with a lowly intern like himself. He wanted to be sure to thank Fran for the opportunity before he left.

Finally, Peter walked back to the trading area. There were six goldfish swimming in the bowl next to the piranha tank. It almost seemed as if they were smiling in Tony's absence. Their world had become a much more beautiful place.

Peter put his face up to the piranha tank. They were natural-born killers. He could detect no sign of a conscience within their steely eyes.

"You guys might be going hungry for a while," Peter whispered.

As Peter was getting ready to leave, he thought about the words he had preached to Terri Tanaka the previous Monday. He shouldn't be mad at the piranhas, he thought. They were just acting on instinct. It's those with a soul, those who lacked a conscience, who should be punished.

He then noticed the blank whiteboard, mounted prominently in the trading area. He remembered Fran Solli's *Animal Farm* analogy on his first day of work. Peter was determined to prevent Tony from altering the commandments of trading, the way the pigs altered the rules in the novel. Peter recalled the conclusion of *Animal Farm,* when the original Seven Commandments were replaced with a single commandment: *"All animals are created equal, but some animals are more equal than others."*

Perhaps that was Tony's ultimate goal, he thought, to be *more equal* than the others. Peter's first inclination was to smash the whiteboard and dispose of it. *Wait—I've got a better idea.* Looking around to make sure no one had entered the office; Peter removed the board from its mount and carried it to his cubicle. He spotted a place under his desk where he could store the board and hide it behind some boxes—it was the same way he used to hide the genie's bottle.

It was just past ten when David Koslow walked over to Peter's cubicle. Without even wishing him a good morning, David told Peter that Fran Solli wanted everyone in the trading area for an eleven o'clock meeting. Numerous thoughts ran through Peter's head. *Is this the announcement about Terri, or is it an announcement about Tony? What if they're trying to find out who stole the whiteboard?*

Looking down at his feet, Peter stared at the whiteboard, hidden beneath his desk. He then looked around his immediate area and noticed that the floor was relatively empty. Now would be the time to act if he was going to do anything. Struggling to determine an appropriate course of action,

Peter finally managed a smile and whispered to himself, "I might as well go out with a bang."

Peter thought back on the various commandments that Tony had posted on the board over the past summer. He was determined to prevent the pig from changing the social rules within the organization.

He pondered how he would re-phrase the first rule Tony had posted: "Lehman Brothers traders are unreasonable and self-centered. Thou Shall Not Trade with Lehman Brothers for two weeks."

A smile came to Peter's face as he re-wrote the first commandment:

"People are often unreasonable and self-centered. Forgive them anyway."

Peter looked at his new commandment and he was proud. With marker in hand, he continued to think and write for the next forty minutes. It wasn't long before it was time to meet in the trading area. Peter had not seen Terri Tanaka or Tony Salami all day.

Feeling a bit alone, Peter apprehensively approached the trading area. He was glad to see Terri standing next to Fran Solli. Terri smiled and gave him a short wave.

Fran immediately took control of the situation.

"Thank you all for taking time out of your busy day. I have a number of things I need to discuss. I thought it would be much more efficient to do this in person than through email. Please feel free to ask me any questions after I'm done speaking."

Everyone simply stood around, looking at each other. Not a word was said. Fran continued.

"First of all, as I think you may know, today is Peter Jangle's last day with us for the summer. I've had the opportunity to get to know Peter a bit this summer, as I think you all have, and I think you would agree that he's done a great job for us. So hopefully you will all take the opportunity to wish him well as he prepares to go back for his senior year at Notre Dame."

"Hear, hear!" David Koslow cheered.

"I'll let you know if I need a place to crash for football weekends." someone else chimed in.

Not wanting to lose control of his audience, Fran continued.

"Unfortunately, there are a couple of other announcements I need to make. I'm afraid that Terri Tanaka is also going to be leaving us. She has decided to accept a terrific opportunity as the Chief Investment Officer for Hoosier Insurance, an insurance company located in Indianapolis. Although it's going to be a loss for us, I certainly hope you'll join me in wishing her well. In fact, I ordered a nice catered lunch for all of us today so that we can get a chance to wish both of these terrific people the best of luck."

Peter looked around the room. He could tell by the various expressions that Terri would be missed. It was evident that Terri had already informed her analyst team, as their looks were more sadness than shock.

"One last item," Fran continued. "As you've probably noticed, Tony Salami is not here today. As you all know, there are very stringent compliance procedures in this business that we all need to adhere to. The Compliance Department is concerned with some recent trades in Tony's personal accounts that were not disclosed. In a nutshell, they want to investigate some of Tony's activities in further detail. Consequently, don't be surprised if some of the compliance folks come to interview you. I have given them my assurance that we will fully cooperate. So if any of you have any concerns over the questions you might be asked, you need to come to me to discuss it. With regard to Tony, he has been suspended from work until the compliance area is done with its investigation. Does anyone have any questions?"

Around the room, Peter saw blank stares on the faces of the employees at American Dinero. They were all in a state of shock.

"When are they going to interview us?" someone nervously asked.

"I don't know. But I suspect it will be soon. There's no need to be worried. This isn't a witch hunt. However, some of the evidence against Tony was pretty damaging and right now we don't know what he's going to tell the compliance folks. As a result, compliance might need some of you to either confirm or deny Tony's story."

Again, no one seemed to know what to say. Finally, Mike Bubnis broke the silence, trying to add a bit of levity to the dour mood. Pointing to the empty wall in front of him he said, "It looks like Tony took his whiteboard home with him."

"Guess he wanted to hide the evidence," Koslow chimed in.

Peter didn't feel ready to talk about his changes to the whiteboard—especially in such an anxious environment. He was hoping for a much more jovial mood. Nonetheless, the issue had been raised. Even though Peter risked alienating some of the traders, he felt it necessary to speak up.

"Actually, I took the whiteboard. I thought it needed a couple of changes."

Immediately everyone turned to Peter.

"What kind of changes did you make?" Terri asked.

Peter sensed an ally. "Just a minute. I'll go get the board."

Peter's comments caused everyone to forget momentarily their concern regarding Tony and the impending investigation. They were now curious to see what the summer intern had done. Peter returned to the murmuring crowd feeling both excited and nervous. He kept his changes hidden, trying to explain his rationale for taking the board.

"I just thought that some of the things Tony wrote while I was here weren't the best principles for conducting business."

Fran smiled and took the board from Peter. "Let's see what you've got here."

He replaced the board in its original spot on the wall so that everyone could read it. Fran then read Peter's revised commandments to the assembled group:

"**People are often unreasonable and self-centered. Forgive them anyway.**"

"**If you're honest and upfront, you'll be eaten alive. Be honest anyway.**"

"**Analysts can do their best work and still lose money. Do your best anyway.**"

"**If you question the consensus, you may be ridiculed and gain new enemies. Question anyway.**"

"**The good you do today will most likely be forgotten tomorrow. Do good anyway.**"

"**What you spend years building, can be destroyed overnight. Build anyway.**"

The room was quiet. Peter looked around nervously, seeking reinforcement and approval. Was it his imagination, or were people purposely avoiding eye contact with him? Even his friends, Fran Solli, Terri, and Dave Koslow were just staring at the board in silence.

Finally, Fran turned to Peter, looked him in the eye, and slowly started to clap. Terri and Dave followed Fran's lead. Within seconds, the room was filled with thunderous applause. Peter smiled with a sigh of relief. Tears of pride welled up in his eyes, and he bit his lip, trying to control his emotion.

"*That's* the philosophy I want to resonate within this firm," Fran Solli boomed over the applause. "That's what sets us apart from our competitors."

One by one, the various employees at American Dinero lined up to shake Peter's hand. Peter realized that this would be a defining day in his future career.

After an enjoyable lunch, Peter said his final good-byes, and went back to his apartment. Within an hour, he had packed all of his belongings. Grabbing his stuffed blue and gold garment bag, he headed for the South Shore station to return to Michigan City. The pleasant memories of the day lifted his mood. Fran Solli had told Peter to contact him if he wanted to work at American Dinero after graduation. David Koslow once again praised him for the work he had done to support the portfolio managers this summer. And Terri Tanaka gave him a long hug and kiss, thanking him for his friendship. A smile crossed Peter's face as he laid his head against the window of the train to rest. The gentle swaying of the train slowly rocked Peter to sleep.

After what seemed like an hour, an abrupt jolt in the ride awakened Peter. Half-dazed from his slumber, he looked around to assure himself everything was okay. *It must have just been a kink in the railroad tracks.* Satisfied, he closed his eyes until he heard the conductor call out, "Next stop, Ogden Dunes."

Reality set in. Peter knew that his world was not perfect. Despite some hesitation, he felt compelled to peer out the window at the Ogden Dunes stop. He looked up and noticed a magnificent sunset. The orange glow of the sun reflected beautifully off the large cumulus clouds that were being gently pushed by the breeze. Peter observed the sparse crowd on the train platform. He saw tired business people returning from a long day of work. He then noticed two young children, each clinging to their mother's hand. They looked directly at Peter as they walked by his train car. Peter smiled, and then noticed the words printed on the back of their T-shirts as they walked past him: 'We survived the New Madrid quake.' Peter closed his eyes. He had ended his first job on a good note, and he couldn't wait to get home and tell his parents. And yet, he knew that his life journey was just beginning.